RHYMNEY VALLEY KILLINGS

A gripping crime thriller

GAYNOR TORRANCE

DI Jemima Huxley Series Book 6

JOFFE BOOKS

Joffe Books, London
www.joffebooks.com

First published in Great Britain in 2023

This book is a work of fiction. Names, characters, businesses, organizations, places and events are either the product of the author's imagination or are used fictitiously. Any resemblance to actual persons, living or dead, events or locales is entirely coincidental. The spelling used is British English except where fidelity to the author's rendering of accent or dialect supersedes this.

Cover art by Nebojša Zorić

ISBN: 978-1-83526-313-6

PROLOGUE

His eyes opened as he returned to the here and now. But it was too little, too late. Someone else held all the cards.

He was trussed. Gagged. Unable to shout. Or protect himself in any way. Disorientated. All he could do was struggle and squeal like a stuck pig. Deep down he sensed it was futile. No one would rescue him. Why would they? After all, there was no one who cared. Panic added to his confusion. It didn't help that the severe blow to the head caused his brain to pulse with pain. He'd never felt so helpless. Powerless; a series of terrifying scenarios flashed through his mind. It was impossible to imagine any good outcome. Yet nothing made sense and he had so many questions that needed answering. Why would someone do this to him? Who were they? What did they want? And where the hell was he?

As a gust of wind struck his face, he flinched as though slapped, and shivered uncontrollably. As air filled his nostrils, he recognised the distinctive scent of animal droppings and soil. From the moment he'd regained consciousness, his vision had been blurred by tears. These smells were the first real clue that he was somewhere out in the open.

Recognising the obvious disadvantage of not being able to wipe his eyes, he blinked rapidly to dispel the tears.

Desperate to see, yet dreading what he would encounter. As seconds ticked by, he sensed he was lying on a sheet of metal.

He jerked at a scurrying sound somewhere nearby, causing the restraints to cut into his wrists and ankles. He hadn't seen the creature that had made the sound but guessed it must be a rat. He hated rodents. Vermin. Filthy creatures. Rife with disease. The very thought of one coming near him made his flesh crawl. As he tried to move his head, straining to find the animal he noticed a human-like shape huddled nearby. It wasn't moving or making a sound.

His thoughts were cut short as people approached. Could this be the moment he found out that this was just some kind of sick joke? They were discussing something, and he strained to listen, but from this distance all he could make out was a jumble of unintelligible sounds, as they were speaking fast and low. Moments later a couple of head torches came into view. They were bright in the darkness, bobbing up and down as two people headed in his direction. As they homed in on his location, he recognised the anger in their voices and his stomach lurched. These people weren't here to rescue him. They were the ones who had knocked him out and tied him up. His captors.

The knot of fear tightened in his stomach. He tried his best to protect himself from what was about to come. Attempted to roll himself into a ball. Reduce his surface area. Like a hedgehog when it perceives a threat. Though he quickly realised that the restraints made it impossible. They were far too tight. With no means of escape, he had to take what was coming to him, and hope he survived.

The thugs were on him before he had the chance to draw another breath. No hesitation. Like a couple of dogs at a fight. They lunged, punched kicked, and stamped. Determined to cause the maximum amount of pain and damage. Showing no mercy. The assault seemed to go on forever.

'Enough!' ordered the taller of the two. He was panting from his exertion. 'Let's get this done.'

The smaller one growled in frustration and shrugged off his companion's restraining hand.

Grabbing both his shoulders, he squeezed the smaller one's bony flesh. 'I said, enough!' He was the dominant of the two and there was no mistaking the sternness of his voice. 'We've a long night ahead of us.'

The warning made his accomplice come to his senses. 'Fine,' he hissed. He nodded his agreement. They clearly had a plan as he dropped to his knees, straddling their prey. A swift movement saw him reach out and tear one of the sleeves from their victim's arm, exposing his shoulder.

Despite being in considerable pain, he tried not to show them the extent of his fear, in case it heightened their enjoyment. Though he doubted that he could keep up the act for too long, as he didn't have a high pain threshold. These were vicious thugs and neither man had taken steps to hide his face. Which could only mean that they had no intention of letting him live. Though he couldn't understand why they hated him so much. He'd never hurt anyone in his life. He was running out of time and hoped that they would end things soon. He couldn't take much more. Not that he wanted to die. He was just a coward.

His eyes widened, as his captor's thighs tightened around his midriff. The pressure was unbearable, making it impossible to breathe. Panting shallowly, he was convinced his already damaged ribs would crack. It was then that he spotted the blade in the other man's hand, as it glinted in the torchlight.

He didn't want his life to end like this. Cut short in such a vicious way without even knowing why. His resolve deserted him, and his squeals took on a new sense of urgency.

The pressure and inevitable sting of the blade was agony as it broke through the skin's surface. Tears flowed, blurring his vision once more, and beads of sweat erupted across his brow. Without hesitation the blade sliced through the fleshy part of his shoulder as though his assailant was carving a piece of ham.

He was disfigured. Bleeding. And what at first were howls of pain soon became pathetic, hopeless whimpers. His bladder emptied at the sudden realisation that was just the tip of the iceberg. These monsters were just getting started and there would inevitably be worse to come. The pain was unbearable. His heart rate spiked and he lost consciousness.

* * *

It was approaching 3 a.m. The time of night when most people were snuggled beneath duvets, unaware of anything going on around them. In general, the only ones out and about at this hour were those unfortunate to pull a night shift, be on an emergency callout, or anyone who was up to no good.

The moon was almost full. Bright. Like a spotlight in the cloudless sky. Far-off constellations twinkled like smatterings of fairy lights against a velveteen backdrop. Out here on moorland, to the north of Pontlottyn and the west of Rhymney, a set of headlights illuminated small patches of the stark scrubland as a quadbike jolted slowly along the uneven surface. The driver and his pillion passenger knew of the dangers posed by the terrain and appreciated that a lapse of concentration could result in disaster.

The Bent Iron was a difficult structure to find in daylight, let alone in the middle of the night. But for what these men had in mind they needed the added sense of security that darkness brings.

An eye for an eye, as they say. They were stepping up. Doing what was necessary. Getting scum like this off the streets. Protecting the vulnerable. The police had proved that they were incompetent, lazy, and most likely corrupt. There was no justice for the innocent. These executions were long overdue. So, let the bastards swing.

CHAPTER 1

There were boxes and black bags everywhere. Until a few days ago, when she'd started packing, Jemima hadn't realised that she and the boys had accumulated so much stuff. It all had to be sorted through and Lucy's suggestion of adopting the three-pile rule made things easier. One to keep. Another to donate to charity. The rest to discard.

Preparing to move out of her sister's house was a daunting task, and Jemima appreciated Lucy's help. Time was short as they were both busy women. As a serving police officer Jemima often worked unpredictable hours. Whereas Lucy ran her own company, sourcing stock for corporate hampers she shipped around the world. There were those who dreamed of working from home, and Lucy loved what she did. But Jemima knew that her sister worked exceptionally hard. Sometimes late into the night and at weekends too.

Jemima schlepped into the kitchen carrying an armful of outgrown baby clothes. She dumped them on the table: 'Guess these are for the donation pile.'

Lucy picked up the nearest one and began to fold it, stifling a yawn. 'Sorry, Jem. I'm whacked. It's been relentless today. And you're only going to the vicarage, so you don't need to move everything at once.'

'I know. I'm just conscious of the fact that we've taken up so much of your space, for such a ridiculous amount of time. Leave me to it. Go have a glass of wine and put your feet up,' said Jemima.

'You sure? I feel as though I'm letting you down.'

'Don't be silly, Luce. You've done more than your fair share. I've taken advantage of your generosity for far too long. I'll never be able to repay you for what you did, taking me and James in. It was only ever meant to be a stopgap to give me time to recover and get myself back on my feet. But as usual, you've gone above and beyond. It's been more than two years.'

'And I'd do it again if it was necessary.' Lucy wrapped her arms around Jemima and kissed her cheek. 'You're my sister. I've got your back.'

Lucy had come up trumps in their hour of need. In a selfless act of generosity, she had taken Jemima and her adoptive son James into her home and went above and beyond to ensure they felt part of the family.

It was a level of support that Jemima was initially reluctant to accept, but one she was inevitably grateful for. Those who knew and cared about her appreciated that Jemima's head had been in a bad place back then. Having been raped and subsequently finding herself pregnant would have resulted in a termination in many cases. But Jemima wasn't like most people.

Indeed, it had raised more than a few eyebrows when she eventually decided to keep the baby. Though the decision had been far from easy, as she battled with the possibility that the child would always remind her of an awful episode in her life. But appreciating that it could be her one and only chance to have a biological child had made up her mind. And she had not once regretted that decision.

'I know it's sometimes seemed as though this house has been full to bursting. But I like that kind of crazy, and I'll miss you and the boys,' said Lucy.

'You won't have time to miss us. You'll still see us most days,' reassured Jemima. 'I'll be dropping Finlay off whenever I'm on shift. It's a godsend you've got Eloise as a live-in nanny.'

'Tell me about it. I couldn't manage without her. She'll obviously include James in the school run and he'll be here until you collect him.'

'It's good she's so accommodating,' said Jemima. 'I wouldn't fancy my chances of finding decent childcare if I had to start from scratch. Moving in here was the best thing to happen to James. It's allowed him to get to know his cousins and finally feel part of something.'

As an only child, James had longed to be part of a large family. And that was exactly what he got when they moved into Lucy's home. When you saw them together, it was obvious that his cousins idolised him as each of them hung on his every word.

When Finlay was born, James had his first real taste of what it was like to be an actual big brother, and despite the significant age difference, he welcomed the arrival of his younger sibling.

Theirs could never be described as a conventional family. James's parents had split up when he was a toddler. Nick Huxley, the man he had believed to be his father had subsequently gone on to marry Jemima. But shortly after James's birth mother died in a traffic collision, Nick discovered that his ex-wife had lied to him.

'I know it must've hit Nick for six when he found out he'd been born with Klinefelter Syndrome,' said Lucy. 'But it's unforgivable that he rejected James when he realised he couldn't possibly be his biological child.' Jemima loved him unconditionally. James adored her too. Despite coming to terms with her own heartbreak, she rose to the occasion and put James first. Through a determined effort not to let him see that she was upset, she kept a lid on her emotions and growing insecurities, only allowing them to surface in rare quiet moments when she was alone.

She showered him with affection. Helped him work through his anger and grief, in the knowledge that she was all he had. She held him when he needed comforting. Wiped his tears and offered reassurance. Did everything in her power to rebuild his confidence.

Jemima appreciated the importance of ensuring that the lad realised that he was not in any way responsible for anything that had happened. She reassured him that his mother's passing was a case of dreadful bad luck. Whereas his father's actions had been a display of selfish idiocy by Nick.

As the days passed, she became the boy's best friend and confidante, ensuring that James was well cared for and knew that she loved him unconditionally. Despite having missed out on his early years, they were closer than many biological mothers and sons.

'So, tell me, sis, is it the real deal with Mason? Is he your happy ever after?' Lucy raised her eyebrows questioningly.

Jemima had first made the acquaintance of Father Mason Roy shortly before she was due to go on maternity leave. When out of the blue, the seemingly idyllic village they now lived in was thrown into chaos, as the body of a murdered woman was discovered inside St Agnes' church. It was the closest building to Lucy's house. This meant that a vicious killer was at large and possibly posed a threat to Jemima's nearest and dearest.

'We're friends, Luce. Close friends, and he's great with the boys. Who knows where this will lead. But at the moment it's a house share which suits both of us. It's all above board. I'll be paying him rent.'

'Is that what you call it?' Lucy shook her head and smiled.

'You've a mucky mind, Luce.'

'Well watch your back, sis. All I'm saying is he's one hot bachelor. And in this village, that's a rare commodity.'

'He's also a vicar, Luce.'

Jemima often teased Mason about his band of female followers. As a red-blooded woman herself, she understood why they did it. After all, she herself found the man to be attractive. Though, unlike many of the women who had seemingly discovered religion in their lives and now regularly attended Mason's services, there was no way Jemima was ever going to throw herself at the man.

Jemima's attitude towards Mason was most likely the reason their friendship developed. Her career and family responsibilities meant that she didn't have the luxury of being self-absorbed and needy. Even while on maternity leave, there were always calls upon her time. So much so that she sometimes didn't even have time to put a brush through her hair, let alone spend hours studying herself in the mirror, applying layers of cosmetics and choosing outfits to attract his attention. When she was working, it was a case of having a quick shower and grabbing whatever clean clothes were available. When she was on maternity leave, whatever clothes she chose to wear inevitably ended up stained by Finlay.

It seemed that fate kept drawing Jemima and Mason together. There was hardly a day that went by without them bumping into each other. Lucy frequently commented how Mason made excuses to be in Jemima's company. The couple were at ease with each other. The man was also a natural with James and Finlay. It was understandable that anyone who didn't know them could easily make the mistake of thinking that they were a family unit.

Jemima was the one to decide that it was time for her and the boys to move out of Lucy's house. There had been no falling out between the sisters.

In the end, the catalyst for Jemima moving out was Lucy's husband, Ellis, breaking his leg. He was a cameraman whose work took him all over the world. It was a demanding job resulting in him spending extended periods away from home. His latest project had been on a movie set somewhere in Italy when a platform on which he'd been standing gave way due to a ground tremor. He hadn't fallen far, but the movement also dislodged equipment which landed on his limb and caused a bad break. It meant that he required an extensive period of recuperation followed by physiotherapy for him to get back to the level of physical fitness to enable him to return to work.

'Well if the bishop gets wind of it and throws a hissy fit, you can always come back,' said Lucy. She and Ellis hadn't wanted Jemima and the boys to move out. Their home was more than big enough for everyone to rub along without getting under each other's feet. But Jemima felt it was time to go, and despite having been on the look-out for a property for her and the children, nothing affordable was readily available.

'It's all above board, Luce. Mason's sorted it. The church own the property, but it's too big for just one person. It's a family-sized home, with four large bedrooms. More than enough room to accommodate me and the boys.'

CHAPTER 2

Recent months had seen seismic changes at work. A series of shocking events and revelations, beginning on the day that Jemima returned from maternity leave, had exposed pervasive rottenness at the core of both the police and the justice system.

Evidence of failures and corruption had been broadcast around the world. This effectively ensured that they were boxed into a corner, and those in positions of power were denied the option of pretending things hadn't happened.

Embarrassment didn't cover the shock and humiliation. Everyone knew that the system was broken, and the cancer needed to be cut out. There was an immediate and extensive investigation, followed by a radical overhaul.

In a reconfiguration of policing in the area, a new team had been set up to investigate major incidents occurring throughout South-East Wales. The initiative combined the geographical area of two police forces and was a pilot exercise for a new way of working. There were plenty of officers in both forces who were hostile to this change, but it had still gone ahead.

Jemima had been promoted to the rank of DCI and had agreed to head up the team on the proviso that DS Dan

Broadbent and DS Gareth Peters formed part of that new team. Having worked together for many years, they had each other's backs. They'd already been through so much together and given the extreme nature of some of the crimes they investigated it was essential to have people you trusted at your side.

With DCI Ray Kennedy no longer on the force, Superintendent Torsten Olsen had been drafted in from the Metropolitan Police and was now Jemima's immediate boss.

'No sign of the cyborg this morning,' said Dan as he placed a mug of coffee on Jemima's desk.

'Thank God. Make the most of it while you can.'

One of the few things Jemima knew about Olsen was that the man was aloof. Having met with him to discuss the remit of the newly formed team, she realised that he had no sense of humour or apparent warmth. He was all about the job and nothing else. It was that lack of humanity that caused her to name him the cyborg. Indeed, she wouldn't have been surprised to discover that there was a circuit board where his heart should be, and wires running beneath the surface of his skin instead of arteries and veins. She had referred to Olsen by that name when she was speaking to Dan and Gareth. It had amused them so much that the moniker had stuck.

The man compelled a wary respect, but they were all seasoned enough officers to appreciate that he was not someone who could be trusted to have anyone's back.

Jemima had a hunch that Olsen was focused on climbing the ranks and wasn't interested in making friends along the way. Whether that was because he had no qualms about stepping on others to get what he wanted, she had yet to ascertain. The only thing she knew for sure at this moment in time was that Torsten Olsen was no Ray Kennedy. And that was a shame. He was the type to hang any, or all of them, out to dry if it suited his purpose.

'What's Nancy up to?' she asked. DC Nancy Chen had also been drafted onto the team. She had joined Kennedy's squad, six months into Jemima's maternity leave. So, Dan and Gareth had the advantage of knowing her better. But Jemima had yet to make up her mind. Chen had played a role in the investigation to locate the missing high court judge, Rory Lawson, and had been there throughout the fallout that ensued. Jemima had no cause for concern over Chen's competence.

What worried her was that she had not selected Chen as a member of this new team. That decision had been made by Torsten Olsen. This was odd in its own way, as coming in from another force he would have no knowledge of anyone's strengths or weaknesses. Yet he had insisted that Chen be given a place on the squad. And when Jemima had tackled him about it the man had fudged the issue by shutting her down and refusing to talk about the reasons behind his decision. All Jemima really knew about Chen was that she had completed a stint as an undercover officer in another police force. It raised concerns about what else was being kept from her.

'Dunno,' said Dan. 'She's been on the phone all morning. Making one call after another. I'm guessing it's something she doesn't want us to know about as she's been talking quietly and making a lot of notes.'

'Keep an eye on her, Dan,' said Jemima.

The other two DCs to join the team had both been selected by Jemima. Firstly, there was Levi Jackson. He was in his late twenties and had been a police officer for four years. This would be his first posting as a plain clothes officer. Having previously worked for the Gwent force at their headquarters in Cwmbran, he had put his name forward to join the team. And when Jemima had read his application, she had to meet him.

Levi's enthusiasm had bowled her over and she sensed he would be a good fit with the other officers. Both sets of his grandparents had emigrated to Britain from the Caribbean, in the late 1950s and early 1960s. The two generations preceding him, along with Levi and his sister had faced instances of racial abuse. It was one of the reasons he had joined the police force, as he wanted things to change for the better.

From what Levi had said, he had not had an easy ride. As although most officers treated him fairly, there had been others who had gone out of their way to make his life difficult. Their hostility had been covert. Never in front of independent witnesses. But it was still an ever-present hostility he had to deal with. He had learned as a child that it was sometimes better not to complain as it often made the situation worse.

Jemima had first-hand experience of just how hateful some of the officers could be. Throughout her entire career she'd had to either ignore or negotiate her way around the misogynists. But she knew that her experience of facing hostility and dealing with underhand behaviour was nothing compared to Levi's.

Just as in the wider population there were a lot of decent people on the force. But the sickening reality was that racism was still very much alive and kicking. Very few officers were stupid enough to act in an overtly prejudicial manner. The stakes were too high as they could end up losing their jobs. But for those who possessed that mindset their prejudices remained, festering beneath the surface. Tolerating, but secretly despising others because of the colour of their skin, their gender, their sexuality, or their religious beliefs.

Levi had a late start that morning as he had a hospital appointment.

Another newcomer to the team was DC Andrew Mackintosh. Or, Mack, as he preferred to be called. A distinctive mop of unruly auburn hair and a Scottish burr set him apart from many of the population in this part of the country. A gold band on his ring finger suggested that he was either married or in a long-term relationship. Though, just like Olsen, he avoided speaking about his personal life. He was far from the typical thirty-year-old. Reluctant to socialise and network. Choosing instead to head off once the shift had ended.

Jemima liked Mack, but he was an enigma. He was personable and well-intentioned, but clearly had his boundaries. And although she was keen to know more about the man,

Jemima knew not to push. For the team to gel effectively it was essential to give everyone space and time to get to know and trust each other. It was only natural that everyone had secrets. She knew that better than most.

'Is it just me or can any of you smell that?' he asked.

'Smell what?' asked Jemima. Their desks were at opposite ends of the room.

'To be honest, it smells like someone's taken a shite,' said Mack. He wrinkled his nose in disgust.

'Yeah, I've got a whiff of that too,' said Nancy.

'Not just me then,' said Mack, as he got up from his chair and moved around the squad room, sniffing the air to locate the source of the offensive smell. 'Seems to be coming from Levi's desk,' he said, as he pulled out the chair and crouched down to examine the floor. 'Probably carried something in on the sole of his shoe . . . No. Nothing there. But the smell's really strong.'

Jemima walked over to where Mack stood. 'You're right. That's bloody awful. What the hell is it?' Glancing at the floor she could see that nothing had been trodden into the carpet, and if the smell was coming from the air conditioning unit it would have been noticeable throughout the room.

For security reasons whenever they were out of the office, they operated a clear desk policy. As such the only objects on display were a keyboard, processor, and mouse. Everything else would be locked away in filing cabinets or the drawers of the pedestal.

With no obvious source visible, Jemima tried Levi's pedestal, and her eyes widened when she discovered it was unlocked. Knowing that every member of the team was fastidious about security, she dreaded what she was about to find.

With the others now gathered at Levi's desk she opened the top drawer to discover that everything was as it should be. But the smell was stronger now, and there was no doubting what it was. As she closed the top drawer and opened the middle one Jemima couldn't help but take a step backwards.

As the five officers stared in disbelief at the faeces smeared across the inside of the drawer, the door opened, and Levi walked in.

'What's up, guys?' he asked in a cheery voice. Though moments later he realised that there was nothing to be cheerful about.

CHAPTER 3

The shocking abuse directed at Levi was proof, not that any was needed, that despite the bad press and the significant overhaul of law enforcement, they still employed people who were an absolute disgrace. Olsen had assured them that the incident would be investigated, but they were all seasoned enough to know that that nothing would come of it. Already twenty-four hours had passed with no updates. Jemima stopped typing and glanced across at DS Gareth Peters who was leaning back in his seat, staring at the ceiling. In all the years she'd known him she had been struck by the fact that little seemed to faze him. He was hardworking, competent, and remarkably level-headed. A dependable officer and genuine all-round good guy. However, for the last few days, it had been obvious that Gareth was not his usual self.

Throughout the last hour Jemima had heard him sigh with increasing regularity. Another tell-tale sign was that he kept rubbing his face. At least three times in the last half hour, he had propelled his chair away from his desk and hurried out of the room. Only to return seconds later to slump back down and stare at the ceiling.

It didn't take a detective to work out that something was up with him. And Jemima knew that whatever it was, must be important, as he was not someone to make a mountain out of a molehill. She decided it was time to take him to one side. Buy Gareth a cup of coffee. Sit him down. Ask what was wrong and offer to help if she could. Whatever was up with him was clearly important enough to distract him when he should be working. Which could be disastrous if they were suddenly given a new case.

Jemima stood up and headed in his direction. 'Gareth.' As he failed to react, she repeated his name. This time more loudly. 'Gareth!' She was practically standing in front of him.

Sensing something had changed, he lowered his gaze and flinched. 'S-sorry, guv, I—' There was no time to finish his sentence as the door was opened with such force that the handle hit the wall, denting the plasterboard.

Every eye was on Superintendent Olsen as he strode purposefully into the room. It was an unusual occurrence for him to venture into the squad room. His preferred method of communication with the team was by summoning Jemima to his office to brief her about information he expected her to impart to the minions. So, for him to appear in person and unannounced meant that some major development had come to his attention that required swift action.

'Gather round!' Olsen bellowed like a sergeant major on the parade ground. This was an order. End of. He made no attempt at social niceties. Or gave any acknowledgement of being one of the team. It was a blatant demonstration that he was the one in charge, and they were merely there to do his bidding.

Olsen came to a halt, positioning himself in front of the white board. As he surveyed the room, he positioned his feet so that his legs were apart, and his shoulders squared, clasping his hands behind his back.

Everyone stopped what they were doing and headed towards him. Apart from Mack, who was just winding up a work-related phone call. The superintendent glared in his direction. 'Get a move on, Mackintosh! I haven't got all day!' He raised his arm, clicked his fingers, then flicked his wrist, pointing his forefinger to indicate where he expected the junior officer to stand alongside the others. It was offensive. Demeaning. Like an old-fashioned teacher setting out to humiliate a troublesome child.

Jemima closed her eyes and silently counted to ten. She disliked the cyborg more than any other officer she had come across, which said something given the significant number of the arseholes she'd had to deal with. As much as she wished she could tear him off a strip and make him acknowledge the fact that he should treat people with respect, she knew that it was merely wishful thinking.

As this was a new squad, there was a lot at stake, and it was her job to make things work. Recently there had been a significant amount of disruption, with far too much bad feeling and mistrust. And with this new way of working across two different police forces, there was a hell of a lot riding on them making a success of it.

For now, no matter how distasteful Olsen's manner happened to be, they all needed to suck it up and rise above his inexplicable and unacceptable antagonism. So instead of rising to the bait she kept quiet. Let the cyborg impart whatever information he felt he needed to tell them. That way he'd be out of their hair in the shortest amount of time, and they could get on with whatever they needed to do.

Mack ended the call and walked over to join the rest of them. Jemima admired the man's composure. Despite the cyborg's overt antagonism, Mack hadn't allowed it to affect him. Or else he had a formidable poker face.

'Fiiinaaaally!' The word was protracted for dramatic effect. 'Now that I have everyone's attention, I'll introduce you to the particularly nasty case which you will be investigating.'

At those words, Jemima's annoyance faded like a shadow in the night, as she was keen to learn about their next challenge.

'Who in this room has heard of the Rhymney Bent Iron?' asked Olsen. His laser-like blue eyes scanned the room. From their blank expressions and the collective shaking of heads he was left in no doubt that they were all just as clueless as him.

'Is it something to do with Rumney, Cardiff?' asked Dan.

'There's no connection with Cardiff, as far as I know. Though you're the locals in this part of the world,' said Olsen.

'Well, there's a town named Rhymney at the top of the Rhymney Valley?' suggested Jemima. She hadn't been there. Just seen the name on a map. Until she moved to Leighton Meadow she had lived in Cardiff her entire life. She'd left the family home as soon as she became a student and never returned. Having initially lived in student accommodation whilst at university, followed by a house-share for a time after graduating.

Many Cardiffians rarely, if ever, ventured into the valleys. Conversely, people who lived in the valleys frequently travelled to Cardiff for work and leisure purposes. As such, city dwellers didn't necessarily have first-hand knowledge or experience of local towns or villages.

Though, in recent years there had been a shift towards younger people accepting that they would never be able to afford to buy or even rent a property in the city they had grown up in. This meant they had to look further afield. Caerphilly, which was located at the southern point of the Rhymney Valley had become a popular choice as it was only a couple of miles away from the northern edge of the city. Transport links were reasonable, making it a quick and relatively easy commute. Though very few were prepared to put down roots further north. And Rhymney was the town at the top of this particular valley.

'It's my understanding that's where you will be heading,' nodded Olsen.

'What's the case?' asked Levi. In his eagerness to learn more, he spoke without thinking.

'I don't appreciate interruptions, Constable!' The reprimand was implicit in Olsen's tone. He glared at Levi, daring him to utter another word at his peril. 'As I was about to say, earlier this morning, two corpses were found suspended from this Bent Iron contraption. I've no idea what it is. Or what purpose it serves. If any. All I know is that it is on moorland to the west of the town, and I've been advised that it's not easy to get to. As you don't have the luxury of off-road vehicles, you'll have to park up and go prepared to negotiate some difficult terrain on foot.'

Jemima opened her mouth to say something, but the cyborg stared her down, and she thought better of interrupting him.

'It seems that these corpses are not fresh. I've no idea how long they've been there, but I guarantee they won't be a pretty sight. The forensic team are on their way and the coroner has been alerted. It's my understanding that given existing work commitments, John Prothero, who's based at the University Hospital of Wales will perform the post-mortems. I appreciate that he's at a different health board. However, it's a strategic decision, based on the need to expedite things as efficiently as possible.

'There's a DI Mike Hughes co-ordinating things at the scene until you arrive. He's aware that you have overall command, Huxley. But feel free to use Hughes and his officers as you see fit. They'll inevitably have local knowledge and contacts. And it'll give you more boots on the ground.

'Well, there you have it. You know everything that I know. Any questions?' There was no warmth in his expression, as he swiftly cast an eye over the officers in front of him. It was apparent to all of them that this had been a rhetorical question. It would be foolhardy to attempt to elicit any further information from the man. 'No? Excellent. I would have thought maggots and the wildlife are having a picnic. So, you'd better get up there while there's still some useful forensic evidence. These are the co-ordinates I've been given. The first is the location of the Bent Iron. The second is where I've been informed you should park up. As I've already said, you'll have to go the rest of the way on foot.'

Olsen transcribed a set of map co-ordinates onto the white board, then turned and marched out of the room without so much as a backward glance.

'He's a real piece of work,' muttered Nancy, shaking her head in disgust. 'He's talking about people who have lost their lives. He should show some respect.'

'And you're going to be the one to volunteer to tell him that?' asked Levi.

'No, I was just saying,' she muttered.

'Let's establish exactly where we're heading to,' said Jemima. She was determined to focus minds and wasn't about to allow any petty argument to get in the way of the job.

'Already on it,' said Mack, as he opened a map on his screen. They all gathered round to ensure that they knew exactly where they were going.

'Be sure to take appropriate footwear. I don't want any twisted ankles or other injuries. We've no idea how rough that terrain is, but I guarantee it's going to take some physical effort,' said Jemima.

'We'll take three vehicles. That should give us the flexibility to split up should we need to. Dan, you go with Levi. Gareth, you're with me.'

Dan and Gareth exchanged glances. Both were clearly surprised by the travel arrangements, as it was usual for Jemima and Dan to travel together. But neither man commented on the decision.

CHAPTER 4

Gareth was uncharacteristically quiet as Jemima negotiated the city centre traffic. So far, he'd made no attempt at small talk, preoccupied by whatever problem he was trying to deal with.

'What's up, Gar?'

'Uh? Sorry, did you say something?'

'I know you well enough to recognise when something's wrong. I can't and won't try to force you to confide in me, but I'm a good listener, Gar. I guarantee that whatever you tell me, won't go any further.'

'It's not work-related, guv. It's to do with my family.'

'Let's get one thing straight. Whilst we're in this car and we're having this conversation, you don't have to call me, guv. This is me. Jem. Your friend. We're talking as equals. Not as a DCI and a sergeant. You know how messed up my personal life has been, Gar. So, you'll know that I won't judge you. But I get the sense that you've got a problem, and as a friend I want you to know that I'll help in whatever way I can.'

'And there was me thinking I was hiding things. I should have guessed you'd notice something was up,' said Gareth. His shoulders relaxed as he spoke. 'You promise it won't go any further?'

'Gar, I just want to help. I know how soul-destroying it can be to keep bottling things up. It won't do you any good.'

Gareth exhaled forcefully. 'OK, if you must know, it's my father.'

'Is he ill?'

'Oh, if only . . . No, no he's healthy as far as I know. He just doesn't know that I'm gay . . . There, I've said it. Now you know that I'm a coward. Too bloody scared to tell my father that I'm gay. I'm pathetic.'

Jemima was surprised. Right from the start, Gareth had been open with them about his sexuality. None of them were in the habit of talking about their relationships, but naturally, things sometimes got mentioned on those occasions when they socialised outside work, and they had all met each other's partners. But Jemima had always presumed that Gareth was comfortable with his sexuality.

'You're not a coward, Gar. Whenever we've worked alongside each other you've always stood your ground. And when you consider some of the situations we deal with, that takes guts. As for parents . . . take it from me that some of them have a way of fucking their kids up. If he's that much of a bigot, then don't tell him. It's none of his business anyway. You don't answer to him.'

'You don't understand, Jem. It's not that simple. We've set the date. Ryan and I are finally getting hitched.'

'That's wonderful news, Gar. Congratulations. I've always thought you and Ryan make a great couple.'

Gareth and his partner, Ryan Blake had lived together for years. Following a chance encounter at a Doctor Who convention, they bonded over their shared love of sci-fi.

'Ryan's my soul mate, Jem. Hell, he even shares my obsession with Dungeons and Dragons.'

That's proof you're meant to be together, if any was needed,' said Jemima. The comment was an attempt to lighten Gareth's mood, and as she glanced across, she spotted him smile.

'Precisely. Ry's family are solid gold. They're so loving and supportive of both of us. He's lucky to have them.

They've never had a problem with him being gay. In fact, his mother said she'd known and embraced it from an early age. Way before Ryan even acknowledged it himself. From the moment he introduced me to his family, his parents, his siblings, they all treat me like I was one of their own. It was, and still is a wonderful feeling. It's such a relief, knowing I'm accepted for who I am. Feeling safe and loved. That I genuinely belong.'

'That's brilliant, Gar. It's all any of us can hope for.'

'Yeah, it is . . . but then there's my family. My mother knew and accepted that I'm gay. Sadly, she passed before Ryan came into my life. My sister's cool with it too. But we all knew how my father would react. The man's a neanderthal. A bigoted bully, who's handy with his fists. Especially when he's got a couple of drinks inside him. He made my mother's life hell. Making sure that she knew her place, which in his opinion was either in the kitchen, or flat on her back whenever he was in the mood. He was a pig of a husband. Good old Dennis is very vocal about his opinions. Hates those who are not white. And despises gays. Says they're perverted and should've been drowned at birth.

'As a kid, I had to put up with that man's bile day-in day-out. Can you imagine what he's going to be like when he finds out that his only son is gay? At best he'll do everything in his power to drive a wrecking ball through my relationship with Ryan. But if I'm honest, I'm more concerned about what the bastard will do to me and Ry. I wouldn't put it past him to get physical and try to teach us one of his so-called lessons.'

'Gar, that's awful.' Jemima's heart went out to him. She knew how crushingly debilitating and longlasting the effects of growing up with a hostile parent could be. Gareth was a genuinely kind, supportive and brave man. Yet here he was, reverting back to childhood and adolescent fears he had fought hard to distance himself from. It was awful to see him so distraught. Especially when he was planning what should be one of the happiest days of his life. 'I take it you're not in contact with him?'

'No. I moved out as soon as I could. Met my mum in secret and had nothing to do with him. Apart from when we inevitably came face-to-face at the funeral. I can't have my father destroying what I have with Ry.'

'So don't tell him about the wedding,' said Jemima. It seemed the simplest solution.

'It's too late. He knows. My sister, Lowri let it slip. I'd sworn her to secrecy, but she let that big gob of hers run away with itself. She doesn't have much to do with him, but he walked into the pub she was drinking in. She was out with her mates and had had a few too many. Dad had a go at her. Telling her she was making a show of herself, and they started to argue. That's when she told him it was no wonder his kids wanted nothing to do with him, and she was glad he wasn't invited to the wedding. She told me she could have cut her tongue out for letting it slip. But the alcohol caused her to drop her guard, and once it was out there, she couldn't take it back.

'He pushed her for information, but she refused to give him any details. In fairness she didn't specifically say it was my wedding that she was referring to. But I know him. He won't let it go, and for all his faults he's not a stupid man. If he hasn't worked it out already, he'll eventually find out, and when he does, all hell will break loose.'

'If it helps, we can all keep an eye out at the wedding. Stop him interrupting the service or spoiling the reception.'

'Thanks, but we won't be able to rely on you guys for the rest of our lives. It's not me I'm worried about. It's Ry. He's self-employed and home alone most days, and he's not a fighter.' Gareth's voice trembled and he gulped as his breath caught in his throat. It wasn't in his nature to over-dramatise things. He was usually the calming influence on the rest of the team. Level-headed. Quietly competent. Yet he was genuinely fearful about what his father was capable of.

'You know there're things you can do,' said Jemima.

'Of course, I do. I worked Violet's case with you and look how that turned out.' This was a reference to a horrendous case they had worked together, when a young woman named Violet Watkins was targeted by an obsessive stalker named Byron Toombes. The circumstances were very different to Gareth's current predicament, but from what he had just said, his father's obsession might prove to be equally as destructive. And Gareth had a lifetime's experience of knowing what the man was capable of.

'Are you saying that you believe that your father's capable of killing you and Ryan?' Jemima wanted to know what Gareth believed could be the worst-case scenario, should his father come after him.

'Possibly. Yeah. No. Oh, I don't know. The truth is I'm scared. I don't want anything bad to happen to Ryan. I love him. He's my world. But this is my nightmare scenario. Which means, I'm too close to it to make a rational judgement and that scares me even more. If I've misjudged my father, I risk turning our lives upside down for nothing. If I underestimate him, I could put Ryan's life in danger.'

'Has your father got a record?'

'No. He's careful to portray a respectable image to the outside world. I'd go as far as to say that most people think he's Mr Reasonable.

'Even as I'm saying it, my accusations sound ridiculous. I bet you think I'm just blowing things out of proportion.'

'Believe me, I don't. Being the daughter of a narcissistic mother, I know all about just how manipulative people can be. She branded me a liar and a troublemaker from a very early age. It got to the stage where I was too afraid to be myself, and I certainly couldn't stand up to her. So yeah, I believe you. I know that if you have concerns about someone's potential actions, then those concerns are genuine. But there's a fine line to tread. Have you spoken to Ryan about this?'

'Not yet.'

'Well, I suggest you have the conversation at the earliest opportunity. He needs to know what he could be up against. What's your security like at home?'

'Pretty good. We've an alarm, movement sensors, cameras, and panic buttons.'

'Well, that's a good start. Do you both have personal attack alarms?'

'No.'

'Then get it sorted, Gar. We all know they're a good way of scaring people off. You've already said that your father's not a stupid man. By the sound of things, he cares about his reputation?'

'He does. I think that's why he'll go ballistic when he finds out I'm gay. He'll see it as a reflection on him. Putting his so-called manhood into question.'

'Umm. I see where you're coming from, but it could also be the case that if it reaches the point where he discovers that you're gay, he could just cut you out of his life completely. Your father lives over Llanelli way, doesn't he?'

'Yeah.'

'And have you kept in touch with anyone from that area?'

'No. I broke all ties when I moved away. I was in North Wales for a while when I first started on the job, and came to Cardiff about a year before I was drafted onto the Llys Faen Hall case, to work with you and Dan. Given the job, I don't have social media accounts, and the house is in Ryan's name. So, there's no way he could track me.'

'Well, there's little chance of anyone he knows, apart from your sister, finding out about you or the wedding. He sounds like someone who only cares about his own reputation. So, I'd have thought he'd want to distance himself from you. Reduce the risk of anyone finding out. In case, in his mind, it'd reflect badly on him.

'I'm not saying, don't take extra precautions. I just think that you shouldn't get fixated on the idea that he's going to do something awful to Ryan or yourself. After all, that wouldn't do his reputation any good.

'So, talk to Ryan. He needs to know. Get those personal attack alarms and make sure you always have them on you. And as for the wedding, Dan and I will have your backs. You're like family, Gar. We'll always look out for you,' said Jemima.

CHAPTER 5

The journey towards the head of the Rhymney valley turned out to be a real eye-opener. Jemima had decided to travel on the minor roads instead of the faster A470 dual carriageway. It wasn't an ideal choice, as it slowed them down. But she wanted to get a feel for the area.

They continued the journey in companionable silence, taking in the view and getting the lay of the land. The further north they travelled the more the valley narrowed. There was less housing stock, and those in the line of sight were older, smaller properties.

Having reached the small town of Pontlottyn, Jemima had a change of heart. The journey along the valley had been a frustrating one, as the local roads were often narrow, poorly maintained, and meandered due to the topography. This made it impossible to travel as fast as she would have liked. She had originally wanted to drive through Rhymney, to check the place out. But as she'd chosen not to travel along the A470 bypass, the journey had already taken far longer than she had anticipated. And given the fact that the crime scene was something called the Rhymney Bent Iron, she was certain that it would be inevitable they would get to visit the town at some stage during this investigation. As time was now of the essence, the most direct route would be to take a left just after Saint Tyfaelog Parish Church and head towards the hillside above.

The vehicle's satnav reconfigured the most direct route as they rose above the houses. Open scrubland, uneven, bleak, and remote, gave a sense of danger, even in daylight hours. The air was undoubtedly fresher, having risen above the valley floor and the polluted rat-run of the only road that provided a route to the other conurbations further down the valley.

It was a steep ascent on the bleakest of hillsides. The landscape scarred. Stark. Barren. Unforgiving. Glancing in the rearview mirror, Jemima noted there was little of beauty in the valley below. This was a harsh terrain, not offering much to the eye and even less to the soul. Yet they were seeing it at its best, with the sun shining and the temperature pleasantly mild.

Jemima acknowledged that for anyone actively seeking solitude this place might hold some appeal. But given the reason for their visit, she could find no upside for being there. This was work. Pure and simple. A harrowing crime scene in the middle of nowhere.

Having eventually turned right and continued some way along a road which was no longer on an incline, she spotted a collection of official vehicles already parked up. They had pulled off the carriageway to prevent the road from being blocked. Jemima and the others followed suit.

A uniformed officer, presumably from the local station, stood nearby. As they parked up, he approached their vehicles. Clearing his throat loudly, he proceeded to speak. 'You can't stop here. This entire area is out of bounds. You'll have to move on.' He was doing his best to convey an air of authority but failed miserably as there was a noticeable tremor to his voice.

'I'm the SIO in charge, and this is my squad,' said Jemima. 'I see the forensic team has arrived.' She nodded at their vehicles. 'Any idea who's heading up that operation?'

The red-faced young constable cleared his throat and flicked through his notebook. 'Ummm, that'd be a Jeanne Ennersley.'

'Excellent. At least the crime scene will be in safe hands.' Jemima and Jeanne had collaborated on many cases. They understood and respected each other, and were both sticklers for detail, which made the entire process and the sharing of information as efficient and comprehensive as it could possibly be.

'Who found the bodies?'

'Couple over there,' he pointed towards a police car. 'They were out walking their dog.'

'Has anyone taken their statements?'

'Not yet. They're a bit shaken up. We all are, to be honest. Things like that don't happen round here.'

'And their names?'

'Don't know. We haven't gone near them, but DI Hughes is over at the crime scene. He'll know more.'

'Not the bodies. The witnesses,' snapped Jemima as she rolled her eyes in despair. If this was the typical calibre of the local plods, she had a feeling it was going to be a very long day. Following a change of footwear, the six officers set off in the general direction of where the Bent Iron was located. There were no signposts or even a well-worn path to follow. There was little doubt that if this was a hillside somewhere in the Brecon Beacons or any other National Park, the area would have been heaving with ramblers no matter the time of year or the weather. But as with most things in the South Wales Valleys, the area was underutilised and largely ignored.

As this was not a popular walking route, the ground underfoot remained treacherously uneven. Clusters of tuffets and hidden divots made it all too easy to twist an ankle should the walker be careless when placing a foot. This was not the terrain to run freely across unless you had little care of the potential consequences.

'There's been people up here, fairly recently,' said Mack. He pointed at a patch of scorched earth and twenty or more crushed cans of cheap lager.

'Probably kids,' said Nancy.

'More than likely,' said Jemima. She sensed that the evidence of a bonfire and binge drinking had nothing to do with the murders they were about to investigate. Teenagers liked to kick back, and out here in the wilds, they were hardly likely to be disturbed, and could party to their heart's content.

As there was still no sight of the crime scene, it was safe to presume that they had a fair distance to cover. No matter how self-assured the killer or killers, they would have surely wanted to distance themselves from the crime scene as quickly as possible. The last thing they would have done was light a fire and sit around drinking, which had the potential to alert others to their presence.

'Just as well they didn't decide to get off their faces over there,' said Levi nodding in the direction of a large body of water known as Rhaslas Pond. 'That really would've been a disaster waiting to happen. Alcohol and water aren't a good idea.'

Jemima left the others to their pointless speculation and strode out ahead of the group. Having already spoken briefly to the middle-aged witnesses, a Mr and Mrs Windsor, she was certain of two things. Firstly, the two deaths were murder. Secondly, the killer had used either a four-wheel drive or an off-road vehicle to arrive at the Bent Iron.

As she gathered her thoughts, she tuned out from the sound of voices. From what she'd already learned, this case was unlike any she'd worked. As a seasoned investigator of murders, she'd come to appreciate that you should approach the case without any preconceived ideas. Yet she was already convinced that there was a reason why such an obscure location had been chosen for these deaths.

There were many ways to end someone's life. Ways far less problematic than bringing the victims out to a remote hillside overlooking a town, to string them up on a sculpture. Whether the victims had been alive when the noose went around their necks, or whether they were already dead and had been strung up to make a statement, needed to be established. And that fact would make all the difference, as whichever of those scenarios had played out, was obviously of importance to the killer or killers.

A labyrinth of tyre tracks of varying sizes crisscrossed the ground in random directions. Given the areas where most of their cases had been located, this setting was particularly quiet. Apart from the six officers, the only signs of life were a few birds circling far above and the occasional sheep grazing unconcernedly on the scrubby greenery. Given the terrain, and the apparent remoteness of the area, despite its proximity to at least four centres of population, it was conceivable that on weekends and holidays this hillside became a playground for mountain-bikers, quad-bikers and drivers of other types of vehicles too.

By the time the crime scene and the forensic team came into view, Jemima had long since began to wish that she had had the foresight to put on an extra pair of socks. The big toe on her right foot was feeling sore, and she knew that when she was eventually able to remove her hiking boots, she'd find that she had a blister. There was nothing she could do about it apart from put up with the discomfort.

CHAPTER 6

Even from this distance it was possible to see the two corpses suspended from a structure which looked like a piece of bent metal. There were four forensic officers in attendance, each clad in the usual protective gear. As one of them raised a hand in greeting, Jemima realised it was Jeanne Ennersley. She smiled and returned the woman's wave.

As they continued their approach, Jeanne pointed towards something. As Jemima and the others looked in that direction, they saw it was a heavy-duty plastic box containing sets of protective clothing and overshoes. 'Put them on before you get any closer!' shouted Jeanne. 'Given the location, I know I'm on a hiding to nothing, but I don't want any further contamination of the crime scene.'

As she slipped the coveralls over her clothes, Jemima stared in the direction of the bodies. From where she stood, they could easily have been mistaken for a couple of sacks, for there were no extended limbs. Though as she moved closer it was possible to see that both bodies had been hog-tied, before being hoisted up into position.

This was no suicide pact. No sex game gone wrong. This was murder. And by choosing this particular location, although it was far enough away from the nearby centres of population, the bodies had been staged out in the open as the killer or killers wanted them to be found.

'Everyone ready?' asked Jemima as she set off towards the crime scene.

'Boss, I need a word. In private,' said Broadbent.

Jemima knew from the tone of his voice that something was wrong. Yet to those who didn't know him so well, he might have sounded almost normal. 'Go ahead, I'll catch up,' she said to the others. Gareth gave a questioning look but said nothing and strode out with the others.

'There's nothing to worry about, Dan. There's not likely to be any blood.' Jemima had known for many years that her sergeant had an aversion to blood. It was a phobia he had struggled to overcome, something he was ashamed of and was keen that no one else should get to know about. However, on the last big case they had worked, Gareth had realised that something was up with him when he acted oddly while they were at the hospital. Broadbent's insistence on secrecy had caused a minor rift and he had been forced to open up to Gareth. Lucky for him, Gareth was very understanding and like Jemima, had agreed to keep schtum about it.

'I know there's no blood. It's not that . . . I thought I could do this. Thought it wouldn't affect me, but it's too much. I can't . . . I just can't.'

'It's OK, Dan.' In all the years they'd worked together, Jemima hadn't ever seen Dan act in such an irrational way. Even with his aversion to blood he had never refused to come to a crime scene or attend a post-mortem. His complexion was grey. As he inhaled deeply the breath caught in his throat and he gulped as he attempted to keep a lid on his emotions.

'Don't as—'

'It's OK. As long as you're not feeling ill, then it's fine. You can stay here. You don't have to follow us down to the crime scene. You're not ill, are you?'

'No, it's not that. Look, I'll be fine. Don't worry about me. Go find out everything you can from the crime scene. I'll be OK.'

There was no point in pushing him. He'd seemed fine earlier on, but something must have happened. And though it pained her to walk away to allow him to get his head together, this was neither the time nor the place to try to get him to explain what had rattled him. Right now, she needed to focus her attention on the crime scene, as even without speaking to Jeanne Ennersley she could tell that this was no run-of-the-mill murder — if ever there was such a thing.

She decided that the best course of action as far as Dan was concerned was to get him to travel in the car with her, once they left the crime scene. That way she'd be able to speak to him in private, and hopefully get to the bottom of what was up with him. After all, Broadbent wasn't just a fellow officer. He was also her friend.

CHAPTER 7

Conscious of the fact that her delay in joining the others might cause some speculation, Jemima jogged the rest of the way towards the crime scene, wincing as it aggravated her blister. Gareth was the only one of the team to raise a questioning eyebrow. Though when she didn't volunteer an explanation, he knew better than to ask about it within earshot of the others.

The three newest members of the squad seemed oblivious to whatever was going on with Broadbent. Instead, they were transfixed by the macabre sight of the pair of hog-tied corpses, suspended like a couple of grotesque pinatas and seemingly attracting every fly in the area.

Another man stood apart from the others. He was far enough away so as not to need protective gear and appeared to be giving her daggers. She raised a hand in acknowledgment, but the gesture was not returned. He was clearly uncomfortable by the sight of the crime scene. There was no doubt in Jemima's mind that his sharp suit and footwear had been chosen carefully. This was someone who was determined to impress. Someone who believed the old adage, "*clothes maketh the man*". Yet he had obviously not had the foresight to dress appropriately for a trek across such difficult terrain.

'Nice of you to join us, Chief Inspector,' said Jeanne. She nodded in Dan's direction and raised an eyebrow, clearly fishing for information about what was going on with Broadbent.

As Jemima glanced back at the way she'd just come, she saw him in the distance, pacing back and forth like a stir-crazy beast. 'So, what have we got, Jeanne?' Despite having a close relationship with the scene of crime officer, she was determined not to comment on her sergeant's personal issues. Not that she had any idea what was up with him.

Jeanne knew better than to push it. 'Well, as you can see, we've two male victims, and decomposition is already underway. Both have been hog-tied. We're just about ready to get them down, but I wanted you to see them in situ first. DI Hughes over there, said we should cut them down as soon as possible, but I told him in no uncertain terms that they were staying there until you arrived.

'My guess is that he's got a bee in his bonnet about being sidelined on this one. Not that he's said anything. Far too canny for that.'

'Yeah, well, there's no room for bruised egos in an investigation like this. And you can see straight off that this isn't some run-of-the-mill killing. That's why we've been called in.'

'Precisely, but I don't fancy your chances of getting a smooth ride with him. You could find the locals close ranks.'

'I've dealt with worse, and I'm not wasting time thinking about what might happen. Anyway, back to these poor buggers, I appreciate you leaving them in situ. Out of interest, have you ever come across this type of murder before?'

'Nothing like this. I've lost count of the number of hangings. Mainly suicide but some murder. I've also examined scenes where victims have been hog-tied. But this combination of the two elements is a new one on me, and there's the fact that there are two victims. What're your initial thoughts, Jem?'

'That there are far easier ways of offing someone. This required organisation and wasn't without risk. Do you know if they were already dead before they were strung up?'

'We'll need to get them down first. Even then, I wouldn't like to hazard a guess. John's the expert. He'll be able to tell you more when he's performed the post-mortem.'

'Any idea how the perp managed to get them up there?'

'With difficulty I'd say. It's far easier to tie a noose around someone's neck and allow them to drop. But this way would require significant strength.'

A dry period had left the ground compacted. Towards the structure, there was no sign of vegetation. The ground was dusty, suggesting that an off-road vehicle might have been driven there.

'Given the number of empty cans we've already bagged it suggests that this could be a bit of a party spot,' said Jeanne. 'We'll do the usual fingerprints and possible DNA on those, but chances are they're not going to be relevant to the case. They'll most likely be kids.

'But take a look at this.' Beneath where each of the corpses hung, were two indentations, just over a foot apart. 'Looks like they used a ladder to fix the ropes into position.'

Until now, Jemima's focus had been on the bodies. But as she took a closer look at the metal structure, she could see that it wasn't a solid iron bar. The structure was more decorative, with gaps through which the ropes had been threaded. 'So, these murders were premeditated. The killer or killers had to have visited this place beforehand to know that they needed to bring a ladder. And as this structure isn't exactly well-known, it suggests that the perpetrators are local.'

'That would be my thinking too,' said Jeanne. 'Luckily, we have our own telescopic ladders. They've come in handy on more than a few occasions. And take a look through these.' She handed Jemima some binoculars.

Jemima adjusted the lenses to zoom in on the corpses, and took a step back as it felt as though her face was only inches away the carnage she was focused upon. She cleared her throat before speaking, disappointed that she had allowed Jeanne to see that the scene had unsettled her. 'What am I looking at?'

'Firstly, the knots on the rope binding the limbs.'

Jemima changed the angle of the binoculars as she studied each of the ropes. 'They're different, suggesting at least two killers,' she eventually said.

'Exactly. Now move around to the other side and focus in on their foreheads.'

Jemima did as she was told. 'Are they cuts? Has something been carved into their foreheads?'

'That's my guess but given the fact that decomposition's already underway and the birds have inevitably turned up for a picnic or two, I can't make out whether they're just random cuts or something else.

'Anyway, that's all I'm able to give you until we can take a closer look. Now, if you're satisfied with everything you've seen so far, we'll make a start on getting the two of them down. Once we've got them at ground level, we'll know more. It'll be a tricky operation as we don't want any uncontrolled drops which could compromise evidence. So, it won't be a quick process. In fact, it could take hours.

'Your best bet would be to head off, do whatever it is you do, and wait for the post-mortems. I'll give you a bell once we're finished at this end. Let you know if I find anything noteworthy. Other than that, John will let you know when he's ready.'

The time had come for Jemima to turn her attention to DI Mike Hughes, and as she strode towards him, she could see that he was scowling at her. His lips were almost non-existent as the set of his jaw was so tight. On the way she stopped to have a quick word with her team. 'Have any of you spoken the local DI?'

'Tried to. Questioned me about my rank, but when I told him I was a sergeant he point-blank refused to engage,' said Gareth. 'Seemed very put out that you chose to engage with the SOCOs before speaking with him.'

'Did he now?' said Jemima. 'Tell you what, get yourselves back to the cars. I'll go speak with him and follow on behind.'

'What's up with Dan?' asked Gareth. His voice was low, so that the others wouldn't hear.

'I don't know, but I want him in the car with me. I need to get to the bottom of it, and quickly. I've no idea what we're up against with these murders, but the level of violence and the staging of the bodies scares the hell out of me. I need Dan focused on the case, giving it his all. Otherwise, it puts all of us at risk. And I don't want to lose another officer.'

'I'll travel with Levi,' said Gareth. 'And good luck with getting him to open up. Dan can be a right stubborn bugger.'

Gareth and the team headed back to their vehicles. As Broadbent saw them approach, he began to walk back to the car too. Whatever was up with him, he seemed determined to keep his distance from everyone until the moment came when he would have no choice in the matter.

'DI Hughes, I presume?' said Jemima. She held out her hand to the man, but the courtesy was not returned.

'What's with keeping me hanging about like a spare part? Do you and your team think you're a cut above?'

'Not at all, but this is our case, and I'm the SIO. So, you can park whatever petty gripes you have and show me some respect.' The inspector's attitude had already started to rile her, but she wasn't about to react in kind. 'I appreciate that you might very well feel as though your toes have been trodden on, but my team are a new initiative on cross-force working. And as I'm sure you're aware, it's been sanctioned at the highest level.'

Hughes harrumphed loudly but said nothing.

Jemima chose to ignore his annoyance and continued speaking. 'This is no run-of-the-mill murder. Anyone can see that. Which is why we've been brought in, as we specialise in complex investigations. However, it's no reflection on your capability. We will still require input from you and your team. You'll inevitably have local knowledge which will be invaluable.'

'Which is code for you expecting us local yokels to do the grunt work while you lot sit back and take all the glory.

Well, I'm telling you now, you won't get an easy ride from me and my team.'

Jemima had expected him to play nice, but as the man clearly wasn't up for that it was time to take the gloves off. 'It's up to you, Hughes. I've told you how it is, and I'm not prepared to waste time or effort on a jumped-up prima donna with a bruised ego. You've been standing here for God knows how long, but have you even taken a look at those bodies?'

Hughes didn't reply and refused to meet her gaze. The man's jaw was so tight that the muscles twitched on the side of his face. A confrontation was only a heartbeat away. But she was in no mood to back down. 'I've asked you a question, Inspector Hughes, and as the SIO in charge of this case I damn well expect an answer!'

Hughes' expression darkened further. He radiated resentment as he refused to answer her. This was a make-or-break moment. One which the investigation could do without. But it was a situation which Jemima was determined would be resolved one way or the other. There would be no overlooking the man's insubordination. Right now, her primary concern was that there was a killer, or killers out there, quite possibly eyeing up their next set of victims.

'OK, well I'll have to take your silence as a "*no*". Which doesn't surprise me in the slightest because I doubt you've got the balls or the brains to deal with a case like this. I've come across many officers like you, Hughes. Men who build their careers on being the big "*I am*". But usually, it's all talk. A front to hide your inadequacies because you've most likely been over-promoted and can't cope with the level of responsibility that you've got.'

'How dare you! You don't know me!'

'Oh, I might not have come across you until an hour ago, but your actions, or should I say, lack of, speak volumes as to the type of man you are. What I'm absolutely certain of is that you've got your head inserted so far up your own arse that you can't see how ridiculous you're being. For God's sake, man, this isn't the bloody Michael Hughes show. This,'

Jemima gestured towards the corpses and the SOCOs preparing to lower them to the ground, 'this is about those two poor bastards strung up there for anyone to see. That's why my team and I have been drafted in. To find their fucking killers before they do this to anyone else. And if you don't understand that and do everything you can to help us, then in my opinion you don't deserve to be an inspector, because you're a disgrace to the force.'

The man's fist bunched at his side as he shot her an angry look.

Jemima continued to hammer it home. 'This is a career-defining moment for you, Hughes. You can either swallow your pride, dust yourself down and get on board. Or I will personally ensure that your Chief Constable knows that you refused to cooperate with this investigation. And believe me when I say that it isn't an idle threat. If you try to obstruct my investigation, you'll be lucky to have a job as a tea boy by the time I've finished with you. Have I made myself clear?'

Hughes finally appreciated that his surly attitude wasn't going to get him anywhere. This was a battle he wouldn't win. They'd all heard about this new unit which had been set up as a pilot for cross-force working. They'd all been told to get on board and cooperate if this team were called to investigate an incident on their patch. It was all very well for the higher-ups to demand their compliance, but it didn't mean that when front-line officers were called upon to provide that cooperation that they would do so willingly. Police officers, like everyone else, had feelings, egos, pride, and when they were suddenly expected to step aside and act as gofers for a team of supposed experts who would take all the glory should they eventually solve the case, it was only natural that it would feel like a slap in the face.

'Now I suggest we put this animosity behind us. I'm sure you'll agree that as police officers we have far bigger concerns. You'll have your chance to shine. To show me and everyone else what you're made of. But I'm deadly serious when I say that there's no room for egos in an investigation like this.

'You can see from those corpses that we're up against a dangerous individual. Possibly even more than one. What you might not know is that one of my officers was killed in the line of duty, because we didn't have all the information to hand, and he let his guard down. He wanted his moment of glory, and it only took a matter of seconds for someone to end his life.'

'I had no idea.' Hughes' voice softened. This was a scenario any sensible officer would dread.

'We hunt down some of the most depraved people on the planet. They take ruthlessness to another level. We've sworn to protect the public, and it's my responsibility to protect every officer working the case too. I need everyone to bring their A-game to this investigation. If you don't, it could end up being your last day. Or you might have to live with the fact that you're the reason someone else has died.

'Now, if you and your officers can play by those rules, then I'm happy for you to work alongside us. If not, then tell me now, and I'll arrange for someone else to take your place.'

'What do you expect of us?' asked Hughes.

'You're the ones with local knowledge, and my feeling is that whatever's going on here is a local issue. It's the only thing that makes sense of choosing this remote location to display the bodies.'

Hughes nodded.

'We both know that there are so many ways they could have been killed. Far easier places to dump the bodies, but whoever's behind this wanted those bodies found. They've made a hell of a statement. We just need to figure out what they're telling us.

'First off, I want you to arrange for a handful of officers to be stationed up here, until the SOCOs have finished with the crime scene and have combed the area. Once word gets out, I guarantee we'll have all sorts up here wanting to take a look, to get some sort of cheap thrill. Your people will need to watch out for drones. I don't want this crime scene ending up on social media or the news channels.'

'I can do that.'

'Good man. Now, walk with me, Hughes,' demanded Jemima. They headed back towards the bodies, staying far enough back so that his lack of protective clothing wouldn't risk contaminating the scene. 'Take a good look. When you leave here, I want you to remember the horror and revulsion you feel right now. Take that and use it. Let it drive you on to do everything in your power to get to the bottom of this. Because if you don't, the next time this person kills again, you could be staring at someone you know and care about.'

'I hadn't thought—'

'I know,' interjected Jemima. 'But that's what every case that we investigate boils down to. We're not doing this because it's some sort of ego trip. Or because we want the accolades. We're doing this because we want to protect the public and the people we love.'

They returned to their cars and were informed by a uniformed officer that the couple who had found the bodies had been taken to a nearby police station to give their statements.

'I'll call ahead and make sure they're expecting you, guv.'

Jemima had to stop herself from doing a doubletake. Had she just imagined it? Or had Mike Hughes just called her guv? 'Thanks, Mike. I appreciate it.' It was quite a while since she'd had to act like such a ball-breaker. But it appeared that she could still cut it.

'No problem. I'll arrange for more officers up here and stay until they arrive. I'll see you at the station as soon as I'm able to get away. I take it that'll be the nerve centre for the investigation?'

'It will, Mike. You'll be stuck with us for the foreseeable.'

'Well, you'll get cooperation from me and my officers. You've made me realise we're on the same side. Any of my lot step out of line they'll have me to answer to.'

CHAPTER 8

As they pulled away from the grass verge, Jemima glanced sideways at Dan. He'd not questioned her decision when she'd said that he would be travelling with her. In fact, he hadn't said anything at all.

'Are you going to make me ask? Because I need to know what's up with you, and I need to know now. I can't have you distracted throughout this investigation. You're my most experienced sergeant, Dan. I expect you to set an example to the others. They look up to you.'

'I know. Look I'm sorry. I shouldn't have allowed my personal feelings to get in the way. It's just . . .' His voice was laden with emotion.

'Just what, Dan? Talk to me. You know you can tell me anything.'

'I know, but this is hard. Real hard. I've struggled with this for much of my life. Tried to stop thinking about it. And I'd managed to do just that. But as we got closer to those bodies, I was back at the worst time of my life. I spent years afraid to fall asleep because of the nightmares. All the guilt. The feelings of helplessness. Playing things over and over in my head, like a circuit I couldn't break. I thought I'd moved on. Forgiven myself, and finally come to terms with what happened. But it seems that I haven't . . .'

'Christ, Dan, what the hell happened?' She was at a loss to understand what could have affected him so badly.

'The week before my sixteenth birthday, my best friend killed himself. I had no idea anything was wrong. We'd walked home from school together. Messed about as usual. He went to his and said he'd call at mine at five o'clock.

'I waited until twenty to six, getting more and more angry that Gwion hadn't turned up. So, I headed over to his. It was only a five-minute walk. Next street over. But when I got to the end of his street, I saw an ambulance and a police car. Blue lights. Some of the neighbours were on their doorsteps. I heard his mother wailing. Sounded like an animal in pain. Back then, I'd never heard grief like it. I knew straightaway that something terrible had happened. I figured that Gwi's dad must've had a heart attack, or something. Anyway, I pushed my way through, towards his front door and that's when I saw Gwi.

'They hadn't even cut him down. He was still there, suspended from the banister.'

'Oh, Dan! No wonder you didn't want to go near to those bodies. Why didn't you say something? You didn't have to be part of this case. You don't have to, now. You can walk away, and no one will think badly of you,' said Jemima.

'I'm not walking away from this case, Jem. I need to work it. I allowed what Gwion did to define me for such a long time. You can't imagine how guilty I felt.'

'But you weren't to blame for what happened to him.'

'That's easy for you to say. If he'd given me a chance, I might have been able to talk him out of it. Instead, he left me with questions that will never be answered. Feeling that I hadn't been a good enough friend. That somehow, I was responsible for him not wanting to live anymore. And just for a moment on that godawful hillside I was right back there. I was that boy about to look up and find my best friend hanging there. I knew it wasn't the case, but I couldn't put myself through it.'

'Like I said, Dan, you don't have to work this case.'

'Oh, believe me, I do. I've got to get past this. You forced me to confront my phobia of blood, and I'm not entirely there yet, but I'm way better than I was. And I need to confront this too. We investigate violent deaths. It's unrealistic to think that I could avoid deaths by hanging. So, I need to dig deep and get on with it.'

'I'll support you all the way.' Taking a hand off the steering wheel she reached out as squeezed his hand.

'I know you will, Jem. Believe it or not, it's helped talking about it. I don't feel like such a coward now.'

'I've never thought you were a coward, Dan. You're my partner, and I've lost count of the number of times you've had my back. Let's face it, my son might not be alive if it wasn't for you. So, as far as I'm concerned, you're my hero, and don't you forget it.'

CHAPTER 9

As they pulled into the car park at the police station, Jemima's attention switched back to the case. It concerned her that what with the unexpected personal revelations from her two most senior officers, and the initial antagonism from Mike Hughes, she had unavoidably spent a significant proportion of her time on issues unrelated to the murders.

With the victims not yet identified and no apparent motive, combined with having to work out of an unfamiliar station, she just hoped that Hughes would be true to his word and become a team player for the duration of the investigation. Solving the case would be hard enough, without having a local DI conspiring against them to score points in a petty vendetta. Especially when that individual would undoubtedly have the support of other officers, who might also see Jemima and her team as being foisted upon them, just so that they could teach them how to suck eggs. She had a feeling that her need for a united and focused team was a big ask.

Walking through the door was like stepping back in time. Not that the building was old. Yet it reminded her of the TV series Life on Mars. The air was musty with dust motes visibly floating around. The middle-aged officer behind the screen was mid-yawn. His mouth opened so wide she could practically see his tonsils. He unashamedly looked her up and down, and finding her lacking, turned his attention to Broadbent who was at her side.

'Can I help you?' It seemed obvious he thought this little lady was incapable of speaking for herself.

'I'm already beginning to doubt it,' said Jemima, as she leaned forward and placed her hands on the narrow ledge.

Dan thought it was good that there was a protective screen separating the uniformed officer from any visitors to the station. He'd partnered her for long enough to know precisely what Jemima's reaction was going to be, and lowered his gaze as he suppressed a smile, the first of the day.

Most people would find the constable's blatant sexism unacceptable. Yet Dan almost felt sorry for the man, as he knew what was about to come. Though he'd put money on it that the oaf's overt rudeness was a mistake he would soon regret and most likely not repeat again. And as far as Dan was concerned it made a welcome relief from the unwelcome trauma of the case.

'Excuse me, madam! Who do you think you are? You can't speak to me like that. I am a police constable, and you are a visitor to this station.' His eyes narrowed.

'Who do I think I am? Who. Do. I. Think. I. Am.' She looked at him with incredulity. When she next spoke, her voice had taken on a dangerous edge. 'I'm your worst bloody nightmare, Constable! That's who I am. I'm Detective Chief Inspector Huxley of the Major Incident Taskforce. It might have escaped your notice but there's been a double murder on your doorstep, while you're sat here, trying to stay awake. So, stop wasting my time. Open the bloody door and let us in!' She thrust her warrant card up to the screen.

'Y-yes, ma'am! Sorry, ma'am!' The constable backed away from the screen. He appeared to shrink as his previous air of indolence gave way to panic. Despite not being the brightest, he appreciated that he had messed up. A sense of self-preservation kicked in as he frantically attempted to redeem himself, pressing the button to allow the door to open. 'Upstairs, first door on the left, ma'am.'

'What a tosser,' muttered Nancy, who along with the rest of the team had entered the station while the confrontation was taking place.

With a mild sense of satisfaction at having metaphorically kicked the constable up the backside, Jemima steeled herself for whatever they were about to encounter on the upper floor of the building. Her expectations were low, as any career-minded officer worth their salt would do their utmost to avoid being stationed in a small area. It was career suicide. If you wanted to make a name for yourself, you had to be where the action was. And having just interrupted the constable's apparent snoozefest at the reception desk, it didn't seem likely that this place saw much action.

Reaching the upper floor, she saw that the door to the left-hand side of the narrow corridor was closed. There were noises from within, suggesting someone was already in the room. Jemima depressed the handle and stepped inside, closely followed by the others, to find a uniformed officer dragging a stack of chairs across the floor.

'DCI Huxley and team?' she enquired.

'That's right.' They introduced themselves. 'Need a hand?' asked Jemima.

'No, almost done thanks. I'm PC Zoe Swann. DI Hughes has been in contact. Let us know you were coming.'

'Us?'

'That'd be Sergeant Wilcox and PC Martin. The three of us have been assigned to this investigation.'

'So why aren't Wilcox and Martin here, helping to get the room ready?'

'It's not their job. It's mine.'

'How long have you been on the force?' asked Jemima.

'Coming up three years. Did a six-month stint as a special before that.'

'Do you have any experience of investigating murders?'

Zoe laughed and shook her head. 'No. Plenty of experience of making the tea, updating files, and cleaning out the cells after the drunks. Oh, and I get to walk around the streets for a couple of hours each day. Just as long as I pick up the cake order from the local café. I think they'd go out of business if it wasn't for us lot. No as I said, this will be my first opportunity of doing something real. To be honest, I can't wait to get started. I'm hoping to learn a lot.'

'I appreciate this is a quieter area than we're used to, but surely there's still crimes committed here?' Mack was the one to voice what they were all thinking.

'Of course, but the lads get first pick. It's just the way things work around here.'

'Seriously? You're a police officer. Not a doormat. If you aren't able to stand up for yourself when it comes to being treated like a skivvy, then God help you out on the streets. Who's your sergeant?'

'Gary Wilcox, but you need to know that this place doesn't run the way I imagine a lot of stations operate. It's best you understand that. It could save you a lot of grief in the end.'

'What do you mean? Come on, spit it out, Zoe.'

'They'll not thank me for saying this, but this place is what you'd call male, pale and stale. If you don't fit into those categories, then you don't stand a chance.'

'Oh, we'll see about that. There'll be none of that bollocks going on while I'm here. I've no time for sexism, racism, or any other kind of -ism these throwbacks have going on. You're about to be dragged into the twenty-first century, Zoe. Now, where's Wilcox?' demanded Jemima.

'He's with Lewis Martin. They're on a break in the rec room.'

Having been told where the room was located, Jemima headed off to find the two officers. These days it seemed that hardly a day went by without reports in the media of misogynism being rampant in police forces throughout the country. It was no wonder that so many people disliked and mistrusted the police. It seemed as if this station was crawling with lazy, self-important men, and she was damned if she was going to put up with it.

As always, Jemima needed team players who gave it their all. Anything else was unacceptable and would ultimately be counterproductive to the investigation. So far, she had no actual evidence that Wilcox and Martin would cause problems. She'd set them straight about what was expected of them. Keep a watchful eye on them and see how they performed. After all, it could just be a case of worrying over nothing. And as for Zoe Swann . . . Well, Jemima would put her through her paces too.

She could hear the music and the sound of laughter as she approached the room. As she opened the door, a dart flew past her face, missing her by inches. 'What the fuck?'

'Hey! You should've knocked. You've no right to be here. Who the hell are you anyway?' The older man's tone was one of annoyance. 'How'd you get past the front desk? You can't be walking around this station unaccompanied.'

Jemima could see from the stripes on the man's uniform that he was a sergeant. 'Wilcox and Martin, I presume?' This was no time for pleasantries.

'Yeah,' said the younger of the two.

'In that case, get your backsides into the incident room now!'

'You can't—'

'Oh yes I can, sunshine.' Sensing that Wilcox was about to interject, Jemima held up a hand to silence him. 'Don't you dare interrupt me, Sergeant. From now on you will both address me as ma'am. I'm Chief Inspector Huxley and it appears I have the misfortune to have you two idle layabouts on my team. Now listen carefully, because if I have to repeat myself, things will not go well for you. Until this case is over, and we've shipped out, all breaks are cancelled. If I catch either of you messing about at work, instead of giving me your full commitment then you'll find yourself on report. Understand?'

There was a moment when they both stared at her blankly. Martin was the first to recover. His cheeks burned with embarrassment as he answered her in a sheepish voice. 'Yes, ma'am.'

Wilcox was yet to say anything when Jemima spoke again. 'Well, Sergeant, I'm waiting. Either get on board, and work alongside my team for the duration of this case or you may find yourself having to look for a job outside the force. The choice is yours.' She stared him down, noting the insolent glint in his eyes. 'I'm not in the business of making empty threats, Wilcox. If you refuse to give me your full cooperation or disrespect me and my team in any way, you'll be out on your backside. Are we clear?'

'Understood, ma'am.' The sergeant's voice was low and laden with disrespect. 'But Martin and Swann report to me.' It was a last shot at saving face and retaining some semblance of control. It was implicit by his tone that this was a deal-breaker. He'd been around the block enough times to appreciate that whilst this bint, who had undoubtedly slept her way up the ranks, was at the station, it would be necessary for him to play the game and show willing. It was in everyone's interests to put this case to bed as quickly as possible. Only then would this band of interlopers get the hell out of his station and life could return to normal.

'You have no authority in any part of this investigation, Sergeant. I'm the SIO and everything goes through me. You are a tool for me to utilise and will carry out whichever tasks I see fit. I'll be keeping a close eye on you, Wilcox. And if I feel you're not up to the job I will ensure that your Chief Constable gets to hear about it. As far as I'm concerned there's no room for dead wood on the force. That goes for you too, Martin. Now move it, both of you!'

Jemima watched as the two officers made their way to the incident room. She felt bad for having demeaned Wilcox in such a way in front of a junior officer, especially by referring to him as a tool. It felt unprofessional. But the man had left her with no choice, and there were far more important matters requiring her attention than pussyfooting around a bone-idle misogynistic relic whose outdated attitudes should have seen him drummed out of the force a long time ago.

CHAPTER 10

The two recalcitrant officers entered the incident room ahead of Jemima. As she glanced around, she was pleased to find that Mike Hughes had arrived back from the crime scene. After a quick round of introductions, the briefing began.

'First off, you need to park any resentments you have and work together as a team. All that matters is that we solve this case. And to do that we need to identify those victims, find the bastards that did this and build a cast-iron case to give the families of these victims the justice they deserve. Have you printed off initial photographs of the crime scene, Gareth?'

'Sure have, guv.' He strode forward and fastened a series of images to the board. The first two were shots of both bodies taken from a distance to show them suspended side-by-side from the sculpture. One was a front view, the other taken from behind. The following four images were close-ups of each individual corpse. Again, from the front and also from behind. Next came two close-ups focusing on the way in which the bodies had been hog-tied. Specifically, the way the ropes had been tied.

'Thanks, Gareth. Now I want you all to take a close look, because these photographs tell us a lot. Even to the untrained eye you can see that it would have taken time, strength, and effort to hoist those bodies up. Those corpses could have been dumped anywhere. But it's safe to presume that these victims were alive when they were strung up. Of course, we'll know for certain once the post-mortems have been carried out.'

'I don't understand. What makes you think they were alive at the time?' asked Lewis.

'Because they were hog-tied, presumably to restrict their movements. It made the victims easier to handle. Which meant that there was less chance of the killers receiving injuries they might subsequently have difficulty explaining away.'

'You said killers. What makes you think there was more than one?' asked Zoe.

'Take a closer look at the way the victims were bound, and knots tied.'

As Zoe, Lewis, and Mike Hughes stepped closer to get a better look at the images, Jemima noted that Wilcox stayed put. It suggested that most of them were keen to learn, which indicated that they could be put to good use on the case. But as for Gary Wilcox . . .

'They're tied differently.' Lewis was the first to speak, and the excitement in his voice was noticeable.

'Yes, they are.' Jemima smiled encouragingly.

'So that's what suggests there are two different killers working together.'

'Well done,' said Jemima. She was starting to think that perhaps her first impression of him was wrong. It seemed the constable might have potential after all.

'Why take them there? I doubt many people know about the Bent Iron. I grew up about five miles from there, and I didn't know it existed,' said Zoe.

'That's what we need to establish, because hanging them from that particular sculpture clearly means something to whoever's behind this.'

As she continued speaking, Jemima looked at each of the local officers in turn, as she wanted them to realise the importance of what she was about to say. 'Somewhere on your patch are at least two killers. They could be people you know. People you regularly say hello to in the street, or drink with at the pub. God forbid, they could even be members of your own family.' Jemima suppressed a smile as she saw the realisation of what they were up against dawn on some of their faces.

'Jeez, people we know. I hadn't thought of that,' said Lewis. The young officer's discomfort was apparent from the way he suddenly shoved his hands in his trouser pockets.

'Though, chances are, the killers are unknown to any of you,' said Jemima.

'But from our experience it could even be a copper. Someone you know and trust,' said Broadbent. He was keen to back Jemima and hammer home a lesson they had been forced to learn the hard way — no one was above reproach.

'Dan's right. It's imperative you always have your wits about you. This case will require commitment. You'll be working long hours. Concentrating far harder than you might have done in the past. Using your brains, not coasting through a shift. So, what do we know so far?' It was a rhetorical question.

'Sod all,' interjected Wilcox.

'That comment shows your inexperience, sergeant. You see, we already know a number of things. Two men were murdered and displayed in a very particular way, out in the open for everyone to see. Whoever's behind this wanted those bodies to be found. Believe me, there are far easier ways of killing someone. Some of which only take a matter of seconds.'

Wilcox glared at her.

'How do you want us to proceed?' asked Hughes.

Jemima was relieved to hear the inspector ask the question. He had been silent up until this point, and she had been starting to think that perhaps he was as resentful as Wilcox.

'First up, I want a map of the area. It's important that given the remoteness of the crime scene each of us familiarises ourselves with the location.'

'Wilcox, go and get one,' said Mike. The lack of friendliness in his tone, and the fact that he hadn't asked either of the two constables to do this, suggested that Jemima wasn't the only one to have a problem with the sergeant.

Wilcox did as he was told, muttering something incomprehensible as he walked out of the room and slamming the door behind him.

'For now, we'll concentrate our efforts on three areas,' said Jemima. She didn't see any point in waiting until Wilcox had returned with the map. 'Firstly, we need to identify the victims. Secondly, the possible routes the killers took to get them to the Bent Iron. Thirdly, we need to find out if any off-road vehicles have been reported stolen recently. Given the landscape and the remoteness of the location it's safe to say the victims were transported there either in an off-road vehicle such as a quadbike with a trailer, or in a 4x4 vehicle. It'd be too risky to take an ordinary car. The slightest lapse of concentration could damage a vehicle, which in turn would have to be abandoned. And if we found the vehicle it could give us the killers' DNA.'

'I agree,' said Mike.

'Once we've identified possible routes, and forensics have given us a timeframe we can trawl CCTV for sightings of likely vehicles.'

'There won't be much CCTV up that way, ma'am,' said Zoe. 'It's not the sort of thing many people would go for. It's not an affluent area. Most of those residents have different priorities.'

'Noted,' said Jemima. 'But it's still worth a try.'

The conversation stopped as Gary Wilcox re-entered the room holding an OS map. He spread it out on the table, and they all gathered around.

'You can do the honours, Inspector.' Jemima's remark was directed at Mike Hughes. 'I'm sure you're more familiar with the area than I am.'

Mike reached for a highlighter, then spent a few seconds studying the map before locating the point he was searching for. 'This is the murder site.' He marked an X on an area of remote moorland, overlooking the town of Rhymney. It was not far from Fochriw and Pontlottyn.

'Do any of you know of any issues in that area which could have led to these murders?' asked Jemima. It was a vain hope, but she still felt her heart sink as each of them shook their head.

'In that case, as we haven't yet identified the victims, Gareth and Zoe will work together to undertake a search of the missing person's database. Start with reports in a fifteen-mile radius of the murder site, possibly within the last month,' said Jemima.

'Sorry, ma'am, but if they were alive when they were strung up, surely they couldn't have been there for that long,' said Zoe.

'They might have been killed recently, Constable, but it doesn't mean that they weren't captured a while back.' Her team would have to keep a close eye on these officers. Lewis Martin and Zoe Swann might very well be keen to learn, but it was obvious that they were out of their depth and unable to make sound judgements. Gary Wilcox had done neither of his young charges any favours.

'Guess I've a lot to learn, ma'am,' said Zoe. Her face glowed with embarrassment.

'Don't beat yourself up. We all started out that way,' said Dan.

'Exactly,' said Jemima. 'Just speak up if you're unsure of anything. It's better to ask the question than get the wrong end of the stick, as that could cause us problems further down the line. The last thing we want is for us to miss something which allows the killers to strike again. Or by not following procedure to the letter, we allow the killers to walk on a technicality.'

'Mike, I want you and Gary to identify possible routes the killers might have taken to reach the Bent Iron. Once you've done that the pair of you should concentrate on possible CCTV, doorbell, traffic camera coverage along each of those routes. You know the sort of thing we need.

'Mack, Levi, trawl through reports on any missing off-road vehicles. It's possible the killers might have had access to their own vehicle, in which case we're not going to get anything useful. But as those vehicles don't come cheap there's a chance that they could have stolen one. While you're at it, look for reports of burnt-out or dumped off-roaders.'

'What about the pond? It's the most convenient dump site,' said Gareth.

'Good point. I'll organise divers,' said Levi.

'Nancy, Lewis, I want you to cast your nets wide. Find out everything you can about the Bent Iron and the surrounding area. That structure means something to the killers. Speak to locals, find out if there's any worrying or unusual activity in the vicinity. Establish what gangs are operating in the area. We need to get a handle on what we're dealing with.

'This is a huge task, and we can't afford to have any slackers.' Jemima looked directly at Gary Wilcox as she said this. 'But for now, I'm aware that time is getting on. So, get yourselves home and have a good night's sleep. I want everyone firing on all cylinders. We'll pick up tomorrow where we've left off. Eight o'clock sharp people!'

CHAPTER 11

As Jemima headed home that evening, she did her best to put the day's events behind her. When her maternity leave had ended a few months earlier, she had promised herself to do everything she possibly could to compartmentalise the various parts of her life and live in the moment. It was something she had failed to achieve in the past. But having reached a stage in her life when it was more important than ever, she was determined to make it work.

She had long ago accepted that her job was a huge part of her life, and her chosen career was not one which easily allowed her to work regular hours. It was a rare occasion when she was able to clear her desk at the end of the day, head home and forget all about it until she arrived back at the station on the following morning. The cases she dealt with were invariably complex and harrowing. It wasn't unusual for her work to take almost everything she had and then some. It wasn't as if she regularly had to pull all-nighters. It was just the nature of the job, that there would be occasions when she would need to work exceptionally long hours.

On the domestic front there was so much requiring Jemima's attention, especially with the impending move to the vicarage. Her life had changed so much in recent years.

James and Finlay needed her to be there for them. Her personal circumstances didn't afford her the luxury of being a stay-at-home parent. It was down to her, and her alone, to ensure that her boys were brought up in a financially stable home. This meant that they all had to make sacrifices. But despite the time she was able to give them being curtailed now that she had returned to work, she was determined to make every second she spent with them count. There was homework to help with. Games to be played. Books to be read. And films to be watched. All before she was able to kick back and relax.

Still, when push came to shove, she wouldn't want it any other way. She was happier now than she'd ever been.

As she pulled up at Lucy's house, it was as though a weight had been lifted from her shoulders. She had returned from the awfulness of the day, and within minutes would see the people she loved the most. As she cut the engine and got out of the car, loud music filled the otherwise peaceful evening air. Reaching out to insert the key in the lock the music suddenly stopped and was replaced with shrieks of laughter, shouts, and groans. Jemima smiled to herself, as she imagined the scene inside the playroom, where Eloise undoubtedly had the kids playing musical chairs. The seasoned nanny always organised some games to tire the children out before it was time for their baths and bed.

Jemima removed her jacket and shoes and headed towards the playroom. Music, laughter, and a great deal of chatter left her in no doubt that this was where everyone had gathered. As she poked her head around the door, James was the first to spot her. The boy immediately stopped what he was doing and rushed over to greet her.

'Mum, you're back. Come and help me.' A partly constructed K'nex model was laid out on the table at the far end of the room. James grabbed hold of her hand and dragged her into the room.

'What're you building this time, champ?' asked Jemima as she ruffled his hair.

'A spaceship. Do you like it?' His enthusiasm for the construction set had lasted over the years. Especially since family members kept adding to it by buying him different kits for birthdays, Christmas and the like. There were now so many pieces that he no longer needed to build the specific things which each set enabled him to do. Which meant he could use his imagination to combine elements and it wasn't unusual for him to create impressive constructions which were entirely of his own invention.

'It's brilliant,' she replied, then kissed his forehead. 'Now give me fifteen minutes to sort myself out and say hello to Fin, and you can show me what to do.'

'You already know what to do,' said James.

'Ah, but you're the chief engineer heading up this project, and I need to follow your instructions to the letter.'

'You mean I'm the boss?' The boy's eyes lit up at the thought of it.

'When it comes to this, you certainly are.' As Jemima turned to leave the room, she caught Eloise's eye. The nanny smiled sadly, shrugged her shoulders and mimed that Finlay was already asleep. Having not seen him amongst the other children, Jemima had already guessed that was the case. However, the confirmation still caused a surge of disappointment. Given the hour, she had known that her little one might already be asleep. But it hadn't stopped her from hoping that she might get to spend a short while with him, and perhaps give him a cuddle and read him a bedtime story.

As she opened the door of the bedroom she shared with Finlay, she saw the nightlight display shapes of stars moving slowly across the walls and ceiling. It was restful, beautiful in its own way, and she appreciated how a small child would find it calming and help them fall asleep. She glanced down at her youngest and gently touched his head. Oblivious to her touch he snuffled in his sleep. It was all Jemima could do not to pick him up and hold him close. She desperately wanted to feel him next to her. But knowing it was selfish to risk waking her toddler when he was so content and relaxed, she fought against the urge. Suddenly realising that she was about to cry, she smiled and gave herself a silent talking-to, questioning how she deserved to have such a wonderful family.

After the day's events she was glad to get out of her work clothes, and distance herself from everything she had been subjected to. Those clothes were for Jemima the detective. The person she needed to be to earn a living. Whereas for the next few hours she could be herself. An ordinary woman. A mother. A sister. A friend.

Pulling on a pair of boyfriend jeans and a comfortable sweatshirt, she headed downstairs to help James with his model while catching up on everything that had happened to him at school that day. As he got ready for bed, she put some washing on. With him safely tucked up, she agreed that he could read for half an hour before switching his light off.

Spotting the outside security light come on, she raced to the door before the delivery driver rang the doorbell and woke Finlay and Lucy's youngest too. Her sister had ordered takeout. As Jemima carried the bags of food through to the kitchen, the smell of Oriental cuisine hit her nostrils. Her stomach growled noisily, and her mouth watered too.

'Anyone want more noodles, or shall I finish them?' asked Ellis.

'Nah, I'm stuffed, said Jemima, as she munched the last of the prawn crackers.

'Go for it, hun. You need to build your strength up, ready for tomorrow's physio session,' said Lucy.

'Is Mason coming over this evening?' asked Ellis.

'As long as he doesn't get called out by one of his parishioners. You know how it is,' said Jemima, as she stacked the empty plates, then swilled the crockery, cutlery, and utensils before loading the dishwasher. It was then time to check that James was asleep too.

It was almost nine o'clock when her phone pinged to say that Mason was on his way round. This meant that it was time to hump some of the full boxes to the front door. Given the day she'd had, she'd have liked nothing more than to curl up on the sofa with a glass of wine. The last thing she wanted to do was transport some of their possessions to the vicarage, and then spend an hour or so constructing flat pack bedroom furniture. But Mason's schedule was as busy as hers, and this was their only opportunity to get organised before the big move on Saturday. Jemima thought that IKEA was a godsend. Though she wasn't crass enough to say so to Mason. But the downside of this popular Scandinavian furniture was having to assemble it, especially when you were tired and pushed for time.

'How did your day go?' he asked, as they worked together on what would be James' bed.

'Busy. We've got a new case. Tilt that a couple of degrees to the right,' she ordered as she picked out the appropriate screw, from the selection to the side of her, and inserted the screwdriver into its head.

'Anything you want to share?' Mason knew better than to push her for details. She often spoke to him about a case in the broadest of terms, but never went into details. Which was fine by him, as he found what she did quite off-putting.

'Just the usual murders,' she began, then thought better of it. 'Actually, that's not true. These bodies were on a hillside at the top of the Rhymney valley.'

'More than one, then?' His brow furrowed at the thought of it.

'Yeah, two males we've yet to identify. Hanging from something called the Bent Iron.'

'Could it have been suicide?'

'Definitely not.'

'What sort of ages were they?'

'What's with all the questions?' asked Jemima. She put down the screwdriver, tilted her head, and stared at him quizzically. She was used to Mason enquiring about her cases in the vaguest of terms. He always feigned a polite interest, but that was as far as it went. She knew that he wouldn't want or expect her to go into detail about any aspect of a case. It was just his way of showing support for her, by letting her know that she could talk to him about anything, should she so wish.

'Oh, it's probably nothing. It's just when you said they were hanging it made me wonder whether it was linked to a spate of suicides in that area.'

'What spate of suicides?' Even though Jemima's case was unequivocally murder, her interest was piqued. She always made a point of not watching the news. Or reading the papers. When she was off duty, she wanted to fill her time with enjoyable things and forget about the horror and tragedy her career forced her to deal with. Since becoming a detective her work life had been filled with far too much doom and gloom.

'Youngsters up that way have been killing themselves. As far as I'm aware it's been going on for a couple of years.'

'And you know this, how?'

'The clergy in South Wales were told about it at a meeting of the synod.'

'Are you saying that these young people were all members of the Church of Wales?'

'No. But with the number of young people taking their own lives in such a small geographical area, there's clearly some sort of problem. As we're in the business of helping people, the archbishop just wanted us to be on the look-out for uncharacteristic behaviour or signs of distress amongst any youngsters in our individual parishes. It was hoped that a show of support, a sympathetic ear, or some timely intervention might help prevent another young person from taking that ultimate step to end it all.'

'Sounds reasonable,' said Jemima.

'The thought was that there might be something going on which no one had picked up on. A sinister problem which if left unchecked could spread like a ripple across water.'

'And have the suicides stopped?'

'I haven't been informed of any in the last three months or so. I guess I've been fortunate. There haven't been any in my parish, but that's not to say that there won't have been.

None of us can afford to be complacent. No one wants to look back and think, if only . . .'

'I guess not,' said Jemima, as a shiver run down her spine. Her thoughts had drifted towards James. It wouldn't be long before he started high school. And shortly after he reached that milestone, he would enter the dreaded teenage years and all the impending problems that could bring. He was surprisingly happy and well-adjusted, despite all the upheaval which had occurred in his short life. It was fortunate that he was surrounded by people who loved and cared deeply about him. But in their desire for greater independence, teenagers were notorious for isolating themselves from family members. When that happened, it would be difficult to spot the warning signs that something might be wrong. But if those crucial signs went unnoticed it could soon become too late to intervene.

Over the years Jemima had seen far too many young people lose their lives for various reasons. Far too often untimely deaths resulted from drugs, gangs, or both. She'd lost count of the number of parents left devastated and bewildered, claiming they had no idea of what their child had been up to. And Jemima had sworn to herself that she would not be one of those parents, pointlessly wishing that they had done things differently. Though, deep down she knew that if an individual, even someone you believed you knew everything about, was intent on hiding something from you, it was an easy thing to do.

No one knew what the future would bring. It was most likely better that way. But being a good parent was like walking a tightrope with your offspring. The path was perilous. Even the slightest change of wind direction, or a lapse of concentration could cause you to lose control and fall. Once you embarked on the journey there was no turning back. You were committed to seeing it through to the end. For every step taken along the way, you needed your wits about you to ensure you were ready to compensate effectively should the need arise.

CHAPTER 12

Following her conversation with Mason, Jemima had been unable to stop thinking about the recent spate of suicides amongst teenagers in the Rhymney area. There was no doubt that the crime she and her team were dealing with was a double murder.

Yet to have so many unnatural deaths in such a small area in a relatively short space of time, made her question whether something sinister was going on in the background, and these two murders were somehow linked to those suicides.

As she walked into the station's reception area she was running through a to-to-list in her head, and her hackles rose when she spotted Gary Wilcox having a laugh about something with the desk sergeant. The first days in a murder case were crucial. Yet here he was, chatting away as though he didn't have a care in the world. It was almost as if he was enjoying a pint at his local.

Only yesterday, she'd set out the ground rules in a forcible manner. The man was going to be a handful. Calling the shots in an unfamiliar station was a difficult line to tread. Some officers embraced the challenge of working with them. Whereas others were resentful and put more effort into making the likes of her look stupid than contributing to the investigation. After yesterday's encounter with Wilcox, she had hoped he would consider the bigger picture and put his resentment and prejudices aside. She'd been prepared to give him the benefit of the doubt. But witnessing this relaxed attitude at such an inappropriate time was a dereliction of duty. As well as being lazy and objectionable, the man was a dinosaur, with no place in the police force.

Jemima took a deep breath. She needed him to toe the line and if he was unwilling or unable to do that, then get the hell out of her way. She decided to give him a short, sharp shock.

'Wilcox!'

The two men stopped talking, and Jemima saw Wilcox stiffen. Though he did not turn to face her. Undeterred she continued.

'Wilcox! Show some respect when a senior officer addresses you.'

It was as though the temperature in the room had risen by at least ten degrees. As Gary Wilcox slowly turned to face her, the man's eyes burned with rage.

'Ma'am.' His jaw was so tight that his lips barely parted as he spoke, Making the word sound more like a growl.

'I warned you yesterday, Wilcox. Do not test my patience. When you're on shift you're here to work. Do you understand that basic premise?' She raised her eyebrows as she waited for an answer. 'Well?'

'Yes, ma'am.'

'Take this as your final warning, Sergeant.' Jemima witnessed the man's shoulders stoop slightly and had to force herself not to let out a sigh of relief. This was aggravation she could do without. Keen to reinforce the order she continued. 'While we're investigating these murders you will undertake every task I set you, in a timely fashion and without complaint. Do you understand?'

Wilcox nodded.

'It's not in your interest to keep me waiting for an answer, Wilcox.'

'Yes, ma'am.' Beads of sweat erupted across on his forehead.

'Good. There's no time for idle chitchat. And that goes for you too.' She addressed this latest comment to the desk sergeant. The man had obviously been listening intently to everything she was saying, and as her eyes bore into him with a laser-like intensity, he appeared to visibly shrink from her gaze.

'Yes, ma'am. Sorry, ma'am.'

'So, there's no further misunderstanding, Wilcox, these are the ground rules,' Jemima counted them off on her fingers. 'Firstly, you will do what I tell you when I tell you. Secondly, you will treat every officer, regardless of rank, with respect. And finally, when I tell you to jump, I expect you to ask how high. Are we clear?'

'Yes ma'am.' As he spoke, his head nodded up and down like the dog in the Churchill advert.

'Good. Now keep up. Chop-chop,' she clapped her hands then pointed at the security door which led to the upper floor. 'There'll be a briefing session in the operations' room in five minutes time. I expect you to round everyone up. No exceptions. Attendance is mandatory.'

Sergeant Wilcox's fingers trembled as he keyed in the access code.

Upstairs in the incident room everyone was busy with their respective tasks. But having learned of the spate of suicides in the area, Jemima needed to establish if there was any connection.

'Good morning, everyone. I'd like you all to stop what you're doing and gather round.'

Members of the core team realised that at this early stage of the investigation, it was unusual for Jemima to drag them away from what they were doing. Though the four local officers were unfamiliar with her style of working.

'Last night I became aware of a spate of suicides in this area. Does anyone know anything about them?'

'Mostly youngsters as far as I'm aware,' said Mike. 'The cases weren't allocated to this station, so none of us would have been involved.'

'You said that our two victims weren't suicides,' said Lewis.

'That's right. They're not,' said Jemima. 'But I'm certain that something is going on in this area. You can expect the odd suicide, but not that many in such a short space of time. I know it's a long shot, but I don't think we should dismiss the suicides until we've looked at those case files.

'Gareth, how are you and Zoe getting on with trawling through the missing person's database?'

'Early doors, guv.'

Jemima's brow furrowed as she thought through the possible implications of reassigning tasks. She sighed before she next spoke. 'OK, I'm making an operational decision here. Gareth, Zoe, I want you both to look in detail at the recent suicides in that area. I can't put my finger on it, but something's bothering me. Could be that there's no connection with our case. Then again . . .'

'Right you are, guv,' said Gareth.

'Levi, Mack, you know what I'm about to say.' As she looked in their direction, they both nodded their understanding.

'No problem, guv,' said Mack. 'We'll add the mispers to our task. It'll just slow things down a bit, that's all.'

'Mike, you and Gary push on with yesterday's task.'

'Right you are.'

'Dan and I will be off out to see John Prothero.'

'Who's he?' asked Mike.

'The pathologist who'll be carrying out the post-mortems. They're scheduled for this morning.'

CHAPTER 13

Following yesterday's reawakening of Dan's childhood trauma both officers were under no illusion that given the method of death, he would find these particular post-mortems distressing.

John Prothero was based at the University Hospital of Wales. Over the years they had attended numerous post-mortems and had got to know him well. He was a short, pot-bellied, middle-aged man who reminded Jemima of the late actor Arthur Lowe.

As a child, her father had loved watching re-runs of Dad's Army, and Jemima couldn't help but think of Captain Mainwaring whenever she saw Prothero. She had not dared mention the likeness to him in case it caused offence.

Having arrived a few minutes early, the post-mortem area was still being set up. John liked attending police officers to arrive on time as he didn't want the process to be disrupted. He frequently described the workload he and his team were expected to get through as a production line, often complaining that there were not enough hours in the day.

Given what many would consider the gruesome nature of the work, it was surprising that Prothero was such a well-balanced individual. In all the years they had dealt with each other Jemima had not once seen him have an off-day.

As they made themselves comfortable in the screened-off viewing area, the door to the working area opened and Prothero strode in wearing his protective coveralls. When he spotted Jemima and Dan, he smiled warmly. 'Jemima, my dear. And, Daniel. It's good to see you both. It's been a while.'

'Sure has, John,' said Jemima.

'How's Ray these days? Made a full recovery?' Prothero was referring to Ray Kennedy the former DCI who headed up the team on which Jemima, Dan, and Gareth had worked, before the entire setup came crashing down in a series of extreme events, which had left Kennedy fighting for his life.

'We don't have much contact with him these days. But as far as I'm aware he's doing much better. Even got himself a new job. He reckons it's better paid and less stressful,' said Jemima.

'Good for him. The events of that day were a rum deal all round. Anyway, look at you. DCI no less, and very well-deserved. Your boss is a right high-flier, lad.' This final remark was directed at Dan.

'Anyway, enough of the small talk. I'll tell you straight off that Jeanne's informed me there were no phones, wallets, credit cards or the like to aid with identification. So, time to get this show on the road. FYI, due to the unusual nature of these deaths I attended the crime scene yesterday. Not a place I've been before. Bleak location to have one's life snuffed out. Jeanne informed me that you'd already come and gone. First off, both corpses were suspended from the structure using what I believe to be Beal Karma 9.8mm climbing rope. It's predominantly orange in colour with a diagonal yellow line running around it. Affordable rope with the strength to hold a body. Pretty much perfect for the job. Readily available online or in outdoorsy shops.'

'Impressive John. I'd no idea you knew so much about ropes,' said Jemima.

'Hardly. That's Adannaya's speciality. Only recently discovered that she's into climbing. Showed her a section of the rope and she identified it straightaway.'

'Always fancied giving that a go myself,' said Dan.

Jemima suppressed a smile. Dan might very well convince a casual acquaintance that he was an adventurous sort, but he was one of the least physically active people she knew. He'd only recently reluctantly agreed that he needed to raise his fitness level and had joined her and Gareth on daily runs at the end of their shifts with the aim of entering the Cardiff half-marathon. His willpower had waned, but they'd refused to accept his excuses, endured his moans, and all but shamed him into competing. They had buoyed his spirits along the course but with half a mile to go he was ready to give up. It was only when he saw the excitement on his young son's face as his wife held him aloft that he managed to raise his game and work through the pain. When it came down to it there was no way he was ever going to allow his little Harry to see that his dad was a quitter.

'In case you were wondering, Adannaya's carrying out the post-mortem on your second victim.' Adannaya Okoro was the junior pathologist who worked closely with John. 'Given the gruesome nature of this particular crime scene we thought it best to bump them up the list. After all, we don't want to keep you hanging around longer than necessary.' He waited to get a reaction, but when none was forthcoming, he laboured the point. 'See what I did there? Don't want to keep you hanging around. Hanging around. Hanging.' He repeatedly looked from one to the other. Disappointment clouded his expression when he finally accepted that he wasn't going to get the reaction he had hoped for.

'Sorry, John. We're just up against it and not in the mood for jokes,' said Jemima. 'Any other time, and your sense of humour would be appreciated.'

'Fair enough,' he sighed. 'Back to business. Jeanne's team photographed the corpses in situ to ensure there was a close-up of the knot used. The longshot is that both corpses were suspended using the same knot, which happens to be a bowline. I'm presuming you don't have an extensive knowledge of knots. These days not many people do. This takes me back to my scouting days, but feel free to stop me if you're already up to speed on it.'

'I'm up for an idiot's guide,' said Jemima.

'In that case, whoever strung these men up knew what they were doing. There are various knots they could have chosen to use, but the bowline is superb for the purpose of suspending someone as it can withstand a substantial amount of pressure. It forms a loop at the end of the rope and the knot tightens as pressure is increased. Now take a look at this,' he instructed.

'Looks like another knot at the end of the rope,' said Jemima.

'That's exactly what it is. It's a stopper knot. Sometimes called a Figure Eight knot. Whoever strung these men up knew their stuff. There's no way that the bowline could've failed, as the stopper's the failsafe.'

'Jeanne reckons that the victims were hog-tied using different knots, suggesting that it was the work of more than one person,' said Jemima.

'Exactly right. One was tied with a square knot. Possibly one of the most common knots, where you place right over left then left over right. The other victim was secured with a single-column knot. Which is perfect as it doesn't tighten or give way under pressure. FYI a popular choice for bondage, so I'm told. Especially if your partner happens to be a wriggler.' Prothero winked suggestively at Broadbent as he imparted this latest bit of information.

Dan had no idea why Prothero should have addressed this latest remark to him, but it left him feeling uncomfortable. Pondering the potential reasons, his mind drifted away from the unwelcome thoughts which had preoccupied him for much of yesterday.

'As you can see, the cadaver is still in the body bag he was placed in yesterday. As is the other. They're still trussed, that's why they look an odd shape. I'll be putting my mask on straightaway as I know for a fact that he would have soiled himself. The smell is bearable out in the open, but as soon as I open this body bag it's not going to be pleasant.'

'From what we saw at the crime scene it appeared there was damage to the forehead of both victims,' said Jemima.

'And I'll get to that in due course, Chief Inspector.' John's voice was unusually stern. Reinforcing the fact that this was his turf, and he was in charge.

Given the nature of their job, Jemima and Broadbent were familiar with the sight and smell of death. 'Will you have to break their limbs to straighten them out?' asked Jemima. She was keen for the post-mortem to get underway. She appreciated that she'd offended him by clumsily trying to call the shots, as in all their dealings, he'd not once referred to her by rank.

'I wouldn't have thought so. Rigor would have long passed so they'll be pliable.'

Jemima spotted Broadbent wrinkle his nose in disgust. 'Do you need to go outside, Dan?' She was relieved to see him shake his head. Over the years John Prothero had taken delight in teasing Dan about his queasiness, and Jemima certainly didn't want that to happen on this occasion.

'Would you like a few interesting facts about rigor mortis?'

Jemima nodded. She was always keen to learn as much as she could about things which could help her when attending a crime scene.

'It begins about three hours after death. Brought on by chemical changes. In general, the muscles are stiffest about twelve hours after death. Though that rule of thumb can be affected by various factors such as external conditions. For example, if it's particularly cold, it can slow down the entire process.

'Following full rigor, the cadaver then goes into a state known as secondary flaccidity. It's a myth that hair and nails keep growing after death. It couldn't possibly happen as the body is dead. What happens is that during secondary flaccidity the skin begins to shrink which makes it appear as though hair and nails are growing.'

'That's really interesting,' said Jemima, and she meant it.

'And once secondary flaccidity is complete, as it is now,' said John as he manoeuvred the cadaver's limbs into the usual formation, 'the muscles, as you can see, have relaxed.'

‘How long does this secondary flaccidity take?’ asked Dan. He had clearly been paying attention to John’s impromptu lesson.

‘That would be anywhere between one to three days. And that’s as much as I can tell you prior to examination. Apart from to say that this is an adult male Caucasian. Right, let’s get him out of the bag so I can take a look.’ He nodded to his team who set to work.

‘Any idea of age?’ asked Dan, keen to demonstrate that he was unfazed by events.

‘Patience, lad,’ said John. ‘I’ll not be hurried. First off, there’re petechiae in the eyes. Significant bruising around the neck and the hyoid bone has been crushed. All of which I’d expect to find in a hanging victim.’ He opened the cadaver’s mouth to its greatest extent. The tongue had already been visible. Black and protruding. ‘Let’s see if there’s any fancy dental work for you to compare with dental records. Might help with identification if we can’t come up with anything else. No luck here. From the state of these teeth, I doubt he ever visited a dentist. There’re a few that look to be reasonably healthy. No fillings but plenty of decay and a significant build-up of tartar. Suggests to me he wasn’t someone who was well off. But the wisdom teeth have erupted so that indicates he’s at least mid-twenties. Though I’d hazard a guess he’s at least ten years older than that.’

Jemima supposed it was something to go on. Then again, having seen the corpse she had sensed that he had been at least in his thirties.

Prothero set about cutting the clothes away. ‘The labels have faded, so the clothes weren’t new,’ said John as he squinted to try to read print that was barely visible. ‘As far as I can tell, looks like Primark, and I think another says George. So, either inexpensive tastes, or not much disposable income.

‘Now let’s take a look at the body.’

Even from this distance they could tell it was breaking down.

‘Take a look at the purplish colour around and either side of the knees.’

They both focused on that area of the body.

'That's a result of livor mortis. When the heart stops beating there's nothing to pump the blood. Gravity takes over and it pools at the lowest point. In this case, as the victim was hog-tied before death, and then suspended, the knees were closest to ground level. Hence the darker colour. It confirms that he was still alive when they strung him up.

'I'll take swabs from under his fingernails in the hope that he might have put up some sort of fight and managed to get some of the killer's skin cells. Though to be honest I'm not optimistic that we'll get anything useful.'

Jemima and Dan waited patiently as John took the swabs and passed them to a member of the team who labelled them. 'Time to make a start on the head. Ah, now this is interesting,' he said, as he bent to examine the cadaver's close-cropped hair. 'There's a noticeable area of damage. Suggesting a blow to the head. I'll know more when I've had a chance to examine the brain, but I wouldn't be surprised if this man was hit over the head to subdue him. At the very least it would have stunned him. Possibly even knocked him out for a while. Either way, it would have given his attackers sufficient time to overpower him and truss him up.

'Before I remove the top of the skull, I want to get some close-up images of the forehead. Given the fact that he's been suspended out in the open for a couple of days, it's not just natural decomposition that takes a toll. From the marks and gouges on the skin which would have been exposed to the elements it's likely that birds and potentially any wildlife able to climb the structure on which the bodies were suspended, treated these cadavers like a platter at an all-you-can-eat buffet. They've gone to town on both corpses making it impossible to have a clear idea of what these men might have looked like.'

Jemima wrinkled her nose at the thought of it. She wasn't a fan of wildlife at the best of times. 'Is there anything that isn't an obviously wildlife-related injury?'

'I think there might be. Looks to me as though something has been carved into the forehead. Though, what it is,

I'm unable to say at the moment.' With the initial images taken, John's assistant set about cleaning the skin on the forehead to allow another set of images to be taken. 'We'll need to take a closer look at these later,' said John. 'All I'm prepared to commit to is that apart from a significant number of bite marks, something has been carved into the flesh. It appears to have been an intentional act as the blade has damaged the epidermis, dermis, and subcutaneous cells.'

'From what we saw when the cadavers were in situ, it appeared that they both had similar injuries on their forehead,' said Jemima.

'I agree that both foreheads had injuries. As to whether they're the same injury I'm unable to say, until I've spoken with Adannaya and we've had a chance to compare these images with the ones her team will undoubtedly take. Best not to jump the gun. Stick to facts, not speculation. We'll know for certain soon enough.'

Prothero's attention returned to the cadaver as he set about removing a sizeable section of skin on the forehead. Far larger than the intentionally damaged area. He had decided it was best to do this before he opened the top of the skull. As he didn't want to risk inadvertently compromising the injury, and so make it more difficult to establish what had been carved into that area. Since at first glance it appeared that both victims had similar cuts in the same place, it suggested that this was somehow important to the killers. As to whether they would be able to successfully identify it and eventually understand what it meant, only time would tell.

The powered saw cutting through the cranium was the part of the post-mortem that Jemima least liked. She'd watched it happen on numerous occasions yet had never managed to feel at ease with the sound it made. Watching John remove the brain from the cavity was no different to watching him remove any other organs. But the sound of the saw slicing through the skull always unsettled her.

'As I expected. There's a large haematoma. This man was hit with some force. It's conceivable that the blow to the head alone could have ended up killing him if it was left untreated. They could have saved themselves some time and effort. Not gone to the trouble of stringing him up. Though it's likely the killers might not have known that,' said John.

Having eventually completed his examination of the brain, he moved on to other parts of the body. 'There's a section of skin been recently removed from the left upper arm. Messy job and decomposition isn't helping. My guess is that it was a tattoo and it meant something to the killer. Fortunately, there are techniques we can employ to establish what the image would have been. It won't be quick or easy as it involves going down through the layers of skin, but we should be able to get a better idea of what it was like in its original state. And if it happens to be a unique design you might get lucky and be able to use it for identification purposes.'

Learning about the possibility of being able to establish what the tattoo had once looked like provided a glimmer of hope for identification, as currently they had nothing to go on. The post-mortem continued in silence for a while, and the hope of finding something useful to the investigation was starting to feel like a longshot.

'Now this really could be the break you're hoping for,' said Prothero.

'What have you found?' asked Jemima.

'There's a lengthy scar on his right leg. Suggests to me that he might have fractured the bone and the injury required a metal plate to fix it together. If that's the case there'll be a serial number on it, and it'll be traceable.' Prothero sliced through the flesh to reveal that his hunch was correct. They finally had a way of establishing the victim's identity.

Satisfied that there was no more to be learned from this post-mortem, and having learned that Adannaya had inadvertently been delayed in starting hers, they headed back to the station to find out what progress the others had made. John had assured them that he would confer with Adannaya at the earliest available opportunity. They would look for any similarities between the victims and compare the images of whatever had been carved on both foreheads.

CHAPTER 14

Back at the station the incident room was a hive of activity. Mack and Levi were on the phones, busily making notes as they spoke. Gareth and Zoe were also doing similar tasks.

Gareth was the first to spot their arrival. He smiled and gestured for them to come over. Ending his conversation, he put down his pen and pushed his chair away from the desk. 'Find out anything useful?' he asked.

'Possibly,' said Jemima. She and Dan filled him in on how things had gone, including the tattoo and that he'd had a metal plate to fix the bones in his leg.

'That's great. Hopefully John Prothero should get back to you by the end of the day.'

'How's it going with the spate of suicides?' asked Jemima. She was hoping that there would be a link to their murder victims. Though, given the fact that Prothero was certain that the cadaver he had just examined had been an adult, it was difficult to imagine what that link could be.

'Zo, come and join this discussion,' said Gareth. In the last few minutes PC Swann had just replaced the handset, having finished her latest phone call.

Zoe remained seated and used her feet to propel the chair across the floor.

'The guv was asking about our progress,' said Gareth. He was keen to involve the young officer, as he appreciated that this was her first experience being part of a team working a major investigation. 'We've compiled quite a list,' he said.

'All teenagers?'

'Mostly, but not all. We've identified fourteen in total, in the last two years.'

Jemima whistled. She hadn't expected such a high number. 'All locals?

'Yeah, we searched for anyone who had lived in the vicinity of Rhymney, Pontlottyn, Fochriw, and Abertwysswg,' said Zoe.

'And these deaths were all thoroughly investigated at the time?' asked Jemima.

'We haven't got that far. It's taken up all our time to identify the victims,' said Gareth.

'Talk me through what you know, and while you're at it get a list up on the board so we know what we're dealing with. It's a worryingly high number of deaths by unnatural causes for such a small area with a relatively low population density. I know it might seem like a long shot but there's a possibility these suicides could somehow be linked to the murders. And until we have definitive proof that they're unrelated to our murders, we should establish exactly what happened to them.'

'I agree, guv. It seems strange that there've been so many suicides in such a short space of time. I'm hoping that once we've seen the case files and spoken to the families, we'll have a clearer idea of what's going on in this area, because whatever it is, something's not right,' said Gareth.

'I hope you'll find that whoever investigated these suicides did a thorough job.'

'Is it possible that perhaps these weren't suicides?' asked Zoe.

'I've no idea, but it's best not to take anything on face value, Zoe. Those deaths have all been ruled as suicides. Which is possibly believable, had there been only a couple in such a short space of time. But fourteen? Come on, that's highly suspicious. You can't tell me that kids in this area are so depressed that they decide to end their lives.'

'It's a deprived area. There's not much for them to do,' countered Zoe.

'Think for yourself, Zoe. Don't look at things in isolation, and don't just accept what other people tell you. There're lots of deprived areas throughout the country. Doesn't mean that kids in those areas routinely take their own lives. Something's off, and even if we establish that those suicides are not linked to our double murder, I'm determined that we're going to get to the bottom of it.

'Let's get those names up on the board,' said Jemima. It concerned her that PC Swann seemed unable to understand that they were faced with an exceptionally high number of suicides. The first few could easily be written off as the actions of desperate individuals. But with the passage of time and more suicides occurring, they should no longer have been considered as individual events. And Jemima felt there was a fair chance that no one had had the nous or inclination to link these deaths and investigate them as such.

'I'll talk you through it. Zoe will write it up,' said Gareth. 'First off, of the fourteen victims, ten were still at school. We haven't yet had a chance to look at these in much detail, so you'll only get the basics.'

'That's fine,' said Jemima.

'The first victim was Luna Watson, aged fifteen. Next was Sophie Tang, aged seventeen. Ruby Morgan, aged sixteen. Lexi Cook, sixteen. Jack Fernández, seventeen. Oliver Palmer, fourteen. Thomas Sidhu, sixteen. Joshua Booth, eighteen. Kai Probert, seventeen. David Haque, eighteen.'

Jemima swallowed hard. Seeing the dead teenagers' names written on the board together with their ages, made her feel queasy. The youngest had been only fourteen. Not many years older than James. She couldn't imagine life without her boys. Yet the families of these teenagers had probably felt the same way too. Most parents had hopes and dreams for their children. Aspirations which grew from the moment you learned of the existence of that tiny foetus inside your body, relying on you to protect and nurture it. For those first few years of life, when they were almost entirely reliant on you, you protected them and helped them to develop into children who could explore the world in comparative safety. Their first day at school was often a bigger wrench for the parent than for the child. It was a final acceptance that the apron strings had been cut. That there would be lengthy periods of time when they would be away from you. Under the influence of others. Unless you chose to home-school, it was inevitable.

'What timeframe are we talking about?' asked Jemima.

'Twenty-seven months. There are also four adult suicides inside that timeframe.'

'Talk us through them.'

'Evan Cook, twenty-six. David Price, thirty-one. Gwilym Bevan, thirty-four. Finally, Alice Shute, fifty-six.'

'So predominantly teenagers. Do you have more details? Such as the method used.'

'Not so far,' said Gareth.

'Well start digging. You know what we need, Gar. Everything these investigations uncovered and more. Especially if you get the impression that the investigating officers only did a superficial job. We need to get to know about every aspect of these victims' lives. Once you've got all the facts to hand, we'll focus on identifying links between the victims. That way we might stand a chance of finding a pattern.'

'I'm on it, guv.'

Jemima turned her attention back to Zoe. 'This will be a steep learning curve for you. But Gareth's just the man to guide you through what's required. As far as your career's concerned, this is an amazing opportunity. It'll be a hard slog. You'll need patience, determination, and an eye for detail. But follow Gareth's lead, and you won't go far wrong.'

'Yes, ma'am. I won't let you down, ma'am,' said the young officer. The enthusiasm in her voice was apparent, and it was the first time that any of them had seen her smile.

Gareth was buoyed by Jemima's ringing endorsement of his capabilities. It was such a great confidence boost.

Further down the room, Mack and Levi were still busy with phone calls. Though fortunately, as Jemima made a beeline in their direction, Mack ended the call he was on and replaced the handset.

'How's it going?'

'Slowly, but we're making some progress,' he said, as he pushed his seat away from the desk. Stretching his arms, he stifled a yawn. 'Sorry. I think the lack of fresh air's getting to me. We've been hitting the phones since you left this morning. There've been reports of stolen quadbikes from a couple of farms in the area. One had a Land Rover taken too. Nothing unusual about that. Farmers are vulnerable. Always get chancers doing that sort of thing. There's also a quadbike and activity centre not too far away. They've had a couple go missing recently. So, plenty to follow up there.'

As Levi finished his latest call, he joined the conversation. 'I've sorted divers for going to hang on a sec . . .' He shuffled his papers until he found what he was looking for. 'Umm, Rhaslas Pond. But it won't be today. It's a small team and they've already got a couple of jobs considered higher priority. They'll give me the heads-up to get ourselves up to the site when they're on their way there.'

'Are they hopeful for tomorrow?' asked Jemima.

'They wouldn't commit. I did everything I could to push them, but the bottom line is they've no idea how long any job will take until they've sent someone down to see what they're dealing with.'

Jemima appreciated that it would be the case, but she had hoped to have a bit more momentum at this early stage. As it was, they were waiting on other people to feed them vital information. And as in any of these investigations the first couple of days were the most important. Yet they hadn't made any real progress.

'I've researched the area and discovered Rhaslas is a popular location for fishing,' continued Levi. 'More of a reservoir than a pond and the perfect place to dispose of an off roader if you needed to make it disappear in a hurry. You wouldn't want to risk it during the day, but the middle of the night might be a different matter.'

'Great work, guys—' Jemima stopped speaking, distracted as the door opened, with the return of Nancy Chen and Lewis Martin. 'Any progress?' she asked the new arrivals.

'As far as we could make out, the Bent Iron monument is pretty special to the town. It represents the industrial heritage of the area,' said Lewis.

'We're awash with cups of tea,' said Nancy. 'This area's so different to the city. The locals we spoke to are such a friendly bunch. Told us that this latest monument replaced the original that had been there for as long as anyone could remember.

'There's also a mural painted on the side of a funeral home in the town. Showing a miner with his lamp and a depiction of the bent iron in the background. Along with a verse from a song by someone named David Alexander. He's dead now. His real name was Derick Ebdon. He was from Blackwood and used to be a miner himself.'

'Did you get the lowdown on any trouble in the area? Anything that could help explain why those two men were killed on that monument?' asked Jemima. The impatience in her voice was all too apparent. It was all well and good that these junior officers had an amicable meeting with some of the locals, but from what they'd just told her, they'd learnt diddly squat. Of course, she appreciated that she was partly to blame. She'd tasked them with finding out about the monument, but that was only with the hope that it might give them an understanding as to why the victims had been killed there.

'There's the usual problems with drugs, unemployment, antisocial behaviour,' said Nancy. 'They also mentioned general concerns about suicides, but no one volunteered any information that could help with our case.'

Jemima was about to speak when her phone rang. It was John Prothero.

'Adannaya's completed the post-mortem on your other victim, and we've compared our findings. The upshot is, I've two pieces of news. Firstly, my team have tracked down that metal plate. Which means we have a name. You watched me carry out the post-mortem on one John Prosser.'

'Thanks for moving that forward so quickly. It's the first lead we have.' Jemima experienced a small sense of relief. Having identified one of the victims gave them something to work with.

'Thought you'd be pleased,' said John. 'Records show it was implanted five years ago at Prince Charles Hospital, in Merthyr Tydfil. I also have Prosser's NHS number, age, and address if you're interested?' It was so like John to tease Jemima. He knew she needed the information but delighted in getting a rise out of her.

'You know I am, John. But hold on.' Jemima scanned the nearest desk for a scrap of paper and a pen. Finding neither she clicked her fingers to get her team's attention and mimed writing. Dan was the first to find what she needed. 'Sorry about that. Hit me with it, John.' The pathologist relayed the information and Jemima hastily scribbled it down.

'Secondly, Adannaya confirmed that the other victim had a tattoo on his upper arm. Just like my cadaver, it appeared as though someone removed that part of the skin recently.'

'So, we're no closer to knowing if the tattoos were the same, or what they depicted?'

'Correct. As I said there are techniques we can employ to establish what they might have looked like. But it won't be quick.'

'Are you talking hours, days, weeks?' pressed Jemima.

'As quickly as possible. Apart from that I'm not prepared to commit to a timeframe. I'm aware of the urgency. Rest assured you'll know when I know.

'Oh, and Adannaya's cadaver was wearing a signet ring, which she cleaned up and photographed. I'll send the image through to you immediately. You never know, it might enable you to identify the mystery man.'

'Let's hope so. We need something to go on. Have you made progress on the forehead injuries?'

'Patience, my dear. Be assured that I'll call you as soon as there's any news.'

'Well?' asked Broadbent as she put down the phone. Everyone in the room was keen to know what the DCI had just been told.

'OK, you're all going to want to hear this,' said Jemima. She waited for everyone to gather around. 'John Prothero's team have identified one of our corpses from the metal plate inserted into his leg. His name's John Prosser. The operation was carried out at the Prince Charles Hospital in Merthyr Tydfil. We also have his NHS number, date of birth and last known address.'

'What about the tattoo and whatever was carved into the forehead?' asked Dan.

'Nothing on the tattoo yet, but it's been confirmed that both victims had tattoos on an upper arm. However, in both instances the skin's surface was removed. He's told me it's possible that they might be able find out what it was originally like but can't give us a timescale.' Jemima knew that some of the inexperienced officers would be frustrated by this delay. 'I'm afraid it is what it is. But if John says they stand a chance of finding out what those tattoos were, then I believe him. He's always come through for us in the past, and I've no reason to doubt him now. It's the nature of these investigations. You very rarely get things handed to you on a plate.'

'At least we've identified one of the victims,' said Zoe.

'Exactly. Though, we're still no closer to finding out whatever was carved into their foreheads. Both men's faces were extensively damaged, so John and Adannaya need to look at them closely and ultimately compare the wounds. There's a possibility the injuries could mean something. But it's also possible that they were inflicted out of anger or frustration.'

'In other words, a form of torture,' said Dan.

'It could be. So, until we've had a further update from John Prothero, we put any speculation about those wounds to one side and concentrate on what we know. To that end, John is forwarding an image of the signet ring worn by the other corpse, and who knows, it just might help us identify him.'

Jemima's email account pinged. A quick glance at the screen told her that it was from Prothero and that it included an attachment. 'This is a photograph of the signet ring,' she said as she opened the file to reveal what appeared to be a fairly wide band of sliver or possibly stainless steel, decorated with series of Celtic knots. 'Enlarge the image and get copies printed off for us, Zoe. I doubt it's unique, but you never know, someone might recognise it.'

'Sure thing, boss.' Zoe set about the task, keen to demonstrate that she was a team player.

'With this latest information, it's time to change the focus of the investigation. Thanks to John and his team we now have the identity of one of the victims. Until we have more to go on, for the rest of the day I'm splitting our resources into two.

'As things stand, there's nothing to suggest that those fourteen suicides were connected in any way. But I just can't shake the idea that somehow, they are. So, Gareth, I want you to continue to take the lead on them.' Gareth appeared surprised, but said nothing, merely nodding his agreement. 'Lewis, Nancy, I want you both to join Zoe and Gareth. They've already compiled a list of victims. You've the rest of the shift to dig into their backgrounds. I want as much detail as you can find about each of their lives. Following that, I expect you to pool the information and establish whether they have anything in common with each other.

'If it ultimately proves to have been a fruitless exercise, at least it will have put my mind at rest. But approach this fact-gathering exercise with open minds, because I've a hunch that something important has been missed. And if one of those suicides was a member of your own family, you'd expect all the stops to be pulled out to investigate what was behind the deaths.'

'Dan, Levi, Mack, get your stuff together. You're with me. We're off to Prosser's last known address. See what we can find. With a bit of luck, he might have lived with someone.'

'Possibly the other victim,' interjected Levi.

'We can but hope,' said Jemima. 'But even if he lived alone, his neighbours might be able to tell us where he worked, and possibly even know who his friends were. We need to find out what Prosser did to wind people up so badly that they did this to him. It's also the best chance we'll have of finding out the identity of the other victim. And to that end, make sure you each take a copy of the image of that signet ring to show to people when you're knocking on doors.'

CHAPTER 15

As the four officers headed out of the incident room, Mike Hughes appeared, with Gary Wilcox a few steps behind. The latter wore a hangdog expression, so different to the cocky belligerence they had previously encountered. It didn't take a genius to work out that all was not well between the two men. Before Jemima had a chance to say anything, Mike spoke to the troublesome sergeant. 'If you know what's good for you, you'll get in there and find something useful to do.' His voice had a hard edge to it, and it seemed that Wilcox wasn't about to argue. The sergeant sloped off without uttering a word.

'Don't ask.' Mike sighed. 'I've had an absolute bellyful of that useless waste of space. I know you want rid, but it's not an option. If it wasn't for the fact that he was the brother-in-law of the police commissioner, he would have been out on his lazy arse years ago. But I've had it with him. From now on I'm not putting up with any of his shit. As far as I'm concerned, he either shapes up or we sideline him. I'm not going to allow the likes of him mess up this investigation.'

Jemima was impressed. From the little time she'd spent with Mike up at the crime scene, she hadn't had any great hope of him coming good. She'd clearly misjudged the man. Perhaps they had more in common than she'd thought. After all, they both held the same opinion of Gary Wilcox. And this latest revelation that Wilcox was the commissioner's brother-in-law certainly explained the man's cockiness. There was nothing like nepotism to make you feel untouchable.

'You've my full support on that, Mike,' said Jemima, as she nodded her approval.

The inspector smiled and relaxed. 'That's good to hear because support hasn't been forthcoming from anyone else around here. Not that it's usually much of an issue. It's often easier just to allow him to plod along doing his own thing. At least that way he doesn't get to mess up anything of importance. But the bottom line is Wilcox should have been put out to pasture years ago.'

Jemima smiled. It seemed that they were on the same page. There was nothing for her to say.

'You must think we're a right bunch of yokels,' continued Mike. 'You caught me on a bad day, yesterday. I certainly didn't cover myself in glory up at the crime scene, and I apologise for coming across as a bit of a prick. It won't happen again. It's this setup with Wilcox. It just gets me down.'

'We get where you're coming from,' said Jemima. Dan, Levi, and Mack each nodded their agreement. 'Everyone needs to pull their weight. Especially on a case like this. There's no room for slackers.'

'Believe me, I'll do whatever it takes. Whatever's going on up there has to stop, before anyone else gets hurt.'

'Agreed. Did you make any progress identifying potential routes?'

'As you know, there's only one road anywhere near the area, and three ways to get to that point. Though if they used an off-road vehicle, they could have travelled a hell of a long way across the moorland. You've seen for yourself the number of tyre tracks and ruts.'

'I agree. It's not going to be easy to establish the route they took,' said Jemima.

'You can say that again. Anyway, we spent time driving around the area to familiarise ourselves with the layout. The upshot is, we can rule out any chance of them being spotted from the north. To get onto the road from that direction, you'd have to either have come off the Heads of the Valleys Road at Rhymney Bridge, or Dowlais Top. After that, you'd take the minor road which heads under the dual carriageway. It's so remote that the chances of being seen are negligible. If you're coming from that direction, you pass a landfill site on the opposite side of the road to Rhaslas Pond.'

'Possible dump site for the vehicle?' asked Mack.

'Wouldn't have thought so. It's gated and locked at night.'

'If the killer's linked to the site, it's possible they could have the keys,' said Dan.

'Good point,' said Jemima. 'Best to take a belt and braces approach to this, Mike. Contact the person in charge of the site and ask if they have CCTV footage.'

'I'll get Gary onto it. Should keep him busy.'

'What about other directions of travel?' asked Jemima.

'A number of routes where they could more or less avoid detection.

All of which need to be looked at. It's a huge task. Any chance of extra bodies being drafted in to help?'

'Afraid not, Mike. The rest of the team have their own tasks. You'll have to make do with Gary.

'Anyway, we'll be out and about for a while, as we've just identified one of our victims. We're heading to his house now.'

CHAPTER 16

Having arrived at John Prosser's last known address, Mack grimaced as he pressed the doorbell, which was sticky to the touch. He was reluctant to press it more than once, appreciating that they might very well be coming face-to-face with the victim's nearest and dearest. Breaking the news of anyone's death needed to be done in a sensitive manner, as everyone should be treated with respect.

The blinds at the front of the property were shut, so they were unable to tell if anyone was at home. As no one came to the door, Mack tried the bell again. Though when that failed, he used his fist to knock on the door, until he spotted a shape descending the stairs through an obscured glass panel.

'What the hell's so urgent that you gotta keep 'ammerin' like that?' The question was asked by a woman in her late twenties. She was wrapped in a towel, with another fixed tightly around her head. Wisps of wet hair had escaped their wrapping and beads of water were visible on her shoulders and upper arms.

'I'm Detective Chief Inspector Huxley and these officers are part of my team,' said Jemima as she showed the woman her warrant card.

'Police? Seriously? What could you possibly want with me?'

'We were led to believe that this is John Prosser's address.'

'Not anymore it isn't. He rented the place, but the landlord sold up, and I bought it.'

'I don't suppose you have a forwarding address?'

'Yeah. I've been here for the best part of a year, but the lazy sod still hasn't notified anyone of his new address. So, muggins here has to keep forwarding on his post. It's doin' my 'ead in to be honest. Hang on a minute, and I'll get it for you.' She returned moments later with an address written on a scrap of paper. 'Since you're goin' to see him, do me a favour and give 'im these.' She thrust a bundle of post into Jemima's hand.

The new address was in the village of Abertysswg. It was somewhere they hadn't yet visited, but even before John Prosser had been identified as one of the victims, it had been one of the areas of potential interest to this investigation. As they typed the address into the satnav it suggested that they should reach their destination in a matter of minutes. One of the positives of travelling in an area such as this was that there was far less traffic than they were used to having to negotiate in the confines of the city and its immediate surrounding areas.

The colliery wheels were visible ahead on the right as they approached the turnoff to Abertysswg. With the pit long gone, the wheels had been erected as a tribute to the area's history. Decades earlier, a large, unsightly gasholder had dominated the nearby area. Raising and lowering as it met the needs of local industry and residents.

Having left Rhymney behind they eventually passed a sign for the Idris Davies School, named after the long-dead local poet, and situated towards the valley bed.

In no time at all, they had reached the address they had been given. The house was mid-terrace, unremarkable in any way from many of the properties they had passed. As before, there was no answer, but a dog could be heard barking from somewhere inside the property. A quick glance through the letter box showed a selection of junk mail littering the floor just inside the threshold.

The door of one of the neighbouring properties opened, and a thickset man, clad in a vest top and tracksuit bottoms appeared. His torso was ripped, and his tattooed biceps looked as though they could easily crack nuts. 'About bloody time! You from the RSPCA?'

'No,' said Jemima as she introduced herself and showed the man her warrant card.

'Whatever you want that daft bugger Prosser for, you need to park it and see to that mutt of his first. It's been goin' mental in there and its doin' my 'ead in. It's not right. I shouldn't 'ave to put up with that noise. I've tried banging on the walls, but it's no good. Damn thing won't shut up.'

'How long has the animal been distressed?' asked Jemima.

'Distressed? Distressed? You've got the wrong end of the stick, luv. I'm the one that's distressed. That constant noise is doin' my effin 'ead in. This is the third day, I've 'ad to put up with it. I got so fed up of the barking and whining that I called the RSPCA, but they 'aven't done anything about it. Call themselves animal lovers. Bone-idle tossers the lot of 'em.'

'Does Mr Prosser have a partner, or anyone living with him?'

'Yeah, right!' His voice dripped with sarcasm. 'Good joke, that, luv. You're a right card. Can tell you've never met the man. Believe me, no one's that stupid or desperate. Truth is, I've no idea which way he swings. But my guess is that 'is wrist takes most of the strain. Cos I'm telling you, anyone with a pulse would 'ave to 'ave the patience of a saint to put up with 'im.'

It was an image Jemima didn't wish to have in her head. 'Levi, put a call in to the RSPCA. Tell them to get around here pronto. That animal's in distress. By the sound of it the dog's been here for three days.'

Levi did as he was asked.

'What else can you tell me about John Prosser?'

'Not a lot. Works in Asda at Dowlais Top. Know that 'cause my missus works there too. She can't stand the man. Says 'e's a right lazy git. Always skiving.'

'Does he have any family or friends living locally?'

'Don't know about family. But he drinks in one of the pubs up in Rhymney. Think it's a regular thing.'

Jemima made a note of the pub's name.

After establishing the location of both the pub and the supermarket, Jemima and Dan headed off. Levi and Mack would speak to the other neighbours as they waited for the RSPCA officers to arrive.

Unlike many city centre pubs and some of the large chains which opened for breakfast and remained open until late into the night, this pub was closed. A sign said it would be open for business at five o'clock.

'It's another world up here,' said Dan.

'You're not wrong there. Something to be said for not staying open all hours. Bet it cuts down on the number of troublemakers. Less drinking time for them to get off their face,' said Jemima.

Next stop was Asda at Dowlais Top. Where, after a few frustrating conversations they eventually got to speak to the HR manager.

'Nah, dun't recall him. Then again, we do employ so many staff I'd only get to know him if he was one of the outstanding ones or one of the troublemakers. I can tell you for nothing, we dun't get many that go above and beyond. And as for troublemakers, well they dun't last long. Why are you so interested in him? Has he got himself into some trouble?'

'He was recently found dead,' said Dan. It was the shortest answer he could give her, and likely to stop her asking for details.

'Oh, I-I'm sorry to h-hear that.' The woman shifted in her seat, as she clearly hadn't expected to have been told that. 'That's awful sad. I'll sort this as quickly as I can. Just give me a few minutes and I'll look him up.' The woman sat at her desk and tapped a few keys. 'Ahh, there's your man, and he hasn't turned up for his last two shifts. It says here that his supervisor tried to call him but couldn't get any answer. I can see that it's out of character. Doesn't appear to have had other unauthorised absences,' she said, scrolling through his record.

As they shuffled behind the woman's chair to stare at the screen, they got their first look at John Prosser before his death. It was sad to see an image of the man when he was alive. Until that moment, they had only ever seen his corpse, disfigured, discoloured and decaying. It was a reminder, not that any was needed, that each victim they were forced to encounter had led a life before it was unnaturally cut short.

'We'll need a copy of that image,' said Jemima. 'What other details do you routinely record on your staff?'

'Next of kin. Address. Bank details. The usual sort of thing. I normally wouldn't give out this information, but under the circumstances I'll print everything off for you.'

'We're trying to build up a picture of what John was like. So, we'll need to speak to his colleagues.'

'His team leader should be out on the shop floor. I'm sure he'll be able to tell you more about John and point out other colleagues who would have regularly interacted with him. Just give me a few seconds to print this off and I'll take you down.'

Jemima did a doubletake when they were introduced to the team leader, as he looked young enough to still be wearing a school uniform. It was apparent the HR manager was keen to leave them to it. Seemingly ill at ease with spending time with people, she headed back in the direction they had just come, walking rapidly, swerving customers and staff whose path she crossed. Stopping abruptly as she reached the doorway locked with a keypad, which would take her away from the fray.

The team leader was affable and spoke with authority. 'I'll put this as diplomatically as possible. If John had put as much effort in his work as he did into skiving, then he'd have been a pleasure to work with.

'He was one of the more challenging members of the team. Had a chip on his shoulder a mile wide. He told me that he'd worked here for twelve years, and during that time he'd never progressed. Which says something in this environment. Staff turnover is high. Hardly surprising. A lot of customers treat us like something they've stepped in. The hours are long. The pay's crap.'

'So why do you stay?' interjected Dan.

'Because I want the money and the experience. This is my third year. I started when I was in the sixth form and I'm taking a gap year before I go to uni. But for people like John, this is as good as it gets.' He swept his arm around in a theatrical fashion. 'God help them. That's all I can say.'

'Were you aware of John having any enemies?' asked Jemima.

'Not as such.' He shook his head and pursed his lips as though considering his next words. 'But he had the habit of winding people up.'

'In a jokey way?' asked Dan.

'No. I heard a few people mention that he had very definite prejudices. I've heard him ridicule anyone who didn't have a local accent. I told him to rein it in, as it was inappropriate behaviour.'

'How'd he take that?' asked Jemima.

'Not well. Thought he could call the shots as he was so much older than me, but I soon put him in his place.'

Listening to this young man, Jemima had no problem believing that he was telling them the truth. 'How serious do you think his prejudiced views were?'

'Are you asking me if John's a racist?'

'Yes, but not exclusively. We just need to get as rounded a picture as possible of what he was like.'

'It's possible, I suppose. Though I got the impression he disliked certain people because of his own inadequacies. You must know what I'm getting at. Feeling hard done by and blaming others for circumstances entirely of your own making. There're a lot of people like that around.'

Jemima couldn't argue with that observation.

'Come and have a word with other members of the team. They might have a different perspective of John. Given the fact that I'm team leader, he was always a bit guarded around me. Ah, there's one of my team now. Roger, these are detectives. They're here about John and would like a word.'

Roger Edwards' brow furrowed with consternation. 'I don't know him that well. What's he done?' It was obvious that he was keen on distancing himself from whatever John Prosser had done to cause the police to turn up at his place of employment.

'I'm afraid he's dead,' said Jemima.

Upon learning of John's death, Roger's jaw dropped and his hand shook. 'Sorry to hear that, but I can't see how I can help.'

'We're trying to build up a picture of what John was like. We'll be speaking to everyone on the team,' said Jemima.

'Well, I didn't know him that well. To be honest he wasn't the sort of person I could take to. He probably spoke to me more than the others, but that's only because I speak Welsh, and that was his preferred language.'

'Did you know any of his friends or family?' asked Dan.

'No. He kept himself to himself.'

'As far as you're aware, did he have any enemies?' asked Jemima.

'Are you saying someone killed him?' Roger's eyes widened.

'I'm not saying anything of the sort.' The last thing Jemima wanted was for John Prosser's death to become supermarket gossip. 'This is standard procedure in any sudden death cases. We're just making routine inquiries.'

'I believe you, thousands wouldn't. The truth is, John had a way of rubbing people up the wrong way. He didn't have much time for most people, and you'd know it if he didn't like you.'

'And who didn't he like?' Jemima struggled to sound emotionless, as Roger was starting to get on her nerves. The man clearly wanted to make a point about something, but so far, he hadn't told them anything useful. 'Just spit it out, Roger. Whatever you tell us, you won't be disloyal to John.'

Roger wrinkled his nose as he considered whether he should say anything. 'I suppose you're right. Okay, well he was chopsing about this family who were shopping here a few weeks ago. It was a mother, father and young ones.'

'Was there an altercation?'

'Not a verbal one. I don't think they said anything to him. But I could see that John was tamping. Anyway, he went outside, and I followed him at a distance, so he couldn't see me. He seemed to be looking for a particular car, a green one I think it was, and he made a beeline for it. I watched him bend down. Moments later he stood up, took a couple of steps and bent down again. Then he headed back to the shop. He was out in the car park for less than five minutes.'

'What do you think he did, Roger?'

'I'm convinced he slashed two of the tyres. You see, shortly after the family finished shopping the guy headed back into the store, and he was angry. He said two of his tyres had been slashed. Wanted to know if there was any CCTV footage of that part of the car park.'

'And was there?' asked Dan.

'No. But the car that was damaged was the one John had bent down beside. And I know for a fact that he was carrying the tool we use to rip open packaging. It would have been perfect for slashing a tyre.'

'Did you report him?'

'No. Why would I do that? I'd only be causing problems for myself.'

'Do you know who this family were?'

'No. But John had to have known them to be able to recognise their car. The only thing I can tell you is that they were a black family.'

Jemima and Dan eventually left the supermarket having spoken to five of John Prosser's colleagues. They came away with a sense that people tolerated rather than liked the man. Some claimed they felt uncomfortable about his views. Particularly about politics and immigration.

CHAPTER 17

They headed back towards Rhymney with the intention of visiting the pub where John Prosser was supposedly a regular. With Jemima at the wheel, Dan rang Mack to get an update on progress. The conversation was on speaker phone so that they could both participate, and the sound of barking and whining was noticeable.

'Still waiting on the RSPCA. I feel sorry for the animal. It sounds distressed.'

'Don't be tempted to go in there, mate,' said Dan.

'No bloody chance. If that dog hasn't eaten for a couple of days, it's going to be ravenous and I've no intention of becoming a starter, main course, or dessert.

'Levi and I have been knocking on doors. Speaking to the neighbours to build up a picture of what Prosser was like. Consensus is that he wasn't the most sociable of people. Terrified the life out of a couple of the young lads a few doors away.'

'What happened there?' asked Jemima.

'Apparently a few of the local kids, and I'm talking primary school age, enjoy kicking a ball about. Harmless fun, always supervised by a couple of parents. Anyway, Prosser has a go at them. In particular he focused on two young black kids. Their mother was so concerned that she went around to have a word with him, and he was very unpleasant. Stopped short of outright racist abuse, but nevertheless, quite nasty.'

'Did she report the incident?'

'No. Reckons they don't need the aggravation. Told the boys not to play outside his house, and to cross the street and walk on the other side of the road.'

'Speak to her again and find out what colour car they have. If it's green, ask her if the tyres were recently slashed at an Asda car park.'

'That's a bit random.'

'One of his work colleagues told us that Prosser slashed the tyres of a green car belonging to a black family. There was no argument preceding it. Apparently, he just didn't like them. It's possible he was a racist. It seems as though he wasn't too keen on anyone who wasn't local, and by that, I mean white and Welsh. It'll be interesting to see what you find inside his house.

'We're on our way to talk to people at the pub. It should be open by the time we arrive. We'll see if that brings anything else to light. Keep in touch. I want to know as soon as you've anything to update us on.'

* * *

The pub was a hive of activity. A group of twenty-somethings were playing darts, with plenty of friendly banter, clapping and groans coming from that section of the room. Some of the more hardened drinkers had taken up what was most likely their usual positions at the bar. All of them male. Middle-aged. Ruddy complexions and heavily paunched. With backsides spilling over the sides of barstools, creaking with the slightest of movements. A couple of the seats looked about ready to give up the ghost and fall apart under the bodies they were expected to support. And it seemed wise not to put oneself at risk by standing too close, when the inevitable eventually happened.

As they strode towards the bar, the man on the nearest barstool tilted his head back and determinedly drained his glass, despite it being over three-quarters full. The amber liquid quickly disappeared, and he belched loudly, waving the newly emptied glass at the barmaid. 'Put another in there, Becca, there's a beaut. I gotta right thirst on me today.'

'Haven't seen you in here before. Can I help you, love?' Having finished serving a customer further down the bar, an older man sidled down to where Jemima and Dan now stood.

They introduced themselves and showed the man their warrant cards.

'Oh, this looks serious. What's 'appened?'

'We'd like to speak to the landlord or landlady,' said Jemima.

'That'd be me. Billy James. It's my name over the door. This is my fifteenth year running this pub and I've never had any trouble.' He was clearly doing his best to reassure them that everything was above board. But the confidence in his voice was waning.

'It's nothing for you to worry about, Mr James. We're just making some enquiries about someone we've been led to believe is one of your regulars.'

'And who might that be?'

'John Prosser,' said Dan.

Billy tilted his head slightly and shifted his gaze to the ceiling. 'Can't in all 'onesty say that that name rings a bell,' he eventually said. As if to emphasise his certainty he pursed his lips, frowned and shook his head.

'Are you certain about that?' asked Dan.

'Sure as I can be. 'Ang on a minute, I'll ask my Becca.' He turned his attention to his daughter, who was busily serving another customer. 'Oh, Bec! When you've finished there, come an' 'ave a word with these police officers will you, bach.'

As soon as Billy mentioned that they were police officers there was a noticeable change of atmosphere in the bar. Conversations throughout the room lowered to no more than a loud whisper. The group of lads who had happily been drinking whilst playing darts ended their game abruptly. Hurriedly finished their respective drinks, they retrieved their coats, and headed for the door as though the place was on fire. What looked even more suspicious was the fact that they each kept their head down.

'How to ruin a happy atmosphere, eh?' muttered Dan.

Jemima smiled. It was obvious that some of these customers had things they wanted to hide. Though whatever their misdemeanours, they were of no interest to Jemima and Dan.

'What's up?' asked Becca. The young woman clearly had no problem with a police presence at the pub and held their gaze as she spoke to them.

'We're making enquiries about a John Prosser. We believe he's one of your regulars,' said Jemima.

'Name doesn't ring a bell. Then again, a lot of them use nicknames. What does he look like?'

Dan showed them both the photograph taken from the Asda personnel file.

'Hang on a mo. I recognise him. Isn't that Jonno?' said Billy. 'Come over 'ere the two of you.' He walked towards a wall, where a collage of photographs was displayed, and systematically scanned the images. 'Yes! Well, damn me! There 'e is. You've been asking about Jonno. If only you'd said. I'd 'ave known straightaway who you was on about.'

Billy's bony finger pointed at a photograph of five people. John Prosser, along with two men and two women. A snapshot of a moment in time when they were clearly enjoying themselves. The background showed that it had been taken inside the pub. Indeed, as Jemima scanned the room they were standing in, it was possible to make out the very table they had gathered around. The group appeared relaxed and happy. Five friends, huddled together, holding drinks aloft as they smiled at the camera.

If they could find these four individuals, they could begin to build up a clearer picture of what Prosser had been like. After all, there was only so much information you could get from colleagues or neighbours, all of whom would have formed opinions based on only a superficial understanding of the man. But people rarely let their guard down when speaking to a neighbour or interacting with a colleague. Though there might of course be the odd glimpse into what the real man was about. Most people were adept at keeping their cards close to their chest, and only revealing their true selves to those in their inner circle.

'Who are those with him?' asked Jemima.

'Oh now, let me 'ave a think. That's Nige, Kay, Flower, and Benno,' said the landlord, pointing out each one in turn, as though they should know who he was referring to.

'We need their full names,' said Jemima. Her voice was firm, but surprisingly controlled given the fact that the landlord was being so annoyingly obtuse.

'Eh, I don't think I know their proper names. We don't go in for formalities. Everyone just calls them Nige, Kay, Flower, and Benno.' The man stared at them blankly.

'Aaw, Dad mun, stop actin' so twp. That's Daisy! Daisy Evans,' said Becca, rolling her eyes in despair. She pointed at the young woman her father referred to as Flower. 'She's a teacher.'

'Do you know where she lives?' asked Jemima. She was conscious of the fact that school would have ended for the day.

'Now let me have a think.' Becca closed her eyes and placed her fingers on her forehead. 'Ummm. I think it's Bryn Seion Street. Shouldn't take you too long to get there. That is, if you wanna go and 'ave a chat with her. If she's not there she could be at her parents' house. It's a right posh place. She house-sits when they're away.' She told them where that house was located too.

'What about the others? Do you know their names?'

'Not really. We only serve them drinks. That's all. But I got the impression Nige has something to do with one of the local factories. Which one I 'aven't a clue. 'Im and Kay might be shacked up together, but I've no idea where.'

'What about Benno?' pressed Dan.

'No.' She shook her head. 'Man of mystery as far as I'm concerned.'

* * *

At Daisy's house Dan pressed the doorbell. Music blared from somewhere inside. With no sign of anyone answering the door, Dan pressed the bell again and eventually resorted to pounding the door with his fist. With each passing second, his impatience became more apparent. The sooner Daisy Evans opened the door the better.

Eventually the young woman could be seen through the door's central glass panel, walking swiftly towards them. She opened the door, looked at them, and held up a hand, palm outwards before they had the opportunity to speak. 'Before you start, I'm not interested in whatever it is you're selling. You're wasting—'

'We're police officers, and we need to speak to you as a matter of urgency,' said Jemima. As Daisy lowered her hand, Jemima thrust her warrant card in front of the woman's face.

'You need to speak to me?' The young woman's voice had taken on an air of uncertainty.

'That's correct. Now may we come in?'

'No. We'll speak out here. It's a mess in there. I'd be ashamed for you to see it.'

'I understand that you know a man named John Prosser?'

Daisy wrinkled her nose. 'Yes, that's right. Jonno and I go way back. Why are you asking about him? Is he all right?'

'I'm afraid not. We have reason to believe that he's dead.'

The young woman paled.

'You're obviously shocked. Take deep breaths. You'll be fine. Shall we take you inside? Get you a glass of water?'

'No, I'm fine. I just don't understand. How could Jonno be dead? What happened?'

'All we're able to tell you is that we're investigating his murder.' Jemima wasn't going to sugar-coat anything. She was inclined to believe that Daisy's distress was genuine. It was unfortunate that this young woman's friend was dead. But as most of the people they had spoken to had given the impression that John Prosser was not a particularly nice man, and as people had suggested that the dead man had held definite racial prejudices it begged the question as to whether Daisy might also have similar views.

Under normal circumstances it would have been easier not to be so suspicious about a friend or family member of the victim. But the very thought of Daisy having such prejudices was too awful to contemplate. After all, the woman was a teacher. Someone who was trusted to help shape young minds. Impart knowledge and give the youngsters in her care a moral compass whereby they could go out into the world and make a difference.

'We need to build up a picture of Mr Prosser. So, I'd appreciate it if you would tell us about John.'

'What can I say? He's just Jonno. We've been friends since school. Jonno left after his GCSEs, whereas I stayed on and did A levels. Then I went to uni. To a large extent our lives went in different directions. But this is a relatively close-knit community and we kept in touch over the years. A group of us meet up at the pub every so often. We went to school together. It's just nice to keep in touch. That's all.'

'Can you think of anyone who would want to hurt him?'

'God, no! He could be a bit of a prick at times. Then again, who isn't? We all have our moments. But I can't imagine anyone would hate him. It's not as if he was the sort to go out every night, getting pissed, or picking fights. He was just an ordinary bloke. That's all.'

'Was he a member of any groups, clubs, or political organisations?'

'Nooo.' Daisy shook her head vigorously. 'He was the sort of bloke who enjoyed the odd night out with people he knew. Having a pint and a chat. Putting the world to rights. He wasn't the most outgoing of people. If he was here now, he'd openly admit that he wasn't the cleverest. Didn't make friends easily. But that doesn't mean that he was some sort of oddball. He was just a normal bloke living an ordinary life. Doing a boring job he didn't particularly like, and watching the pennies because it didn't pay much.'

'Was he resentful of people having better jobs and more money?' asked Jemima.

'No more than anyone else.'

'What exactly do you mean by that?'

'I don't mean anything. It's just a turn of phrase. Jonno was happy being Jonno. Look, you don't sound as though you're from these parts. So, I guess you don't have a clue of what it's like living in a town like this. It's not like the city, where you can pick and choose what you want to do. There's not much going on up here, at the best of times. Hardly any nightlife.

'Most people don't have the money or time to waste on expanding their so-called horizons. What you see is what you get in this area. A few pubs. A couple of clubs and that's it. It makes for a close-knit community. One where we look out for each other. Say hello to people in the street. Talk to our neighbours. If you live in the city, you just wouldn't understand.' Daisy's voice had taken on a note of irritation.

'Now if you don't mind, I'd like you to leave. I've got a lesson plan to finalise and homework to mark. There's nothing more I can tell you about Jonno. Other than the fact that he was a decent man, and I for one will miss him. I just hope you do everything you can to find out who killed him.'

'What about the other people in this photograph?' asked Jemima. She showed Daisy the photograph that had hung on the wall of the pub.

'As I've already said, we were all in school together and have remained friends. That's Nigel Davies and Kayleigh Bevan. They've been a couple since they were fourteen. They live close by. The other man's Ben Jenkins. He rents a place in Pontlottyn. I can't tell you anything else. It's not as though we're in each other's pockets. We're all busy with work and our own lives, but we make a special effort to stay in touch and get together occasionally at the pub.' Daisy gave them the two addresses and Dan made a note of them.

CHAPTER 18

A quick search on the satnav told them that their nearest destination was the property which Nigel Davies and Kayleigh Bevan shared. Jemima hoped that this couple would tell them something useful about John Prosser. As they still hadn't been able to build up a clear picture of what the man had been like.

As Jemima drove, they used the time to catch up with Levi and Mack. They could tell straightaway that something was happening back at John Prosser's house. An unmistakeable series of growls, yelps, crashing sounds, raised voices, and various expletives provided a concerning background sound. They managed to ascertain that the RSPCA officers had just arrived and were in the process of trying to secure Prosser's distressed canine.

'The mutt's in such a state they're going to have to sedate it,' said Levi. 'It was the right call to wait for them. God only knows what the animal would have done if we'd forced an entry.'

'Once the dog's out of there, carry out a thorough search of the place. We've spoken to one of Prosser's friends and are on our way to a property shared by another two. I hope that pair give us something to go on, because as things stand, we're none the wiser. After we've spoken to them, we're going to head to Ben Jenkins' place. Dan will text you the address. We'll meet you there when you've finished at Prosser's.'

'We spoke to the neighbour again,' said Mack. 'They've got a green car and the tyres were slashed in the Asda car park.'

'Do you think Prosser was a racist?' asked Levi.

'It's looking as though he could've been. But it's too early to say,' said Jemima. 'He could just as easily have taken against that family for another reason. We need to look into it.'

'That's it, over there,' said Dan, pointing at a property up ahead.

As they pulled up a young woman was getting out of a car whose bodywork appeared to be more rust than paint. She had car keys in one hand, the strap of her bag in the other and was holding a phone in place between her shoulder and ear. 'Yeah, OK, as soon as I—' It was apparent from those few words that she had spent most, if not her entire life living in the area as her voice had a strong local accent.

'Kayleigh Bevan?' asked Dan. He was the first out of the vehicle, as Jemima was still engaging the handbrake.

'Rude! Can't you see I'm on the phone?'

Dan was oblivious to her annoyance and kept closing the gap between them.

'What's your problem?' Her voice changed from mild irritation to confrontational.

Dan held his warrant card out, and as the woman glanced at his hand her body language changed.

'Kayleigh Bevan?'

'Yeah.' There was now a hint of uncertainty in her voice. 'What's 'appened? Are you a copper or somethin'?' Despite being of a similar age to Daisy, Kayleigh appeared older. She was short, stocky, with a forehead which despite her relative youth, was displaying the signs of becoming lined. Her voice sounded weary, and there were dark patches beneath her eyes. She wore a uniform, the buttons of which strained to hold the well-washed material in place. There was a substantial, unsightly stain down the front of the tunic.

'That's right. We're the police,' said Dan. 'I'm Sergeant Broadbent and this is Chief Inspector Huxley.' Jemima stepped forward to join her colleague.

'Has something happened to Mrs Owen?' she gasped, covering her mouth with a hand as though to stifle her emotion.

'Not as far as we know. Who's Mrs Owen?'

'She's one of my charges. I'm a carer. I look after people who live at home but can't fully see to themselves. Look I don't have time to waste. I've still got three more calls to make, and I've had to come back to change my top. Someone tipped soup down me. Whatever it is you'll have to tell me inside. I can't afford to waste time; I have to get moving.'

She locked the car and headed towards the house. Jemima and Dan followed.

'We're here to ask you about John Prosser,' said Jemima.

'Jonno? What's he gone an' done?' Kayleigh stopped abruptly. Her interest piqued.

'I'm afraid he's dead.'

'No, he . . . Jonno . . . dead?' Her legs gave way as the words sunk in. Thankfully both Jemima and Dan, who were standing close by, reacted quickly and were able to support her weight. Otherwise Kayleigh would have undoubtedly hit the floor. She groaned, as though in pain, clearly distraught by this unexpected revelation.

The door opened. 'Kay? Who the hell are you?' He glared at Jemima and Dan. 'Let go of her. What have you done to her?' He stepped forward to grab hold of Kayleigh. 'Have these people hurt you, Kay?'

Kayleigh shook her head. Too upset to talk, she reached a hand up to her face and wiped tears from her cheeks.

'Bugger off the pair of you, before I call the police.'

'We are the police,' said Jemima as they both showed him their warrant cards. 'And you are?'

'Nigel Davies. Kayleigh's partner. What's this about? Why's she in this state?'

'May we come inside?' asked Jemima. 'Kayleigh's just had a shock and needs to sit down.'

The immediate section of the house appeared unremarkable, with no sign of anything amiss. Nothing to suggest that Kayleigh or Nigel were anything other than ordinary people.

'S'pose so.' He guided Kayleigh towards the lounge, where she dropped heavily onto a chair. It was obvious he cared deeply for her as he fussed about her and placed a protective arm around her shoulder. 'Go on then. Tell me what's happened.'

'I'm sorry to have to tell you that John Prosser was recently found dead.'

'Dead? He can't be. He's our age. We grew up together. What the hell happened? A car accident? What?'

'He was murdered.'

'This is some kind of sick joke. It has to be. Why the hell would anyone want to murder Jonno? I'm going to call him, now. Put an end to this once and for all. You can't go around to people's houses like this and make up things about their friends being murdered. It's sick. That's what it is.'

'I'm afraid it's the truth, Mr Davies. We're here because we're investigating John's death.'

'What! You think we killed him?' His eyes were wide with incredulity.

'Absolutely not. We've been told that you were his friends. We're trying to find out as much as we can about John. Build up a picture of his life so we have a clear understanding of the man he was. We're in a race against time to find out who did this to him.'

'Where was he killed? Where did it happen?'

'I'm afraid we can't reveal details of an ongoing enquiry. Just tell us about John and we'll be out of your hair. We understand you were close and don't want to intrude on your grief.'

'First off, he wasn't John. He was and always will be Jonno. At least to those who knew him best. Those who cared about him.'

'Please, we need to know what Jonno was like,' pressed Jemima.

'He was one of us. One of our mates from school. Salt of the earth. Wouldn't harm a fly.'

'Do you know of anyone he'd upset?'

'Not enough to make someone want to kill him. Have you spoken to Flower and Benno?'

'We've just come from Daisy's house. When we've finished up here, we'll be going to Ben's.'

'Well take it easy on Benno. He's had a hard time of it recently. Lost his brother in a motorcycle accident a couple of months back. Their parents have long gone, so it was only the two of them. They weren't that close, but blood is blood, and he took it hard. Me and Jonno offered to help him clear out his brother's rental. Benno seemed grateful for the offer, but then all of a sudden, he didn't want our help. Kept pushing us away. Making excuses about why he should do it by himself. It wasn't like him . . . Grief does funny things to people. Still, given time and space I'm sure he'll work it out,' said Nigel.

'Yeah, I'm worried about him too what with all these suicides. I don't want him to get ideas like that. You've noticed it too, haven't you Nige? Benno's not been himself since his brother passed. It's difficult to explain. He's right there with us, but he's not. Sounds mad I know. But he's not letting us in. Won't talk about things or let us help.

'Him and Jonno stuck together like glue from the time they started school. So, he'll be devastated when he finds out about this,' said Kayleigh.

'We'll bear that in mind,' said Jemima. 'Tell me, had Jonno had any run-ins with anyone?'

'He's not like that. He's a bit of a joker, but not a fighter. It's not who we are. We keep our heads down. Keep to ourselves, and certainly don't get into scraps. Never did.'

'Was he a member of any organisations?'

'Like what?'

'I don't know. Any clubs. Sports teams. Political parties. Anything which could point us in the direction of people he might have interacted with.' Yet again they weren't getting any useful information. It was beginning to feel like pulling teeth.

'Jonno wasn't interested in anything like that. He'd watch the rugby, same as the rest of us, but that's all. He was a bit of loner. Shy.'

'This photograph of the five of you, taken at the pub. What was that about?' asked Jemima.

'We won the quiz that night,' said Nigel. He smiled at the memory. 'Only time we ever managed it. Came second a few times. But that was the night we actually won. Best night ever, eh, Kay? Best night ever.' He gently squeezed her shoulder and bent to kiss the top of her head.

Kayleigh stopped crying for a moment and nodded her head in agreement.

'Is the pub quiz a regular thing?'

'Yeah. We'd only ever meet up once a week. Difficult to find the time for us all to get together. Kay doesn't get much time to herself. Works her fingers to the bone for a pittance. Always on the go with the number of people she's expected to see to. A bit easier for me I s'pose. I'm at the factory. Benno's worst off. Poor bugger's on a zero hours contract. He's a delivery driver. At their beck and call all hours of the day just trying to scrape by. But despite everything, there's not many weeks when we didn't make it to the pub for quiz night. Best mates. Happy times. Putting the world to rights. Guess it won't be the same without Jonno.' Nigel's voice caught in his throat.

'Do you know John's next of kin?' asked Jemima. The entry had been blank on his employment record.

'He didn't have anybody. Didn't know his dad. Think it was a one-night stand or something, and his mother died, must've been at least six years ago,' said Nigel.

They left the couple to their grief. Clinging to each other for support. There was no doubt in either officer's mind that the reactions they had witnessed were genuine. Kayleigh and Nigel had both been shocked to the core to hear of the death of one of their friends.

Levi contacted them as they headed to Ben Jenkins' address in Pontlottyn. 'Just finished up at John Prosser's, and we're on our way to Jenkins' place.'

'So are we, mate,' said Dan.

'It was a good call waiting for the RSPCA,' continued Levi. 'He had a bloody pit bull in there. Dread to think what damage that thing could do. Not a fan of dogs at the best of times.'

'Did you find anything useful in there?' Jemima sensed it was a pointless question but asked it anyway. If there had been anything of interest, her officers would have contacted them immediately.

'Nothing. Apart from the mess and destruction caused by that dog of his, it's safe to say that Prosser was a neat freak. Not that he had many possessions to mess the place up. We did a thorough search, but there wasn't anything of interest.'

CHAPTER 19

Ben Jenkins' house was situated towards the bottom of a steep side-street, which would no doubt be treacherous in icy conditions. There was no answer when they knocked on the door, and the curtains were drawn, preventing them from getting a look inside the property. When Mack opened the letterbox and peered inside, he spotted a selection of junk mail and flyers littering the floor just inside the door. It suggested that Jenkins was not at home, but he still called out the man's name on the off chance that he was inside. Dan was also making enough noise to wake the dead as he repeatedly rapped on the downstairs window with his knuckles.

'What's going on?' The question was asked by a bewildered-looking man from a nearby property. 'Keep the bloody noise down. We've a baby in ours, who's only just gone to sleep. You carry on like that and she'll be screaming the place down again.'

'Sorry,' said Jemima as she crossed to the other side of the street to speak to him.

'What're you doing anyway? He's not there. Haven't seen him for a few days. Thank God. Pain in the arse when he's around.' Up close the man appeared to be quite young. Though it was apparent from his bleary bloodshot eyes and dishevelled appearance that he was suffering from the almost inevitable sleep deprivation that a newly arrived baby brought to family life.

Jemima explained that they needed to speak with Ben and asked the neighbour if he had any idea where he was.

'None whatsoever. His van's there,' he pointed further up the street. 'Which is unusual as he's always out and about in that thing. Think he's one of those delivery drivers.'

'Hard on him,' said Jemima.

'Hard on the rest of us more like. Comes and goes at all hours. Always with his bloody reggae music blaring. I swear I'll swing for him one of these days. Then again, there'll be plenty others in this street queuing up to have a go at him. Antisocial bastard.'

'Go back inside, we'll keep the noise down so as not to wake your baby,' said Jemima. As the exhausted new father closed the door, she headed back towards the others. 'That's Jenkins' van,' she said, pointing to the dented white vehicle parked ten yards away. 'The neighbour said it's been parked up for a few days. Which is unusual, as Jenkins is out and about on deliveries at all hours. Nigel Davies has already told us that Jenkins is practically living hand to mouth on a zero-hours contract. Which means he doesn't have the luxury of taking time off on a whim. And if he'd gone off somewhere for a legitimate reason, you'd think he'd have let his friends know.'

'What're you saying, guv?' asked Mack.

'First off, we've reasonable grounds to force entry to the house. His friend's just been murdered. It's not unreasonable to think that Ben Jenkins could either be the killer, or possibly the unidentified corpse. Either way, we need to get inside, and depending on what we find, also search the van.'

'Leave it to me,' said Mack as he put his shoulder to the flimsy wooden door. With only the most basic of locking mechanism in place, it didn't take much effort to separate it from the frame.

The atmosphere inside the house was unpleasant. It was as though no fresh air had entered the property for long time.

Yet they were under no doubt that Jenkins had been living there, at least until recently.

Jemima turned to Levi and Mack. 'Check upstairs. We'll search down here.' Jemima and Dan opened the door from the hallway and entered a small living room. 'Let's get some curtains open to give us some light.' She headed towards the nearest window and did just that. As they looked around, they saw that the room they were standing in was shabby but clean. In the tiny kitchen, washed crockery and cutlery were stacked on the draining board, where they had long since dried. The items confirmed that Jenkins had been alone when he had last eaten. A small amount of milk remained in its plastic container, inside the fridge. It was past its sell-by date but had not yet curdled. A microwaveable lasagne, again past its sell-by date and two cans of cheap lager were the only other things in the fridge. It suggested that Jenkins was indeed living hand to mouth.

A quick look in the bathroom, showed the downstairs to be completely empty. And apart from their footsteps, the only sound came from a showerhead which slowly dripped water into the bathtub.

'Guv! Guv! You need to come up here!' Mack's voice sounded urgent.

Jemima raced up the stairs, taking two at a time. As she set foot on the landing, she found the two officers standing by an open door.

'What's up?' She sounded breathless, and barely had time to look from one to the other before her eyes widened and settled on what they had found. 'Oh shit!' She gulped as bile rose to her throat.

The sight confronting her was sickening. Much like her own bedroom, there were partially filled boxes everywhere. But unlike her own innocuous possessions, spilling out of the top of many of Ben Jenkins' boxes was a copious amount of Nazi memorabilia. It seemed that everywhere she looked there were items emblazoned with swastikas. Flags. Military uniforms. And even more worryingly, a stash of weapons.

'Well, that's an undeniable link to the far right.' The thought that people could harbour such prejudice and hatred towards others made her blood run cold.

'Hey, take a look at this,' said Dan. The sense of urgency in his voice broke through Jemima's thoughts. Having been so entirely focused on the grotesque tableau laid out in front of her, it was only now that she realised that he hadn't been standing beside her.

As Jemima turned her attention to Dan, she saw that he was holding a photograph. 'What've you got there?' It was a photograph of Prosser and Jenkins, taken in happier times. More importantly they were posing near the Bent Iron. 'Shows that the place meant something to them. Perhaps it's the reason the killers chose it.'

'That was my thought too,' said Dan. 'But take a closer look there.' He pointed at Ben's hand.

'It's the ring,' said Jemima. 'Which means that the other corpse is probably Ben's. Bag up his toothbrush and anything else that's likely to contain his DNA. If they can match it to the corpse, we'll have a positive ID. We need to undertake a thorough search of the place. It's possible he could just have been a collector of Nazi memorabilia, or even buying it to sell on. After all, life would be financially tough as a single man on a zero-hours' contract. He'd have to shell out a fair bit to buy the stuff in the first place, but I'm sure there's a good mark up on it if he off-loaded it to some serious collectors.

'Of course, it's also possible that he could be an active member of a far-right cell. Which is not something I'd naturally associate with people from this area. But who knows? It's something we'll look into. So, look for computers, bank statements, anything we can use to get the bigger picture of what he was up to.'

'I hope to God we're not dealing with an active far-right cell,' said Levi.

'You and me both,' said Mack.

'Given the apparent animosity between John Prosser and his black neighbours, it could very well be the case.'

Knowing that it would take a long time for them to thoroughly search the premises, Jemima rang Mike and told him to make sure that everyone went home as soon as the shift ended. She explained that they would be late getting back to the station, but when he questioned her about how things were progressing, she kept her answer vague. At this time of the day, there was no point in filling him in on the latest worrying turn of events. And she certainly didn't want the team back at the station to have to stay on shift longer than necessary. The way it was going, they would almost certainly be working long hours soon.

CHAPTER 20

The previous night's search of the property had taken far too long, and even when they'd completed it the evidence had to be taken to the station and logged. Jemima had been so late getting home that the kids were in bed, and even James was sound asleep. It was just as well that she had a support network willing to take up the slack whenever she had a shift like that.

Jemima's phone rang as she headed to work. Stifling a yawn, she glanced at the hands-free display which identified the caller as John Prothero. Her heart beat a little faster in anticipation of what the pathologist was about to tell her.

'Good morning, Jemima. I hope you had a refreshing night's sleep, because I've a feeling you're going to be rushed off your feet today. Got a few updates for you, my dear girl, and I know you'll want to hear them ASAP.'

'Hi, John. What've you got for me?'

'First off, the DNA results from the toothbrush you came across yesterday are a match to our previously unidentified male corpse.'

'Excellent. I was almost certain that'd be the case. Thanks for prioritising it, John. I know how busy you are, and I really appreciate it.'

'No problem, Jemima. FYI, no progress with the tattoos as yet, but I've got someone working on it. Moving on to our next breakthrough. Being the diligent professionals that we are, Adannaya and I spent a considerable amount of time trying to work out what was carved onto the foreheads of the corpses. Our initial assessment was that the wounds looked the same. But, as you know, the state of the bodies didn't allow us to easily see what it was. Anyway, I digress. Adannaya and I are finally in agreement that the wounds weren't random. Make of this what you will, the letters aitch-aitch was carved onto those foreheads.'

Jemima swallowed hard as the possible implications of this latest information sunk in. No one had told either John or Adannaya about the Nazi memorabilia they had discovered at Ben's house. So, they would not have been predisposed to actively look for any link to neo-Nazis. Yet after this latest independent assessment by the pathologists a link had been established, and there was a distinct possibility that these murders involved a far-right cell operating in the area.

Throughout her career as a detective, Jemima had yet to investigate a case driven by a political ideology. This was a whole new ballgame. One where officers under her command could easily be put at risk, by the colour of their skin, their sexual orientation, or their religious beliefs. It was not what any of them had signed up for when they joined the force. And it was certainly not what they had expected to face when they had been assigned the case.

Lost in her thoughts, it was all she could do to mutter a thank you before disconnecting the call. If indeed this case was about a neo-Nazi group operating in the area, then she was out of her depth.

Even with the passage of time, having lost an officer in the line of duty still weighed heavily on Jemima. DS Ashton's death had been unforeseen, and in no way her fault. Or the fault of any other officer on the team. Yet it didn't stop her feeling that if things had been done differently, Ashton might still be alive. And less than a year ago Jemima's mentor DCI Ray Kennedy had almost lost his life too.

These days she was far more circumspect than she had once been and was determined to do everything in her power to keep her officers safe. As she was heading up this investigation it was her call to make. If the cyborg didn't like it, he could call her out on it later.

Jemima's mind was made up. The only sensible course of action was to inform the team of Prothero's findings, and for obvious reasons ensure that Gareth, Levi, and Nancy were allocated tasks that would not put them at unnecessary risk. Levi had already voiced his concern. And rightly so, as if the investigation was to bring them in contact with such a group of people, it posed a real threat to his safety.

Knowing the three officers, she sensed that they would object to desk duty, but their protestations and possible resentment was the least of her problems. The other thing she needed to do as a matter of priority was to identify someone on the force who would be able to advise her on the best way to approach things. Extremism came from many sources, and despite being a novice in this kind of crime, Jemima knew that there would inevitably be officers who had already encountered it, and likely those who specialised in it.

One of Jemima's strengths was that she was unafraid of asking for help. In any walk of life there were people who would prefer to bluff their way through situations where they have little or no knowledge of what they're dealing with. Often people get away without making a fool of themselves. But in a career where your life could depend upon those around you, adopting such a brash and reckless approach could come with a high price tag. Though unfortunately, denying your knowledge gaps was the favoured course of action for some people. She'd been a police officer for long enough to have encountered many bullshitters on the force. Ultimately, some of them got found out, while others went on to rise rapidly through the ranks. All-in-all, it didn't bode well.

* * *

When everyone was assembled in the briefing room, Jemima observed relatively relaxed body language and noted that various conversations were taking place. It was a good sign. It appeared, at least on the face of it, that these officers were coming together nicely. Which was just as well, as it seemed as though they were all going to have to face some tough challenges and look out for each other along the way.

'Good morning, everyone!' She raised her voice to get their attention. 'Right let's make a start. We've a lot to get through.' Placing her jacket and bag on the nearest surface she headed towards the whiteboard. With all eyes on her she began to fill them in on the latest developments, then allocated tasks for the day ahead.

'We followed up on John Prosser yesterday, spoke to his neighbours, work colleagues, and friends. We've learned he wasn't a popular man. He's had run-ins with a black family who live in the same street. It's highly likely he slashed two of their car tyres.'

'Racially motived?' asked Mike.

'It's pointing that way, given things we subsequently came across. Though before we accept it as a fact we need to dig deeper. But I'll get onto that in a moment.'

Having subsequently filled the entire team in on the identity of the other victim and the stash of Nazi memorabilia found at Jenkins' house, she went on to tell them what the pathologists had discovered.

'I spoke to John Prothero on my way into work. He and Adannaya now believe they've identified the wounds on both corpses' foreheads, and they're convinced they're the same. It seems the killers took the time to carve the letters aitch-aitch.'

There were gasps and expletives from the assembled group of officers.

'Far-right then,' said Lewis, shaking his head in despair.

'It certainly adds weight to that theory,' said Jemima. 'And it is a line of investigation we'll be following. But at this stage I don't want anyone closing their minds to other possibilities. That said, these are the tasks for today.

'Mike, you know the area. I want you to partner up with Zoe and get out there. Knock on doors. Speak to the locals. Do whatever it takes to find out as much as you can about John Prosser and Ben Jenkins. We've tracked down some of the obvious links, but I'm sure their lives were far wider than we've identified, and so far, we haven't scratched the surface with them. The one thing we can say for certain is that to be killed in that way, those men must have pissed people off and we need to know who wanted them dead.

'Start off with Prosser's neighbours. We've heard about the beef with the black family. But was there more to it? Was it a racist issue? Did he target them specifically because they're not white? Or was there more to it? Is it possible it could have been a dispute between two sets of neighbours, which had nothing to do with race?

'As for Jenkins, we learned that his brother's recent death knocked him off-kilter. So, I'd like you to make enquires about him too. You know the sort of thing I mean. It could be they were both part of a fascist cell.'

'Will do, guv,' said Mike.

'Gary, I want you and Lewis to follow up on the Nazi memorabilia angle. I've arranged for a techie to do a forensic examination of Ben's laptop. I've no idea how long that will take. Or if it will yield anything useful. But Jenkins obviously acquired that stuff somehow. So, trawl social media. Put the word out locally. Approach local fences. Do whatever it takes to find out what Ben was up to.'

'Sure thing,' said Gary. 'And thanks for showing some trust in me, ma'am. I appreciate it. From now on I won't let you down. I'll give one hundred per cent. I know I've given you and your team a hard time. I've been an idiot. But no more. I'm not about to allow this area to become a stomping ground for a bunch of racist thugs. Makes my blood boil to think we have scum like that living alongside us.'

'Fine words, Gary, but I'm only interested in actions. If you want to impress me, go out there and show me what you can do.'

'Fair enough, you're absolutely right, ma'am. But first off, I'm sorry everyone.' Looking directly at Mike he said, 'Sorry for years of not pulling my weight.' Turning his attention to Zoe and Lewis, he continued, 'Sorry for failing to be the sergeant I should've been. Not leading by example and acting like a prick.' He sighed, then continued. 'But from this moment on, everything changes. I'm fully committed.'

There was a glint of determination in his eyes. 'Detective Chief Inspector, I swear that I'll do whatever it takes to shut down this far-right element. Let's face it, I doubt there're any of us here that haven't had a family member make the ultimate sacrifice to stop fascists destroying our way of life. We owe them, and I'm damned sure I'm not going to allow them to take hold in this valley. Not on my watch, anyway. So, I say, let's do our job.'

'With you on that one,' said Gareth. 'United we stand.' He held out his hand to Wilcox, and the older man shook it without hesitation.

Jemima felt a small sense of relief. It was early days, but it seemed as though the news of a possible neo-Nazi cell operating in the area, had united the two teams in their desire to root out the problem. They needed to show a united front if they were going to confront such a formidable enemy.

'So, we're definitely dealing with a far-right cell?' Along with the tremor in her voice, everyone could sense Zoe's obvious concern.

'Nothing's definite in this game, Zoe. We're at a very early stage of the investigation. At this moment in time, all I'm prepared to commit to saying is that the evidence we've uncovered would suggest that these murders might in some way be linked to right-wing extremism. It's something I will personally be looking into. But for now, I'm not prepared to narrow the focus of the investigation entirely down to that line of enquiry.

'If there is a far-right cell operating in this area, it has obvious implications for some of you.'

'Well, at least three of us,' said Gareth. Nothing more needed to be said, as Levi, Nancy and Gareth obviously appreciated that they could quite easily become targets of such a group.

'That said, for today I want the three of you to remain at this station, focusing on the recent spate teenage suicides. Gareth, I want you to work alone. Given what you did on the Rory Lawson case, you've proved you have an eye for detail and can sift through enormous amounts of information effectively. So, go through each of those case files in detail. Check to see if each of those deaths were thoroughly investigated. Look for links between the victims and establish whether any of the investigating officers attempted to find a link between the deaths.'

'Will do, guv.' Some officers might have thought that Jemima was sidelining them from the main investigation. But Gareth knew that the DCI was asking him to do this because she trusted him.

'I've a worrying feeling that those suicides were treated as isolated incidents, and if that's the case, something vital could've been missed. Of course, it might turn out that they weren't linked.'

'You don't need to explain, guv,' said Gareth. 'We owe it to their families to ensure that no stone's left unturned. Dig deeper into the circumstances surrounding those deaths.'

'Exactly. No parent wants to lose a child in such tragic circumstances,' said Jemima. 'Nancy, Levi, we've fourteen suicide victims. It's a big ask but I want you two to do deep dives into their socials. You know the score. Look for anything they might have in common. I'm talking friends, sites they regularly visited, group chats. Ten of those fourteen were of an age that live their lives online. They lived in a relatively small geographical area. Life in that area offers far less choice than the city.'

'What're you getting at, guv?' asked Nancy.

'I'm saying public transport is limited and there're not hundreds of pubs, clubs, or whatever kids of that age are into. It's likely that at least some of them must've interacted at some time or another. Find out what they have in common, because I'd put money on it that there's some obvious link that's been missed.'

'On it, guv,' said Levi.

'Excellent. In the meantime, I'll be heading to the Counter Terrorism Unit with Dan and Mack. We're going to gen up on right-wing activism and find out if anyone knows about active cells in this area.

'I'll be contactable at all times, and want to know of any developments as and when they happen. Any questions?' Jemima looked at every officer in turn, only to see each of them shake their head. When no one responded, she continued. 'Right, get to it, people. And for those of you heading out of the station, just remember, there's someone out there who knows something, and we need that information. Your job is to find that person, or persons, and get them talking. But keep your wits about you and stay safe out there.'

CHAPTER 21

Later that morning, Jemima, Dan, and Mack were directed along a dimly lit corridor to a room at the police HQ. They entered to find two people inside, already deep in conversation. They stopped speaking abruptly.

'DCI Jemima Huxley, DS Daniel Broadbent, and DC Andrew Mackintosh,' she said by way of introduction.

'Ahh, excellent, then we can get started. Welcome to the Counter Terrorism Unit. I'm DCI Maldwyn Thomas. We spoke on the phone. You can call me Mal. And this is Lee Mortimer.'

Jemima looked at the man who was seated next to the DCI and sensed that it was possible he was not a police officer. He was dressed too casually for one thing. Then again, he could be an undercover officer.

'You've probably guessed I'm not one of you lot.' Lee's voice was surprisingly soothing.

'I used to be a member of a far-right cell. And there you have it. My shameful past laid bare. I've said this so many times over the years and it still doesn't get any easier.'

'What doesn't?' asked Dan.

'Acknowledging what I was and what I did. But I'm lucky, I've got the chance to make amends and I'm making it my life's work to limit the damage these hate groups do.'

'Limit the damage. Why not stop them?' asked Mack.

'Because it's an impossible task. Like playing whack-a-mole. You shut one cell down, another opens up.' His facial expression and the tone of his voice left no doubt in their minds that the man was ashamed of his past.

'Lee was deradicalised five years ago,' said Mal by way of explanation. 'You can probably tell from his accent that he's not originally from these parts. I'm sure he'll tell you more about himself in a moment. But first you need to know that you can trust what he says. He's put his life on the line on many occasions. My team and I have been collaborating with him for the best part of four years, and Lee's the best asset I've ever had.'

They listened in silence to Lee's story which gave them a unique insight as to why and how people could become drawn into the orbit of extremism.

'Don't get me wrong. I'm not trying to justify my actions,' said Lee. 'I did what I did and I'm ashamed. But that's how these extremists get you. They exploit vulnerabilities. When your life's turned to shit and you've given up looking for answers, they swoop in and offer you support. I've seen it time and time again since it happened to me. You're just grateful to have someone on your side.

'They suck you in by making you think they're your mates. But they're not. They're grooming you, and you're so desperate to belong to something. To fit in. Feel safe. Understood. Believe that you matter. All you feel is the warm glow they give you, because for the first time in a very long time you're with people who understand your anger and frustrations. And that's when they get inside your head.' Lee squinted as he tapped his forefinger repeatedly against his skull.

'Once you're part of it, it's like a hive mentality. The cell becomes everything you need. You feel validated. They're your family. They open your eyes to the supposed lies society teaches you. Their propaganda becomes the truth. You're brainwashed. Drilled like soldiers to fight a war against the invaders.'

'Invaders?' Dan was unable to hide his sense of revulsion at the term just used.

'Yeah, that's right. To most ordinary people, that sounds disgusting and mad. But when you're brainwashed into living and breathing an ideology, that's what it's like. You're fighting a war. A war that's going on all around you, but most people are blind to it. I became a far-right fascist thug. I did some awful things. Things I'll never be able to atone for. No matter how hard I try. It doesn't matter that I was deradicalised and that I'm spending my days working every hour I can to stop this from happening to others. I've no choice but to live with the knowledge and shame of what I was back then. And believe me, it wasn't pretty.'

'What made you stop being one of them?' asked Mack.

'To be honest, it was me mother. She was long dead by then. But our cell was carrying out an attack on a community centre a stone's throw from where my brother was killed. Only the intelligence we had was faulty. I was led to believe that the place would be full of young men who were part of a gang who were behind my brother's death. Only it wasn't. It was some kid's birthday party. There were women drinking tea and playing games with little kids. They were just people. Ordinary people going about their lives. Posing no threat to anyone. The only difference was that most of them didn't have the same colour skin as you and me.'

A shiver ran down Jemima's spine, as her thoughts turned to her own boys and her sister's children too. Birthday parties were part and parcel of life. They were occasions to look forward to. With never any thought given to them turning into bloodbaths. The very idea was sickening. 'What happened?'

'Our leader, Jez was a man on a mission. He was obsessed with the cause. It seemed that every waking thought of his was about how he was going to drive forward his plans for the cell. He'd been planning the attack on the people in the community centre for some time. Said some contact had recently made him aware of an imminent threat to life by the same gang who killed my brother, Peter. Kept spouting on about how this Somali gang was planning to drive a car at white kids as they were coming out of a local school. And after what happened to Peter his words resonated with me. I kept thinking of how those thugs had cut him down like he was nothing, and I didn't want something like that to happen to anyone else.'

'I can imagine how that must have influenced you,' said Dan.

'Oh, you've no idea. It was like I was back in those early months after Peter's death. I wasn't in my right mind. I felt like storming into that community centre and ripping their heads off with my bare hands. It was like someone had filled me with hatred. I couldn't think about anything else. I just wanted . . . no that's not the right word . . . I *needed* to destroy them.'

'Jez radicalised you,' said Jemima.

'He certainly did that all right. Truth is, I went tooled up. With a metal pipe shoved up my sleeve. Ready to beat the shit out of them. At that moment in time, I thought that if I killed any of them then so much the better.' Pursing his lips, he had a sharp intake of breath, before shaking his head. 'Looking back, I can't believe that that was me. It was utter madness. But I wanted to send a message. Let them know that this was our country. Not theirs.'

'I take it that you didn't go through with it?' asked Mack.

'I almost did. Put it this way, I was this close.' He held a thumb and forefinger millimetres apart. 'There was a group of us. Nine or ten, I can't honestly remember now. I was towards the back. I had the pipe in my hand. Ready for the fight. I was determined to give as good as I got, and then some. I heard a scream coming from inside, but by the time I made it through the door I saw an old man with blood pouring from his head. He was on his back. Cowering. Whimpering. I knew that even before he was attacked, he wouldn't have posed a threat.'

Jemima shivered. Lee's description made it all too easy to visualise the scene.

'The others were out of control. On a high. And as I stared at the old man, I realised that the screams weren't coming from him. They were coming from women and children. It didn't make any sense. Jez had told us that we were going to confront gang members. But these were pre-school kids and their mothers. It was a soft play party, and they were terrified.

'I was shouting. *"This is wrong. Leave them alone. Don't hurt them. We've gotta get out of here!"* but it was as though the rest of them didn't care. I saw one of ours about to kick a pregnant woman. That was the defining moment for me. I just couldn't let that happen. So, I raced towards him and knocked him off balance. Then my group, people I'd thought of as family, were kicking the shit out of me and I blacked out. Long story short, someone must've called the emergency services, 'cos next thing I knew there were sirens, lights, and I was carted off to hospital.

'There was no going back. That incident opened my eyes to the fact that my cell was made up of a bunch of low-life thugs who were no better than the gang who killed my brother, and I was sickened by what I'd become.'

'Thanks for sharing, Lee,' said DCI Thomas.

Lee sat back in his seat and allowed Maldwyn Thomas to continue.

'It's important for you to hear first-hand what it's like to be part of one of these extremist cells. There're no halfway measures for anyone who joins up. They live and breathe it. Indoctrinated to believe that they're fighting a war to protect their way of life. Lee is one of our success stories. He was arrested after that incident but agreed to testify against every member of his cell. His evidence helped put quite a few of them away. In return, he was given a new identity and relocated to this neck of the woods.'

'Since then, I've made it my mission to work alongside the police. I'm part of a small team helping to deradicalise people their undercovers have identified as having the potential to be turned. Of course, it doesn't always work out. Though, we've had our share of success stories over the years.

'It's relentless,' said Lee. 'You dismantle one cell, and another one springs up somewhere else. They spread dis-information on the dark web. Making it virtually impossible to get a handle on the level of interest or activity.'

'So, basically you're saying we're on a hiding to nothing?' said Dan.

'Not exactly. We've run the two names you gave us, but they weren't on our watchlist. So, we're taking the next step and putting feelers out. We've assets out in the field. They're our eyes and ears on the ground,' said Maldwyn.

'Which obviously won't be quick,' said Jemima.

'Exactly. They're treading a fine line, living with danger every second of the day. Nothing happens fast in that game. Until the moment it does and then all hell breaks loose.

'All I can tell you is that we're not aware of any far-right activity in that region. There was some a few years ago at Caerphilly Castle, when some images appeared online of some youngsters posing with a Nazi flag. But no known activity further up that particular valley. That said, we'll put some feelers out and keep you in the loop if we receive any relevant intel. I trust you'll do the same?' Maldwyn raised an eyebrow questioningly.

'Naturally,' said Jemima.

CHAPTER 22

Back at the station, a quick glance around the incident room showed that Gareth, Levi, and Nancy were each engrossed in their tasks. 'Time for a short break, people,' said Jemima. 'Back here in ten for a progress meeting.'

With everyone assembled, Jemima got the meeting underway. 'Who wants to kick off?'

Gareth was the first to speak. 'Given the number of cases, I've still a long way to go. I started with a high-level sweep of the case files. But what jumped out at me is that for each of these fourteen cases, a different investigating officer took the lead.'

'That doesn't bode well,' said Jemima.

'It doesn't, guv. And it gets worse. From what I've seen, each case was treated as an isolated incident. Investigated without any thought being given to the possibility of a link to any of the other cases. Which given the relatively close geographical proximity of the victims, the closeness of the age range of many of the victims and the frequency with which these suicides occurred, is shocking.'

'I agree,' said Jemima. 'It's bad enough that not one of those officers thought to interrogate the database, when they were assigned their own case. But it beggars belief that no one further up the chain of command picked up on the fact that there's potentially something seriously wrong in those towns and villages. Not only have they let down those families, who have undoubtedly faced one of the most awful things any parent could face, but I'd go as far as to say it's a complete dereliction of duty.

'Before computers became part and parcel of investigative techniques there might have been an excuse for not appreciating that something was wrong. Even then it would have been doubtful given the small geographical area we're talking about. But as for these suicides . . .' She sighed in frustration. 'All anyone would have to do is type in the search terms. For God's sake, it's basic bread and butter procedure when you start any investigation. I wouldn't expect to have to tell even the most junior of officers to do it. After all, it's basic common sense.'

'I know, I couldn't believe it either. It's shocking. If we find that any of these cases are linked and that following a basic procedure could have prevented some of those deaths . . . Well, those families would have every right to sue the force,' said Gareth.

'If you haven't already done so, compile a list detailing the next of kin and any other information readily available on the case files. Perhaps we should be looking for links or similarities that are wider than just the victims themselves.'

'It'll be my next task, guv,' reassured Gareth.

'How're things going on the socials?' enquired Jemima as she turned her attention to Levi and Nancy.

'We decided to start with the kids,' said Nancy. 'As you'd expect there's plenty of information out there. Without exception they were far too keen to live their lives online. Posting selfies. Desperate for likes, instead of getting out there and enjoying living in the moment.'

'It's sad that so many people believe that social media likes equate to actual friendship,' said Mack.

'When my Harry gets older, he's not going down that route,' said Dan. 'Me and Caro will make sure he has so many other activities that he won't have time to think of social bloody media.'

'Best of luck with that one, mate,' said Levi.

'Yeah, an admirable sentiment, but I think you'll be on a hiding to nothing,' said Gareth. He smiled and shook his head.

'You'll—' began Dan.

'Come on, people! Stay focused!' Jemima's raised voice was laden with irritation. 'We've a lot to get through.' As she spoke, she made eye contact with each of them to emphasise the urgency of the situation. 'We're under the cosh. Running a main investigation which is possibly linked to far-right extremism. While it's looking increasingly likely that these suicides haven't been investigated as thoroughly as they should have been.

'Has anyone checked if the connection between these kids is as simple as them all attending the same school?'

'It's definitely not that,' said Gareth. 'That thought occurred to me from the get-go. So, it was one of the first things I checked out. Of the ten kids, three attended a Welsh medium school. Four went to a Catholic school, and three attended the local school.'

'Thought Catholics didn't agree with suicide. Mortal sin and all that gubbins,' said Dan.

It was a crass statement and Jemima shook her head in despair. 'Religious beliefs notwithstanding, I would have thought that it's a given that anyone contemplating taking their own life is in a very bad place emotionally. And with the hormonal changes they're having to cope with it's hardly surprising that teenagers struggle with their emotions. So, I doubt that some religious doctrine is going to have much effect on their thought processes, when they're feeling that desperate.'

'Fair point, I s'pose,' said Dan.

'So not a straightforward link . . . Then again, there's nothing to say that there has to be a common factor linking every one of those suicides,' mused Jemima.

'What're you thinking, guv?' asked Nancy.

'What if a few of them were just random events. The desperate act of some unhappy teenagers. Entirely their decision. With no one else involved. It still doesn't mean that there's not a connection between some of the others. Group the victims on the board, by the school they attended.'

Gareth stepped forward. 'I printed off photographs of each victim from their files. Thought it might come in useful.'

'Helps to keep everyone focused on the fact that these were real people. Not just names on a list or in a case file,' Jemima nodded her approval.

Gareth wrote three headings on the board. Under the section for the Catholic school, he wrote the names Luna Watson, Sophia Tang, Jack Fernández, and Joshua Booth. Allowing sufficient room for a photograph to be placed next to each of them. For the Welsh medium school, he wrote the names Ruby Morgan, Oliver Palmer, and Kai Probert. While the names Lexi Cook, Thomas Sidhu, and David Haque were recorded under the heading for the local school.

'So, what does that tell us?' asked Jemima, as she and the others stared at the board. 'The obvious thing is that there's a mixture of ethnic backgrounds. Perhaps I'm going soft. But I was really hoping for a lightbulb moment on this.'

'Do you want us to keep digging?' asked Levi.

'Absolutely and include any social media accounts of those schools. You and Nancy have plenty of potential evidence on those social media sites. So, keep going. I'm not prepared to accept that each of these suicides was carried out independently by an act of self-will. All areas have the odd suicide. But the number we're looking at suggests that there's something going on. And we need to find out what that is before any more teenagers decide they've got nothing worth living for. Get back to it, the pair of you. Look for links between any of those young people.'

'On it, guv,' said Nancy.

'Gar, was there any mention in the case files that the victims' electronic devices were examined?'

'Yes, but I got the impression that it was only done at a superficial level.'

'Meaning?'

'They looked at the victims' social media posts to see if they were being bullied. Or it was obvious that they had mental health issues. But nothing more than that. There was no suggestion that any effort was put into recovering deleted files. It'd be the first thing I'd want to do. After all, it's human nature to hide or get rid of anything you're ashamed of. And anything like that could be the root cause of why they decided to end their lives. I get the impression that instead of putting in the effort to thoroughly investigate the deaths they did a superficial job so they could just write them off as suicides.'

'Were the devices returned to the families?'

'Yes.'

'In that case we need to retrieve them. That is, if the families still have them. Though I bet there'll be some that haven't kept them.' Jemima sighed. 'Why don't people do their jobs properly? I'm sure they'd be the first to make a fuss if someone undertook a half-arsed investigation into the death of one of their loved ones.'

'Do you want me to do the rounds? I've got a list of the addresses,' said Gareth.

'No. You're better off doing what you're doing. Dan, get the list off Gareth and head out with Mack. Take the time to have a chat with the families. I know you'll both be sensitive. Explain that we're coming at this from a different angle, given the numbers involved. Ask them if they had picked up on any concerns. Such as changes in routine, or behaviour in the months leading up to the deaths. I don't need to spell it out for you. You know the sort of thing we need.'

'Will do, guv.'

As the two officers were about to head out, Jemima had another thought. 'Oh, and show them photographs of the other teen victims. There's always a chance they might know of some link between them.'

CHAPTER 23

While Jemima waited for the four local officers to return and update her on their findings, she busied herself with trying to come up with a scenario which might explain the number of suicides.

The photographs of the dead teenagers confirmed that most of them were either bi-racial or of non-white heritage. And Jemima wondered if the Nazi memorabilia they had recently found could suggest that these apparent suicides might in some way be linked to any far-right activity in the area. Though from what she'd learned from their visit to the Counter Terrorism Unit it seemed unlikely as it would be such a significant change in the way they operated. She also appreciated that it would help justify her decision to commit investigative resources to re-examining the suicides, should there be a link between the two.

Every area, whether rich or poor, had its own share of problems. But at the head of this valley, these small towns and villages which were less than thirty miles away from the city were an unknown quantity.

Mike and his team were the ones with local knowledge. They were recognised faces, and in some cases, were trusted by the locals. Whereas there was every chance that she and her team would be treated with suspicion. After all, some city folk held prejudicial views about people who lived in the valleys. And given human nature, it was just as likely that such prejudicial supposition was a two-way street.

To get an impartial overview of the area Jemima needed to think outside the box. As she mulled over this thought, it occurred to her that perhaps the Census of Population might be a good way to start. At least it would provide her with a high-level breakdown of ethnicity in the area. She recalled a conversation with a fellow officer who had been brought up in the valleys. He had told her that the city was so different to the town in which his parents still lived, insofar as the population had remained predominantly white and Welsh. Jemima noticed that this had been the case in both the supermarket they had visited and the pub too. Then again, she hadn't seen or spoken to many residents.

However, they had found the Nazi memorabilia at Ben Jenkins' house and heard that John Prosser had been angry with two young black children. Whereas it did not appear that he had so much of a problem with the white children who were playing with them. Perhaps there *could* be racial tensions in the area.

A quick call to an acquaintance who dealt with demographic statistics confirmed Jemima's suspicions. Data from the census did indeed reveal that an overwhelming proportion of the population in that area classed themselves as both white and Welsh. This was a marked difference to what she knew was the case in the city. It appeared that the area was behind the curve when it came to racial integration. Though that didn't necessarily mean that there were racists in the area.

It was conceivable that there was less racial integration in the valley because there were fewer career opportunities. Residents would have to travel further to work. Which given the poor state of the public transport system, meant that it would add an inordinate amount of time on to the working day, and could easily not be cost-effective.

Jemima's concentration was broken when she heard a couple of voices, and she glanced up to see Gary and Lewis enter the room. 'Any luck with tracking down where the Nazi memorabilia came from?'

'Not as such,' said Gary. 'We visited every known fence in the area. They're the same old faces that've been here for God knows how long, so I've had numerous dealings with them. I know how they operate and can tell if they're lying to me. But there's no suggestion that any of them would touch stuff like that with a bargepole. Each of them, without exception, was offended when we told them what we were on the lookout for.'

'And you believed them?' asked Jemima.

'As a matter of fact, I did. It's one thing being dodgy. Quite another buying and selling that shit. As I just said, I've known these fences for years. Know what each of them are into, how they operate and which lines they wouldn't cross. Ted Francis has been in the game for twenty or more years, and he summed it up perfectly. When we told him what we were enquiring about I thought he was going to have a stroke. He was apoplectic. Said no amount of money would tempt him to deal in that filth. Reckoned that most of his customers have standards. Lines they wouldn't cross, and if he was to deal in that sort of stuff, it'd be like shitting on his own doorstep. Word would get around and people would blacklist him.

'I think he's right. People from these parts don't go in for that kind of thing. We're all about community. From what I've heard that's something that's missing from the cities. Everyone knows everyone up these parts. Some people might find that a bit claustrophobic, but it has its advantages too. Neighbours talk to each other. Not stick their heads down and walk past pretending they didn't see you.'

'Sounds great, Gary. But what about newcomers to the area? Are they made to feel welcome too?' asked Jemima.

'Uhhh . . . Can't say I know many people who weren't born and bred in this area. We all appreciate the sense of community. Familiarity. For a lot of us it's like one big extended family. You're an outsider, so you wouldn't understand. After all, I bet you don't have bopas in the city.

'Bopas?' asked Jemima. She wrinkled her nose in puzzlement, as the word was unfamiliar to her.

'See, I was right,' said Gary. His expression became almost childlike as he grinned broadly, knowing he'd proved his point. He knew something that she didn't. 'A bopa is what kids in the valleys call an auntie who's not really their auntie. For instance, if there's an older woman living next door to you. Instead of a child calling her Mrs Thomas, she'd be called bopa Thomas.

'Fair enough,' said Jemima.

'But in answer to your question, most valley people are the salt of the earth. It's in our genes. So, I don't see why they wouldn't welcome strangers who decide they want to experience our way of life.'

The arrival of Mike and Zoe cut short Gary's enthusiastic extolling of the virtues of the local population. Telling Gary and Lewis to write up their recent findings, she turned her attention to the most recent arrivals.

'We've quite literally been around the houses. Going door-to-door, speaking to Prosser's and Jenkins' neighbours, said Mike. His face was etched with exhaustion, and he slumped in his seat, vigorously rubbing his palms across his face as he attempted to reenergise himself.

'What did you find out?'

'Not a lot. The consensus was that both men came across as socially inept. Reluctant to engage in conversation. Or even have any sort of superficial positive relationship with their neighbours. Antagonistic was a word often used. The only exception was one couple living a few doors from Prosser. They said that he came across as quite amiable whenever they saw him. Not that they went out of their way to have any dealings with him.'

'Any idea why he treated them differently to the other neighbours?'

'I don't know how relevant it is, but the couple are Welsh speakers. They're happy to converse in English too, but apparently, whenever they spoke to Prosser, he always made a point of speaking in Welsh.'

'Any suggestion that the other neighbours spoke Welsh?'

'We didn't ask, but none of them raised it with us, which suggests they didn't have strong feelings about it. But this couple stood out. After we introduced ourselves the first thing they asked us was, *"Sairad cymraeg?"*'

'Which is?' asked Jemima.

'They were asking if we spoke Welsh. It's their preferred language. Though they were more than happy to converse in English, when we told them we didn't,' said Zoe.

'Did you question Prosser's neighbours about why there was bad blood between him and the black family?'

'We did,' said Mike. 'Don't think it was anything to do with racism. Seems that woman took a dislike to Prosser's dog and made it her mission to get the dog taken away from him. Was worried it might get out and attack the kids when they were playing in the street. So, she reported him.'

'Natural concern, I suppose,' said Jemima. 'The number of dog attacks are frightening. There're not many weeks when you don't hear about some innocent person being mauled or even killed by one. It could easily explain the animosity.'

'Thing is, although a lot of his neighbours didn't seem to like him, most of them agreed that Prosser was a responsible dog owner. There was no suggestion he ever let it out unsupervised. Or that it had attempted to attack anyone. He lived alone and that dog was his life.'

Jemima looked at her watch. Time was getting on, yet they had made little progress on either of the cases. Having told everyone to pack up and get themselves home, she contacted Dan and Mack and told them to call it a day after they had brought the teenagers' electronic devices back to the station and logged them into the evidence room. There would be time in the morning for them to update her on anything which had come to light from conversations they had with the family members.

CHAPTER 24

The following morning, Jemima was up and out early. She arrived at the station in record time, missing the usual commuting tailbacks. As she busied herself by making notes of the tasks that needed to be taken forward that day, her phone rang. It was John Prothero.

'I haven't caught you driving again, have I?' he asked.

'No. For once I'm actually sat at my desk.'

'Excellent, in that case I've a few images that'll ping their way to you in the next couple of minutes.'

'The tattoos?'

The tattoos,' he confirmed.

'Swastikas?' Jemima was convinced that that's what they'd be.

'Absolutely not. For once, my dear girl, you're way off the mark. You need to see these for yourself. I'm sending the images through now.'

As the call ended, Jemima eagerly awaited John's email. 'C'mon, c'mon, c'mon,' she muttered, drumming her fingers on the desk. As her impatience grew, she heard the door open and looked away from her screen to see Dan arrive.

'Morning!' His voice was cheerful. When she didn't respond he knew that she was focused on something. What's up?' he asked.

'Prothero's sending some jpeg files over. Images of what the tattoos would have looked like. He reckons both victims had the same image.' There was a ping to announce the arrival of the email. There were a series of images. Three each from both victims. 'Come and take a look at this.'

Dan deposited his coat on the nearest desk and moments later he was staring blankly at the images on Jemima's screen. 'That's gross. What the hell are they supposed to be?' The images of the subcutaneous tissue were blurred and grainy.

'Search me,' said Jemima, as she wrinkled her nose, trying to make sense of what she was looking at. 'Looks like a horse with a barrel for a body.'

'I know this is stereotyping, but it doesn't seem likely that people linked with far-right extremism would have something like this tattooed onto their body. It looks almost cartoonish. Hardly the look I'd imagine a fascist thug would go for.'

'The same thought struck me.'

'So where do we go from here?'

'Off the top of my head, I've no idea. I need a moment to think. This bloody case is driving me crazy.'

'I know you won't thank me for saying it, but you'd better come up with something soon, because the others will be here any minute.'

'Print off those images for me, will you, Dan? I'll need a copy for the briefing session.' Jemima headed to the ladies. She needed to focus her mind, and this was one area of the station where she was guaranteed some peace and quiet. She headed for the nearest sink unit. Placing her hands either side of the bowl, she leant heavily on the substantial fixture, gripping the ceramic so tightly that her knuckles turned white. The coolness of the surface grounded her thoughts and she somehow managed to formulate a plan.

She entered the briefing room to find the others already assembled. Dan looked at her and almost imperceptibly raised an eyebrow. It was a subtle unspoken question. She smiled and nodded in response, to tell him that everything was back on track. With her shoulders squared, and her head held high, the momentary wobble was a thing of the past. When she spoke, her voice once again exuded confidence and commanded respect.

'Good morning, everyone. I'm pleased to see you're all looking refreshed and raring to go, because there's a busy day ahead of us.' She looked at each of the assembled officers in turn to reinforce the message.

'First off, I've just spoken to John Prothero. It seems that Adannaya has worked her magic and as a result they've finally managed to reveal those tattoos which the killer tried to destroy.'

'Nazi related?' asked Gary.

'Afraid not. Dan, could you stick those images up on the board?'

'Right you are, guv.' Dan stood up and did as he was asked.

'What are they? asked Gareth. He leaned forward in his seat, squinting to get a better look.

'Beats me,' said Levi, who was doing the same.

'Apparently, both of the victims had the same tattoo. So, it had to have meant something to them, and to the killers. It's difficult to make it out, but it's of a horse with a barrel for a body. It's being ridden by someone wearing a cap, jacket, and trousers.'

'Seriously?' said Zoe.

'First off, does that description mean anything to any of you?' asked Jemima. The smaller glimmer of hope was almost extinguished, as she looked around and saw everyone apart from Gary shaking their head. His lips had narrowed, and his brow was furrowed as he tried to recall something from the dark recesses of his mind. 'What're you thinking, Gary?' A flutter of excitement built in the pit of her stomach. Could this be the moment when they had a much-needed breakthrough?

'Umm . . . I dunno. I've a feeling I've seen something like that before. But I haven't a clue where. No . . . it's out of reach and there's no point in me concentrating on it. You know what it's like, the harder you try the more elusive it becomes. Sorry, guv. I'll let you know if it comes back to me.'

'Never mind.' Jemima smiled at the sergeant, determined to hide her disappointment from the assembled officers, as she needed each and every one of them to remain focused and bring their A-game to the shift. 'Thought it wouldn't be that simple. Put it out of your mind for now. If you're anything like me, you'll have an epiphany when you least expect it. OK, we'll park that one for now. I'll follow up on it myself. As things stand, we're still running two investigations.

'Dan, Mack, did you find anything useful when you went to speak to the parents of the dead teenagers?'

'We only got to speak to four of the families. But each of them felt let down by the investigations. There was an overwhelming feeling that the officers only did a superficial job. The consensus was that despite being sympathetic, no one was prepared to look beyond the obvious,' said Mack.

'And the obvious was?' pressed Jemima. She pursed her lips and scowled. Annoyed at the thought that the families of these teenagers had been given cause to think that the officers assigned to investigate, had not done a thorough job. Every member of the public deserved an absolute commitment from the police whenever a tragedy like that occurred.

When you thought about it, suicide was a death sentence for those left behind. Life would never be the same again, as the living would often struggle to put one foot in front of the other for the remainder of their lives. No one imagined their child would ever take such drastic action. It was unthinkable. The ultimate nightmare.

The very least these grieving families deserved was for a thorough investigation to be undertaken. As so many suicides had occurred within such a small geographical area, common sense should have made someone question whether there was a common link. Two suicides in such a short space of time could possibly be written off as coincidence. But the number was already into double figures. For any officer doing their job properly it should have set alarm bells ringing. Yet, until now, no one on the force had made the connection or even seemed bothered that these just might be more than a series of unrelated, but tragic events.

Jemima had an unsettling feeling there was something, or someone malign operating in the background. If she was correct, then she needed to get to the bottom of it before more teenagers took their own lives.

'I think it's possible that there could be a racial element to these suicides. You've only to look at their photographs to see that there're quite a few bi-racial and non-white kids,' said Mack. 'As the victims had already been grouped by the school they attended and we didn't get started until late in the day, we concentrated our efforts on the victims who had attended the Catholic school. Our thought process was that those kids might be less inclined to kill themselves as the Catholic religion regards suicide as a mortal sin.'

'Meaning?' asked Jemima.

'Meaning that if you take your own life, you'll be damned, and won't go to heaven. It might sound strange to anyone who is not brought up in a religious household, but for a practicing Catholic, it might be a greater consideration,' said Dan.

'We had this conversation yesterday.' Jemima sighed. 'Look, in theory you could be correct. But I don't believe that religious doctrine would be a consideration for anyone who'd reached the point of wanting to end their lives,' said Jemima.

Unperturbed, Dan continued to make his point. 'That's as may be, but the point is that none of us know. You'll recall from yesterday's briefing that four of the teenage victims attended a nearby Catholic school, and we got to speak to each of their families. First off, three of them were bi-racial. Whereas, the other pupil, Joshua Booth, and his parents were white. But they weren't local. The family moved into the area just over four years ago. They're originally from Whitby, and their Yorkshire accent marks them out as different.'

'But surely Joshua wouldn't have been targeted by neo-Nazis?' said Levi. 'The others, maybe, but not him.'

Jemima ignored the young detective's remark. This latest piece of information about Joshua Booth was interesting. It was possible Dan could be on to something. 'Could it be that we've allowed ourselves to become fixated upon a possible far-right connection and got it wrong? It was sickening to find the Nazi memorabilia at Ben Jenkins' property. And it was a logical assumption that both men having the letters aitch-aitch carved into their foreheads was another link to the far-right. But what if it wasn't? What if it was just a coincidence?'

'But the aitch-aitch obviously means something. Whoever killed them was angry enough to carve it. It must be linked in some way to the reason for their deaths,' said Nancy.

'I agree. But it doesn't necessarily mean that aitch-aitch is a far-right reference. At this stage in the investigation, it'd be a mistake to allow ourselves to become fixated on the obvious. So, we must explore the possibility that it could mean something entirely different.' As Jemima looked at the group of assembled officers, she could see that some of them were clearly frustrated by this latest statement. 'This isn't up for debate. I'm running these investigations. It's my call.

'Have the diving team searched that . . . What's it called?'

'Rhaslas Pond,' said Mike.

'Levi? You were organising that,' said Jemima.

'Last I heard they were still tied up on those other two cases which they said were a higher priority. I was planning on checking again as soon as this briefing session was over. I'm confident they wouldn't have forgotten about us, guv. It's just that their resources are limited,' said Levi.

'Don't worry, Levi, I want you focused on the teenagers. Give the contact details to Gary and he can chivvy them along.'

The two men made eye contact and nodded their agreement.

'Make sure they understand the urgency of the situation. If that off-road vehicle has been dumped in there, we need to retrieve it and see if there's any chance of getting useable forensics from it. Chances are there won't be, but as things stand, we're clutching at straws,' said Jemima.

'Will do, guv,' said Gary, puffing out his chest. He was pleased the DCI had moved on from their bad start and was now content for him to run solo on an important task.

'And while we're at it, did you find anything on that CCTV system from the landfill site near Rhaslas?'

'No guv. I went through it in detail, and there was nothing. I'm confident that the killers didn't travel along that road either to get to or from the Bent Iron.'

'Excellent work, Gary. At least that's one thing we can tick off the list. Now go get me a definitive answer about whether that off-road vehicle is at the bottom of Rhaslas Pond.'

'Will do, guv.'

'Do any of you have connections in Rhymney, Pontlottyn, Abertysswg, or Fochriw areas?' As she looked around, she was surprised to see Lewis tentatively raise a hand. 'And you didn't think to mention this at the start of the investigation?' She sighed in frustration.

'N-no, guv. It didn't seem to have any bearing on things.' He refused to make eye contact, fixating instead on some elusive spot on the floor. 'Is it important?'

'It could be. I want details, Lewis.'

'My cousin, her partner and their kids live in Ponty, that's Pontlottyn, not Pontypridd. But they won't have anything to do with either of these cases.'

'What ages are the children?'

'Fifteen and twelve.'

'So, they attend one of the local schools where some of the pupils died?'

Lewis looked at the board where the photographs of the teenagers were displayed. 'Yes, oooh . . .' It seemed the penny had dropped.

'You muppet,' said Mike.

'Sorry, ma'am. Sorry, sir. I didn't think. Do you want me to go and talk to them? See if they've heard anything?'

'Yes, Lewis, I want you to go and sound them out. It's possible those children either knew or have heard things about those dead teenagers. Things they wouldn't normally tell their parents and certainly not speak to the police about. Are they trustworthy?'

'Absolutely. Whenever I go there, I have a kick about with Nathan. He's the eldest. Looks up to me. Reckons he wants to join the force.'

'Well, what're you waiting for? Go and find out if they know anything. Even if it's just rumours . . . No scratch that, especially if they're rumours! If anyone's going to know about something going on with those suicides, it'll be the kids. Zoe, you go with him. Listen carefully, read the subtext, follow up on any leads, and keep me informed.' The young constables wasted no time in gathering up whatever they needed before heading off.

'Mike, you're on your own today, I want you to identify any community groups in that area and go speak to as many of them as you can. Find out what they know, or think they know about Prosser and Jenkins. Those men have spent their entire lives in that area, so there's more to know and find out. And while you're at it, ask them about this spate of suicides too. Someone must know or have heard something.'

'Dan, Mack, go and retrieve everything you booked into the evidence locker last night. Then get back out there and talk to the rest of those families and collect any electronic devices they still have.

'Gareth, once Dan and Mack have brought up yesterday's haul, I want you to make a start going through those electronic devices and record everything you find. I want a forensic trail for each device, so that they can be cross-referenced against each other. There must be some links that were missed.

'Levi, Nancy, it's going to be a repeat of yesterday for you. Continue with the social media accounts.'

With the day's tasks allocated everyone knew exactly what was expected of them.

CHAPTER 25

With the team going about their respective tasks, Jemima set about doing some research of her own. There had to be a reason why Jenkins and Prosser had the same tattoo. And whatever the reason, it had sufficiently riled the killers enough to make them hack the artwork from their victims' bodies.

Jemima began with the most obvious search term and typed "*horse with barrel body*." As she hit the return key, she was informed that there were more than four million results. It was way too many. First up were photographs of actual horses. They looked nothing like the almost cartoonish horse depicted on the tattoos.

Next, Jemima discovered that barrel racing was a type of horse race, where Appaloosas were the most favoured equine to compete in the sport. The animal's ancestry went back to prehistoric times. Knowing little about horses she scanned the information to see if it could have any relevance to the case. Having no knowledge of barrel racing, she discovered that its roots were in American rodeos. It was a timed event where the rider had to race the horse in a clover-leaf formation around three barrels which were set out as a triangle. Although interesting, it had no obvious connection to Wales.

Refusing to give up so easily she changed the search terms. Taking the four urban areas in alphabetical order she typed in "*horse with barrel abertysswg*". There was nothing of interest. Next up was "*horse with barrel fochriw*". Same result. Feeling it was a waste of time she typed in "*horse with barrel pontlottyn*". For the sake of being thorough she changed the search to "*horse with barrel rhymney*". Though by this stage had no expectation of it returning anything of significance. The result was much the same as the others apart from an entry for *Hobby Horse.*

Being unfamiliar with the term Hobby Horse she clicked on the link only to see a drawing which looked very much like the tattoos. And it suddenly occurred to her that the letters aitch-aitch carved into the men's foreheads could just as easily refer to Hobby Horse. And if that was the case, it meant that any far-right extremist connection was nothing more than a red herring.

Jemima's heart beat a little faster as she realised she was on to something. Leaning forward in her seat she felt a flutter of excitement at the possibility of making a real breakthrough. A few more clicks and she ascertained that this distinctive artwork was the logo for Rhymney Brewery.

But despite the momentary elation she realised that Rhymney Brewery no longer existed in Rhymney. As she scanned the information, she discovered that the town's brewery was originally founded by the chairman of the Rhymney Iron Company. Then, just over a hundred years ago when the ironworks were sold, the brewery became a separate company. Almost three decades later its name was changed to Rhymney Breweries Ltd though it was later acquired by Whitbread and eventually ceased brewing in 1978.

It seemed that the brewery had been a major employer in the area. Though, in more recent times a new enterprise had set up in another part of South Wales, trading under the name Rhymney Brewery.

The sound of familiar voices broke Jemima's reverie, and she glanced up to see Dan and Mack heading towards Gareth's desk. Between them, they were carrying the collection of electronic devices they had borrowed from the bereaved families.

'About time. I'll get cracking on this lot,' said Gareth as they placed the packages on his desk.

'Mack, there's been a change of plan. I'd like you to go talk to the rest of those families by yourself,' said Jemima.

'Sure thing, guv.'

'Why are you pulling me off that?' asked Dan.

'Because there's been a development. You and I are off to Rhymney.'

'We are?' Dan looked surprised. 'What's happened?'

'I've just found out what those tattoos were. Take a look at this.' The others in the room heard what she was saying. Everyone stopped what they were doing and headed towards her desk, eager to see what she had found.

'Well bugger me, Rhymney Brewery!' exclaimed Gary. He'd just got off the phone from talking to the dive team. 'That's where I'd seen it. I'd forgotten about that. This's a right blast from the past. Before my time, but they did have a brewery there. In fact, come to think of it, I've a feeling my uncle might have worked there for a while. The brewing side of things had shut down, but there was a distribution warehouse, run by Whitbread. Served all the pubs for miles around. They didn't have that horse logo. As I recall, Whitbread had a different one. That's why I didn't put two and two together.'

'While Dan and I are out, I want the rest of you to continue with your tasks. We're still running two investigations and need to keep the momentum up.'

* * *

'Where exactly are we headed?' asked Dan. Jemima was behind the wheel, and despite adhering to the speed limits was, as usual, going far faster than he found comfortable.

'Back to the pub where we found the photograph of Jenkins and Prosser. I don't know whether it has any direct link with the former Rhymney Brewery, but it seems like the best place to start. And Gary's already told us that when the brewery was up and running in the town, it supplied beer to pubs throughout the area.'

As they pulled up outside the pub, Becca, the daughter of the licensee was watering the display of hanging baskets. Jemima and Dan wasted no time getting out of the car and making a beeline towards her. At the sound of approaching footsteps, she turned around, put the watering can down and looked at them. From her quizzical expression it was immediately apparent that she was trying to remember where she had seen them before.

'Detective Chief Inspector Huxley and Sergeant Broadbent,' said Jemima.

'Aah yeah. You was yer a couple of days ago.'

'That's right. We'd like to speak to you and your father.'

'Sounds serious.' She gave them a questioning look, but when neither officer responded, she continued to speak. 'Dad's doin' the books at the moment. Truth be told, he'll probably be glad of the excuse to stop. Always says that part of the job does 'is 'ead in. Come in, 'ave a seat, and I'll give him a shout.'

While they waited for Billy and Becca, Jemima and Dan used the time to study the array of photographs displayed as a collage on the nearby wall. The sight of so many smiling faces gave the impression that the pub was a popular place to be. As Jemima studied the photographs, she spotted various faces posing with different groups. But however hard she looked, she couldn't find another photograph of Jenkins and Prosser.

There seemed to be two possibilities. Either this group of friends liked to keep to themselves, or other regulars chose to avoid them.

At the sound of an unseen internal door opening somewhere behind the bar area, Jemima turned to see the landlord approach.

'Back again I see. Becca said you wanted a word with us. Now then, what's this really all about? Twice in one week is a bit excessive. You'll be givin' us a bad reputation. We're not used to 'aving the police come knockin' on our door.'

'We're after some background information, Mr James,' said Jemima.

'Aye, and what exactly do you want to know about?'

'I suppose you've heard about the recent deaths up at the Bent Iron?'

'Aye. Rumours 'ave been flyin' about the place. People 'ave been sayin' those blokes were murdered.' He looked at the detectives.

'Sadly, that's correct, and it's the reason we're here.'

'Now 'old your 'orses, love. Before you get carried away with yourself, I want it on record that me and my Becca 'ave got nothin' to do with those murders.' Billy James' eyes widened with alarm.

'We're not suggesting you have.' Sensing that the man was about to interject, Jemima raised her hand to silence him. 'If you'll allow me to continue, Mr James. I was about to say that we've identified the two victims as Ben Jenkins and John Prosser, and we know that they were regulars at this pub. We're just after some background information on them, along with any other information about a couple of other issues relating to the case.'

'Oh, go on then. I'll 'elp if I can. What do you want to know?'

'First off, what can you tell us about Rhymney Brewery?'

'Which one do you mean? The original Rhymney Brewery, or the new one?'

'The original. The one that was in this town.'

'Well, let me think . . . You're going back a bit there. It was a real big employer in these parts, back in the day. Eventually bought out by Whitbread. In fact, they used to brew their beer not far from 'ere. Just down the road it was. If you 'appen to take a drive down that way, you'll still be able to see some of the old cobble stones. They was a bugger when it'd rain. I 'ad many a bruise from coming off my bike when we was racin' 'round as kids. Slippy as anythin' they got when it was wet. Come to think of it. I remember from the time I was a little dwt that you could tell when it was goin' to rain, from the smell of the hops.

The wind would pick up and fill the air with the smell. Very distinctive it was. Oh, those were the days.'

Billy James had a faraway look in his eyes. His voice had softened, with a noticeable hint of nostalgia. Despite his recollections being mildly interesting, Jemima was determined to drag his attention back to the here and now.

'That's very interesting, Mr James. But we're up against it, investigating a double murder, and there are very specific things we are interested in.' Looking directly at the man, Jemima raised her eyebrows to reinforce the point.

'Yeah, sorry. It just brought back a bunch of 'appy memories, that's all. So, what exactly do you want to know?'

'Tell us about the hobby horse logo.'

'It's what Rhymney Brewery used.'

'And is it still used in this area?'

'No. The new Rhymney Brewery over in Blaenavon use it. They must've done some sort of deal when they took over the name. But I could be wrong. I'm no expert.'

'Did you know that Ben Jenkins and John Prosser both had tattoos of that logo?'

'Did they indeed? Can't say I'm surprised. Right daft buggers they was. Twp as anything.'

'I wonder if the others have them too?' said Becca.

'The others?'

'Yeah, the rest of their team.'

'What're you talking about?' asked Jemima.

'Their quiz team. You know. That photo you borrowed. It was from the only time they won the pub quiz.'

'And what's the link between the quiz and the tattoos?'

'Well, they called themselves the Hobby Horses. It's their team name.'

'So, to be clear, the photograph of Jenkins and Prosser is one of the Hobby Horses quiz team?'

'Yeah. As I said, as far as I can recall, it was the only time they won.'

The implications of what Becca had just told them was not lost on Jemima. She glanced at Dan, who clearly had the same thoughts too. As the tattoos had been hacked from the skin and the letters aitch-aitch carved on the men's foreheads, it suggested that at least two people had it in for the members of the quiz team. Which meant that the other team members could be in danger too.

'I'll make some calls,' said Dan. He didn't even need to wait for Jemima's approval as he knew it was what she would suggest. As he stood up the chair legs scraped across the floor. He headed outside without a backwards glance, determined not to have the conversation in earshot of Billy and Becca.

'What's happening? Where's your sergeant going?' asked Becca.

'It's nothing to concern yourself with,' said Jemima. 'Now, I'd like to know more about your quiz nights. Specifically, about the Hobby Horses team members.'

'Can't say we know that much about them,' said Billy. 'They set themselves apart from the likes of us. Look down their noses.'

'Why would they do that?' asked Jemima.

'That lot have always been the same.'

'Which lot are you referring to? I've no idea what you're talking about.' Jemima was eager to hear what the man had to say, but was finding his seeming inability, or perhaps it was reluctance to get to the point, rather irritating.

'The Welshies.'

'But you're Welsh. You said yourself that you grew up in this town.'

'Yeah, we're Welsh all right, and proud of it too. But the likes of that lot are different. They've got a chip on their shoulders a mile wide and look down on us as traitors to their cause.'

'Aw, Dad, that's a bit harsh,' said Becca.

'Let me finish, Becca.' Billy gave his daughter a stern look. She cast her eyes skyward, sat back in the chair and folded her arms.

'As I was about to say, from the time that lot were kids they were sent to a Welsh school. No idea why. As far as I can recall, at least two sets of parents didn't even speak Welsh. But whatever their reasons, the parents didn't think the local comp was good enough for them.'

'Surely there's no animosity just because of language preference?' asked Jemima. It seemed a ludicrous suggestion. There were very few people who only spoke Welsh. Especially in this part of Wales. She knew people who were bilingual. Whose first language was electively Welsh. But they lived and worked alongside English speakers.

'Not usually. Most people on both sides are reasonable and tolerant. Truth be told, most of us don't give a damn about what language someone chooses to speak. It's only a big thing for the die-hard nationalists, but they're a tiny minority, always harking back to the past and bangin' on about how hard done by they are.'

'So, what in your opinion makes the Hobby Horses members different?' pressed Jemima.

'Because they're a bunch of nutters, and nasty with it. They've got a reputation in these parts. Lived 'ere all their lives, but don't fit in. They don't usually want to be part of things. Not unless their dealin' with Welsh speakers.'

'But when we were here the other day, your customers were speaking English,' said Jemima. 'So why do that group attend the quiz nights? Presumably the questions are all in English?'

'Course they are.' Billy laughed and shook his head. 'None of the staff speak Welsh, and if we went down the route of holding the quiz in Welsh, we'd only have a couple of teams. In these parts, there's not that many interested in the Welsh language. People have more important things on their minds. Like trying to put food on the table and heat their homes. They come yer to forget about things for a couple of hours. Enjoy themselves, have a pint or two and spend some time with their butties.

'When that lot first came in yer they started bangin' on about how I should have bilingual menus. I almost split my sides I was laughin' so hard. I told them straight, my pub, my rules. If you don't like it you can bugger off out the door and find somewhere else to drink. Daft buggers even tried to get a petition going. As if anyone would put their name to somethin' like that.'

'It obviously didn't put them off coming here,' said Jemima.

'Wouldn't have cared if it did. Could do without the likes of them tryin' to stir things up. Perfected the art of playin' the victim. Pointin' the finger. Usually at the English. Though, more recently at other newcomers too.

'What I'm tryin' to say to you is that we've got other regulars, perhaps about a dozen or so, who are Welsh speakers. But to them, language isn't an issue. They'll just as easily gab away in English. They don't make a big thing about it, and certainly don't let it come between friendships. They respect people's choices.

'Not like that Hobby Horses lot. If they had their way, we'd be an independent nation, forced to speak Welsh while the place went down the pan.' Billy sighed and ran his fingers through his hair.

'The other Welsh speakers in these parts keep their distance from them. People like Wyn Hughes and his wife Ceinwen, well, they've lived in this town for years. The only way to describe those two is Welsh through and through. Salt of the earth. Would help anyone and expect nothin' in return. Now, they're both big on the language and the culture. Even take time off work to go to eisteddfods. Not my cup of tea I grant you, but each to their own I say. Anyway, they both think that lot in the Hobby Horses team are not the full shilling.'

'So, people don't like them?' asked Jemima.

'That's an understatement. I've lost count of the number of customers who've begged me to bar them. Believe me, no one in these parts will be losin' any sleep over Benno and Jonno ending up like that. Wouldn't be at all surprised if once all this commotion has died down, someone suggests we throw a party.'

Billy was just finishing speaking when the door to the bar opened and a svelte middle-aged man with a mop of grey curly hair strolled into the room. 'Not interrupting anything am I?' he asked, looking from Billy to Jemima.

'Nah, plonk yourself down. We were just chattin' about you and Cein.'

'Oh aye? And why's that like?'

'Nothing to be concerned about, but introductions first. This is the Wyn Hughes I was telling you about. He's got a day off work and come to have a natter before we open up. Wyn, this is Detective Chief Inspector Huxley.'

'And why would the police be interested in me?' Wyn sat back in his chair and folded his arms.

Billy jumped in with an explanation before Jemima had a chance to say anything. 'They're not. We were talking about those daft buggers, you know, the youngsters in the Hobby Horses quiz team.'

'Oh, dear me,' Wyn's posture relaxed as he smiled and cast his eyes skyward. 'A bunch of daft buggers right enough.'

'I understand they might have extreme views,' said Jemima.

'No love. You've got that wrong. They've definitely got extreme views. Get decent folks' backs up and set back the Welsh language cause no end. I'm first language Welsh, but live and let live I say. We're all people at the end of the day, and we need to get on. Don't matter what language you speak.'

Jemima couldn't fault the sentiment.

'If you ask me, they've all got a screw loose.' Wyn tapped the side of his head. 'Want everyone in the country to have to speak Welsh. Compulsory like. No thought of personal choice. Like a bunch of modern-day crusaders. Full of self-righteousness with their heads up their own backsides.'

'Do you have any reason to believe they'd resort to violence?' asked Jemima.

'What? Like that lot that went around firebombing holiday homes? Nooo.' Wyn shook his head as he thought it over. 'They're an annoying bunch. There's no doubt about that. But they're not terrorists. Just try to bully people into speaking

Welsh, that's all. But no one takes any notice of them. People do what people do. They should have learned the lesson by now. No matter how hard you try to change people's attitudes they end up making up their own mind about things.'

'And can you think of anyone who would want to hurt them?'

'I wouldn't have thought so. Apart from getting on peoples' nerves, I wouldn't have thought anyone would be wound up enough to have a vendetta against them. As I said, they're harmless but annoying all the same. Still, it'd be better for everyone if they gave it a rest once in a while.'

CHAPTER 26

Jemima's head spun as she returned to the car. Billy's point of view was markedly different to Wyn's, and the truth was likely to be somewhere in between. Dan was already at the wheel, and she buckled up. 'Did you get through to the station?' she asked.

'Yeah. Spoke to Gareth and told him to arrange for Nigel, Kayleigh, and Daisy to be picked up immediately and brought in for questioning.'

'That's good. If Billy was to be believed, there's no shortage of locals who dislike that group of friends. And given the extreme level of violence inflicted upon Jenkins and Prosser shortly before they were killed, it's quite possible that the others could be at risk too.'

'The hobby horse tattoos being sliced from the skin and the fact that aitch-aitch was carved into their foreheads all point to the fact that two people have it in for that quiz team. It's bizarre. What could they have possibly done to piss people off so much?'

'Billy said that a lot of people in this town don't like them. From what I understood, it seems as though the Hobby Horses members set themselves apart from a lot of people. Apparently, they're antagonistic towards newcomers, and even with people who've lived here all their lives. Especially if they don't speak Welsh.'

'This can't just be about language. It doesn't make sense. I know people who are bilingual, but they're not like that,' said Dan.

'Exactly. Most people are level-headed and accepting of differences and personal preferences. Billy was saying that some of his other regulars are fluent Welsh speakers, but even they wanted him to bar the Hobby Horses lot.

'I just spoke to one of Billy's friends whose first language is Welsh. He agreed that the Hobby Horses team were annoying, but seemed to think they were harmless enough.'

'They seemed ordinary enough when we spoke to them,' said Dan.

'But if they've got an extremist agenda, they're hardly going to let it slip in front of us. And it sounds to me as though Jenkins, Prosser, and the others could be extremists. It's not unprecedented. I remember my dad talking about the Welsh nationalist movement, Meibion Glyndŵr,' said Jemima.

'I've not heard of them.'

'Well, back in the seventies and eighties some of the members of that group carried out a firebombing campaign. They targeted holiday homes, owned by English people. Blamed them for inflating property prices so that locals couldn't afford to live in the area.'

'But that happens in so many locations. Holiday homes are not just a Welsh phenomenon. You've only got to look at places like Devon and Cornwall. It happens all the time,' said Dan.

'I agree, but the worrying thing is that there were recent reports in the media that that sort of thing could happen again. With the shortage of housing, tensions are rising. It's inevitable that some people will eventually resort to violence. And when that happens it'll be the likes of you and me who'll be expected to deal with the fallout.' Jemima sighed.

'Makes you wonder where an acceptable level of nationalism ends, and extremism begins,' said Dan.

'That's a very profound statement, Dan. And I've an awful feeling that the way some politicians in the Senedd are stoking the fires, it won't be long before there's a major incident somewhere.'

'You can bet your life that when that happens, they'll all be shrugging their shoulders and issuing denials that they played any part in it.'

They arrived back at the station to find Gareth, Levi, and Nancy still hard at it. 'Where's Gary?' asked Jemima.

'He said to tell you that he's gone up to Rhaslas Pond. He was back on the phone after you left. Said he was getting the run-around, and eventually called in a favour from someone they've used before. Promised them a couple of tickets to the next International at the Millennium Stadium. It'll cost him an arm and a leg. Anyway, a dive team was supposed to be heading there about an hour ago, and Gary set off to make sure that they carry out a thorough search,' said Gareth. 'So, I doubt we'll see him for the rest of the day. Unless they find something that is.'

'Have Nigel Davies, Kayleigh Bevan, or Daisy Evans arrived at the station yet?'

'No, but uniform have been dispatched to pick them up.'

'Any developments with the teenagers' electronic devices?' Jemima knew it was a longshot, but if anyone could find something it would be Gareth. Before Gareth's promotion to sergeant, he had worked closely with DS Finlay Ashton who, with a degree in computer forensics, had exceptional skills in that particular area. With Finlay's help and encouragement, Gareth had learned a lot, and had also gone on to undertake more formal studies in his own time. With Finlay sadly out of the picture, Gareth had become their go-to person for IT-based tasks.

'I've looked at three of the devices so far. Run diagnostics to identify files and sites they visited. I'm currently in the process of running a comparison of that data between the devices to establish whether there are any common site visits.'

Jemima glanced at Gareth's screen. Reams of data scrolled so rapidly that it was impossible to focus on any words or characters.

'How'd it go—' Gareth stopped mid-sentence as his machine pinged to announce that the program had ended and the search was complete.

As the three officers focused their attention on the screen, they saw that a single common website had been identified among the hundreds, if not thousands of those visited by three of the dead teenagers. The name seemed innocuous enough. Simply called "*LookAfterYourself*".

'Guys, have you come across any mention of something called "*LookAfterYourself*" on any of those social media sites?' asked Gareth.

'Possibly, hang on a sec . . .' said Nancy.

Gareth drummed his fingers on the desk as he waited for Levi and Nancy to check their findings.

'Yeah, I've got one here,' said Levi.

'Me too,' said Nancy, moments later.

A quick comparison of the names clarified that at least five of the dead teenagers had visited the site. It was a link that hadn't previously been made and gave a focus to the investigation.

'Levi, Nancy, carry on going through the social media accounts of the other victims. Specifically looking for any mention of that website. We're on to something. This surely can't be a coincidence,' said Jemima. 'Great work, Gar. Very impressive.'

Gareth experienced a warm glow of satisfaction at Jemima's words of praise. 'Thanks, guv. While I'm waiting for other devices to come in, I'll start investigating that site. See what I can find. If there is anything sinister about it, I doubt it'll be obvious from the interface. So, I'll probably end up having to do a deep dive. First off, I'll look into the IP address and try to establish who's behind it and work my way from there.' He was so keen to get on with the task that he started typing away before he finished speaking.

CHAPTER 27

It was starting to feel as though they were making some progress. At least on one of the cases. The one Torsten Olsen was unaware that they were investigating, and soon Jemima would have to face the inevitable flack.

Jemima's thoughts were interrupted by a call from the front desk to announce that Nigel Davies had arrived at the station. She asked that he be placed in an interview room.

'Do you want me to sit in with you?' asked Dan.

'Not really. Go give Gary a ring and find out what's happening up at Rhaslas Pond. While you're at it, chase up Lewis and Zoe. They were only going to his cousin's house, and they seem to be taking a long time. If it turns out to be a dead end, then I don't want them skiving and taking the mick. Not when there's plenty they could be getting on with back here.'

'While I'm at it, do you want me to touch base with Mike and Mack?'

'You could do. It'll be good to have updates from both of them.'

Jemima headed towards the interview room. From the moment she entered the corridor she could hear the sound of raised voices.

As she neared the door, Jemima heard an angry tirade in what she presumed was the Welsh language. She took a deep breath and opened the door to see the young PC standing there, red-faced and uncomfortable.

'What's going on here?' she asked. With hands on her hips, she looked from one to the other.

'I've no idea what he's shouting about, ma'am.' The young man was clearly frustrated but had managed to remain calm. 'I told Mr Davies to take a seat. Said you'd be here shortly.'

'Thank you, constable. That'll be all. You can go now,' said Jemima before turning to face Nigel Davies. She placed a notepad and pen on the desk, pulled out a chair and sat down.

'Take a seat, Mr Davies.' The man ignored her instruction and continued to shout in his chosen language. Jemima was having none of it. She stood up abruptly. Sidestepping the table, she closed the distance between them. Davies, who had clearly not expected this, took a couple of steps backwards. Unfortunately for him, he soon found himself against the wall with nowhere left to go.

'Enough, Mr Davies. I will not be bullied by you, or anyone else. I acknowledge your passion for the Welsh language, but right now we're in a race against time to find those responsible for the murder of two of your friends before they have the opportunity to kill anyone else. Now, I don't speak Welsh and we both know that you're perfectly capable of speaking English. It's the language we conversed in when I visited you at home. So, I'm asking you respectfully to sit down and cooperate.'

Anger blazed in Nigel's eyes. This was a fight he believed in. His beloved country and language were everything to him. A point of principle. Though one he was forced to abandon, on a daily basis. He had learned over the years that there were very few people who felt as he did. It seemed that everywhere he went, the use of the Welsh language, Welsh culture, his very essence was being diluted.

As Nigel went to speak, Jemima interjected. 'If I were you, I'd think very carefully about how you act and what you say, Mr Davies. This is a murder investigation. Not a forum for whatever views you might hold.'

Nigel had got the message loud and clear. 'Fine,' he hissed, as he slumped onto the chair. 'I guess I owe it to Benno and Jonno to allow you to do your job.'

'Thank you,' said Jemima. Even though she had not yet questioned the man, the encounter had proved useful and informative. It backed up Billy James's assertion that most of his customers were wary of the Hobby Horses group, as if Nigel was anything to go by, they would be viewed as people who tried to force their chosen way of life upon others.

Jemima sat down, picked up the pen and moved the empty pad of paper towards her. 'Tell me about the quiz team that you're a member of.'

Nigel's eyes narrowed as he tried to work out why she was asking him about this. 'We're just a group of friends. Same as any of the other teams. Why are you asking?'

Jemima ignored the question. 'Who are the other members?'

'Well, there's only me, Kayleigh, and Flower now. Used to be Benno and Jonno as well.' The overriding angry tone of voice was replaced with a tinge of sadness.

'And what is your team name?'

'The Hobby Horses.'

'What made you choose that particular name?'

'Look I don't see how this is going to help you find the bastards who killed my friends.' The anger had returned.

'Answer the question, Mr Davies. The sooner I have the information I need, the sooner you'll be out of here,' Jemima's voice was steady.

'It was the logo for the original Rhymney Brewery. We called our team that as a tribute to the past. A time when all these valleys were alive. When people had jobs nearby. Pride in their community.'

'Surely you're talking about a time before you were born?'

'Of course I am. The brewing operation shut down a long time ago. Big business came in, bought it up and spat it out. Didn't care who got tossed aside in the process. You wouldn't believe it now, but that town was a hive of activity. Hundreds of men worked in local manufacturing jobs. They built things. Big, beautiful machines like Hymac. Things that were useful. Things to be proud of. But that disappeared too, along with all those well-paid jobs. Of course, JC bloody B kept going. Hardly surprising though. It's an English company, after all. That wouldn't be allowed to fail, would it?

'And now look at us. My generation were sold out before we were even born. Maggie Thatcher closed the mines and signed the death warrants for future generations.'

Jemima couldn't believe the self-pitying tirade spewing from Davies' mouth. Spoken with such conviction, it was evident the man had spun this line this many times before. There was no acknowledgement that other areas of the UK had been forced to evolve, reinvent themselves, move with the times. Nigel was full of excuses about why his life was so hard, blaming events which had happened before he was even born. As though he was a leaf blown on the wind, with no choice over his life's trajectory. Asking her to believe that there would never be any hope again.

Jemima couldn't let Nigel's remarks go without setting him straight. Despite having the ability to keep her cool, even with the most provocative of people, the man had a knack of pressing her buttons. 'You're griping about events that happened decades ago, and it wasn't just a Welsh issue. It affected areas of England too.'

'I don't need an English person lecturing me!' His voice was raised. The mask of reasonableness had slipped, and his eyes blazed with contempt, focusing on her with a laser-like intensity.

'I have a different accent to you, Mr Davies, but I'm just as Welsh as you are. Though, no matter an individual's heritage, or their life choices, when all's said and done, we're just people. The very nature of living in a democracy means that we are each responsible for our own destiny. Our choices make us who we are, and as a nation we are richer for it.

It's clear we've taken different paths in life. I wanted to be a police officer. You chose to work in a factory. Different choices. Different life experiences.'

'You condescending cow!'

'Mr Dav—'

'You've come here with your pseudo-superiority. Looking down your nose at me. Well, let me set you straight. I don't just work in a factory. I own the bloody place. I run the place. I employ people. Pay them a living wage. And spend most of my time trying to turn a profit so that local people will have a reason to get up in the morning.

'You've made assumptions about me, because of where I live. You looked at my house and saw it's run-down. Kayleigh works as a carer. I'm a factory worker. Therefore, we're a couple of no-hopers. Well, you couldn't be more wrong. As things stand, every penny we have goes to keep that factory running.

'You get paid whether you get a result or not. Oh, to have such an easy life with a guaranteed income. Perhaps you should get a job in the real world and then you'd realise how tough things are.'

Jemima wasn't often shocked. But she had to admit that she had been too ready to believe that Nigel Davies was someone who had chosen to coast through life. Doing as little as possible to get by.

Appreciating that she needed to dial down the tension in the room she continued. 'It wasn't my intention to condescend to you. It's apparent that we've both allowed unconscious biases to cloud our perception of each other. So, I'd like us to start again. I asked my officers to bring you in here for a reason and it's important that I speak to you.'

'Fine, ask your questions.'

'Evidence found during the course of the investigation into the murders of Ben and John, has led us to believe that there is a very real possibility that they were killed as a result of them being members of your quiz team.'

Nigel's body went rigid. Jemima's words had shocked him to the core.

There was a moment when it occurred to Jemima that she just might have to press the emergency button and ask for medical assistance, as she was worried that the man was about to have a heart attack. But before she took such a drastic step, she needed to make sure. 'Are you all right, Nigel?'

At first, he stared at her blankly. Then, as her words sunk in, he nodded.

'Take a slow deep breath. In through the nose. Out through the mouth. That's it.' As she talked him through what was usually an autonomic response, he regained some self-control.

It took almost ten minutes, during which time Nigel sipped slowly from a beaker of water. He concentrated on his breathing, until he was able to continue with the interview.

Having witnessed the man's incapacity to deal with the unexpected, Jemima wondered if he bullied others as a defence mechanism. Though it was equally conceivable that by attempting to make others feel inadequate for not being able to converse in or understand the Welsh language, gave him a perverse sense of superiority. What she did know for certain was that the realisation that he could be on the killers' hit list absolutely terrified him.

'Are you able to continue?' asked Jemima. She was conscious that his panic attack had resulted in wasted time. When he nodded, she continued. 'Is there anyone who might have it in for you and your friends?'

'Get real. Why the hell would anyone want to kill us? I admit we've never been popular. Most of the people I employ resent the fact that I'm so pro-Welsh language. People like me are often seen as misfits, despite the fact that it's our country, our language. And as for outsiders moving into the area wanting to take what's ours and change things to suit themselves . . .' He stopped talking abruptly when he realised that Jemima genuinely had concerns about his safety. 'Are you seriously saying that there're some nutters out there who want us dead?'

'As things stand, it's a theory we're exploring. Which is why I need your cooperation. I appreciate you're grieving the loss of your friends, and you're also scared. But believe me when I say that we will do everything we can to find out who's behind this and stop them before they do it again.'

'Has Kayleigh been brought in for questioning? She spends a lot of time travelling around by herself, which makes her more vulnerable. I need to know she's safe.'

'An officer has been dispatched to bring her in,' said Jemima.

'Thank God for that. I can't lose her. But you must have got it wrong. It's insane to suggest that someone would kill us because we were in the same quiz team as Benno and Jonno. It's not as though we lived in each other's pockets. We only get together for quiz nights. Apart from that we don't have anything to do with each other. Kay and I have lived together for years. We work ridiculously long hours and keep to ourselves.

'On a superficial level we stayed friendly with the others after we finished school. But the only thing we have in common with them is our love of the Welsh language. I don't even know what the others are into these days. I think Benno and Jonno might have hung out together sometimes. But I don't know for certain. And as for Daisy, well I haven't got a clue. She was always a bit of an enigma. Can be quite aloof at times.

'Why the hell would someone target us? We're just one of ten or so quiz teams in an ordinary pub. Your theory makes no sense.'

Unperturbed, Jemima continued with the interview. 'Ben and John had a hobby horse tattoo on their shoulders. Do you have one?'

'Yeah.'

'What about Kayleigh and Daisy? Do they have the same tattoo?'

'Yeah. Outside of quiz night it was the only time we did something together as a group. Actually, it was my idea. I'd had a tough couple of months and was fed up being Mister Sensible all the time. It started off as an off-the-cuff remark while we were waiting for the quiz to start. Jonno loved the idea and kept banging on about us getting it done. In the end we all just did it for a laugh.'

'I see. And would anyone outside of your group know about those tattoos?'

'We didn't show them off, or anything. Let's face it, it would only give other people another reason to laugh at us. So, no. The only person who would know about the tattoos would be the bloke who did them.'

'And that would be?'

Nigel gave her the name of a local tattoo parlour but only knew the first name of the individual who had created the tattoos.

'So, what happens now?' asked Nigel.

'In what respect?'

'Will Kay and I be protected until you arrest whoever's doing this?' asked Nigel.

'So far, we haven't identified any likely suspects. I was hoping that by talking to you, I might have made some headway. But as you've been unable to give me the names of people who might hold a grudge against your group, I'm afraid we're no further forward.

'Are you and Kayleigh able to take a couple of days off work? Do either of you have any family you could stay with. Family out of the immediate area that is?'

'No and no. It's not that simple. It's my factory. My workforce relies on me. I can't just drop everything.'

'And it's not an option for you to manage the place remotely?'

'No.' Nigel shook his head. 'As it is I'm going to have to play catch up for the disruption caused by you dragging me down here. And as for Kayleigh, well there're a lot of people who depend on her just to get them through the day.'

'The best I can do is issue you with a panic alarm which will alert us immediately should you be in danger, and I'll get an officer to take you back to the factory. But I will try to find someone to keep an eye on Kayleigh, as I agree, her job makes her more vulnerable. I'll reassess the situation at the end of the day. As a minimum you'll have the panic alarm, but should I have reason to believe there's an imminent threat to your safety, I'll see about getting you both to a safe house.

'In the meantime, stay vigilant, and if anything occurs to you about who could be behind this, then get in touch with me immediately.' She handed Nigel her card.

CHAPTER 28

As Jemima headed back to the incident room, she found herself thinking about Dan's earlier observation –

"Where does an acceptable level of nationalism end and extremism begin?"

She had to admit that devolution had all but signed the death warrant for the country. Almost a quarter of a century with the same party in power had resulted in a seemingly never-ending merry-go-round of no accountability.

No one acknowledged her when Jemima entered the incident room. In the furthest corner, Dan, Levi, and Nancy were huddled together, discussing something in low tones, so as not to disturb Gareth. The sergeant's desk was nearest the door. He was engrossed in his objective of finding out everything he could about the suspicious website, *LookAfterYourself.*

When Gareth was determined to do something, God help anyone or anything that got in his way. His steely determination and agile curiosity to master new skills were an admirable and formidable combination of qualities. Being entirely focused upon the task he had set himself he furiously tapped away at the keyboard. Stopping occasionally to absentmindedly tug at strands of hair, he stared at reams of data scrolling on the screen.

'Any developments?' she asked, standing only a few feet away from him.

'Ummm?' He looked up and almost jumped when he saw her. Having been so engrossed in his work he'd failed to hear her approach.

'Sorry, Gar. Didn't mean to creep up on you like that.'

'That's OK, guv. Did you want something?'

'Just wondering how it's going?'

'I did an initial sweep of the website and looked at the source code. For the most part, it's pretty standard stuff. But I've come across one section that looks dodgy. It doesn't appear to relate to anything you see on the user interface, and I've a feeling it might be a backdoor.'

'Give it to me in simple terms, Gar, because I've no idea what you're talking about.'

'The site's aimed at teenagers. It's set up under the guise of supporting them. Giving positive reinforcements about self-image and life in general. You can tell from the IP address that it's registered in the UK. On the face of it, it's legit. I've established who owns the website and no worries there.

'However, there's a section of code that I think might be an add-on.'

'And that's a problem because?' Jemima had no idea where this was leading.

'Whichever language they're using, every programmer has their own way of doing things. It's like speech patterns. For instance, if everyone in this room was asked to give a written account of something you'd probably be able to make an educated guess about who had produced each account. That's because we all favour the use of different words, syntax, et cetera. Which means there would be some very obvious and also some subtle differences between those written accounts.

'It's the same with programming. As we all think differently and approach things in different ways you can identify amendments and add-ons in the source code. Especially when they've been done by someone other than the original programmer. That's why I spotted one particular section. If you've any knowledge of code, it'd jump out at you.'

'I'll take your word for that, Gar. As far as I'm concerned it all looks like a load of gobbledegook.'

Gareth smiled. 'Trust me on this, guv. This section wasn't part of the original source code. It was added in by someone else.'

'So, what does it do?' asked Jemima.

'That's what I'm trying to find out. I can't see that it has any relevance to any of the visible options available to the users. Which makes me think it's a back door.' Observing the puzzled look on Jemima's face he continued. 'To put it in layman's terms, I think someone is piggybacking on the website, without the website owner's knowledge. And I think that this section of code allows certain users to access a hidden layer. Most likely hosted on the dark web.'

'And how would users access that?'

'They'd need a password. Which is why I've asked Nancy and the others to see if they can find any sort of chatter on the socials. I've also informed the website owner of what I believe has happened and they're putting some people on it, to work at it from their end.'

'Excellent work, Gar. Finlay would've been proud of you.'

'I hope so, guv. I wouldn't have got into this if it wasn't for him.' Gareth smiled sadly.

'If someone has hacked into that website, they're obviously up to no good,' said Jemima.

'My thoughts exactly. Anyway, must get on.' The data had stopped scrolling. Gareth squinted, as he stared at the screen and moments later began to type instructions so quickly that Jemima was unable to keep up with the movements of his fingers.

Jemima headed in the direction of the others. 'Found anything of significance?'

'First off, Gary's confirmed the dive team has arrived and were getting ready to make a start. That was about twenty minutes ago. He'll keep us informed of any developments,' said Dan.

Jemima nodded her acknowledgement. 'Gareth's just told me that he thinks someone has piggybacked onto the source code for that *LookAfterYourself* website. Thinks they might have created a hidden section which takes users to the dark web.'

'Sounds sinister,' said Dan. 'Especially when the website's been created to help teenagers feel better about themselves.'

'Exactly. You'd only visit that site if you were emotionally fragile. If you were confident and on an even keel you wouldn't feel the need to take a look at *LookAfterYourself*. You'd just get on with living your life,' said Jemima.

'I've had a look at it and there's nothing obviously dodgy on the webpage,' said Levi.

'There wouldn't be,' said Nancy. 'If they wanted to keep it a secret, and it's something they only wanted certain users to access, whoever was behind it would give their targets a password to enable them to enter that section. Chances are that they'd change the password for each person. That way, it would restrict access, and make it next to impossible for anyone to enter without permission.'

'How would they be able to do that?' asked Dan.

'It'd be easy enough by text,' said Jemima, as her thoughts raced ahead. 'Do you have to sign up for full access to the website services that are offered to anyone who looks at the site?'

'Yeah,' said Levi.

'What sort of things do they ask for?'

'Usual things. Name. Age. Ethnicity. Phone number. Email address. They also ask for the school you attend, but no surprise there as they're specifically targeting teenagers, and it's linked to an educational welfare initiative.'

'Umm, I wonder . . .' As the seed of a hypothesis began to germinate, Jemima's brow furrowed. With one arm folded across her midriff, she rested the elbow of her other arm upon it. Slowly tapping her lips with her forefinger, her footfall matched its rhythm. She strode back and forth and allowed her thoughts to flow.

All eyes were upon Jemima, but Nancy, being the most impatient of the officers was keen to know what the DCI was thinking. Unable to keep quiet any longer, she broke the silence.

'What're you thinking, guv?'

Upon hearing the junior officer's voice, her thought process was broken, and Jemima turned to see the three of them looking at her expectantly. With insufficient time to think everything through she hoped her idea had legs. Currently it would be a leap of faith. But as things stood, she was prepared to back her hunch. After all, if she'd called it wrong, the worst that could happen is that she made a fool of herself. However, if her hunch was correct, she could end up potentially saving some lives. It was time to instruct her team to set up a sting.

'What if some, or all of these teen suicides, weren't suicides at all? What if they were proxy murders?' said Jemima. The room was silent as the others stared blankly at her as they tried to make sense of what she was saying.

'No, you've lost me there,' said Dan.

'Well, Gareth thinks he's found someone piggybacking onto the site. Using a backdoor that they've created to hide the fact that they're accessing it. I think it's possible we might have a tech-savvy psychopath treating this government sponsored platform as an online marketplace. Where from the safety of their own home they can browse potential victims at leisure.

'A crude analogy would be that it's like going on ASOS to look for a dress. You might only have a vague idea about what you want. You could have very specific requirements. But when you come across the perfect dress you place it in your shopping basket and proceed to checkout.

'If my hunch is right, that's the point at which the killer makes contact. Possibly by text. Sending the potential victim, a personalised code to access a specially designed site on the dark web where they can be groomed at leisure. Pushing them further and further down the rabbit hole until the feel they have no choice but to kill themselves.'

'That's a sick theory, guv, but I think you could be on to something,' said Nancy. 'Sounds like something you'd see on Criminal Minds.'

'I say we set up a sting. Present this bastard with their perfect victim. Make them salivate at the thought of grooming them. Play their sick game. Keep them online so that Gareth has a chance of tracing them. Then we catch them in the act and end this once and for all.'

As Jemima looked at each of them in turn, she smiled. They had a plan. The team was united, re-energised and raring to go.

CHAPTER 29

The door opened as Lewis and Zoe entered the room. They ignored Gareth who was still engrossed in his task and headed towards the others.

'Did you learn anything useful?' asked Jemima. She was determined not to waste any more time.

'We had an interesting discussion,' said Lewis.

'Let me stop you there, Lewis. I need bullet points from you. Just cold hard facts, or speculative information which might be of use.' Jemima appreciated that she was denying him his moment in the spotlight and experienced a slight pang of guilt. She could still remember what it was like to be a junior officer. Keen to impress. Make a difference. Still, time was of the essence . . .

Colour rose on Lewis's neck and flushed his cheeks. He dropped his gaze and took a deep breath before relaying the information. 'In general, there's not any significant tensions in the area. Most people have lived there for donkey's years. Wouldn't move out if you paid them. There've been a few newcomers moving into the area, but as it's not one of the so-called honeypot areas, they're very few and far between. Especially since there're not that many job opportunities up that way, and it takes too long to travel to areas where there are jobs.'

‘Not exactly breaking news,’ said Dan. ‘We knew all of that stuff before we arrived.’

Jemima shot her sergeant a disapproving look, and he fell silent. She understood his frustration. Lewis hadn’t yet told them anything relevant, but he was new to this, and she sensed that he was just trying to give them a thorough background to the area. It was already apparent during the few days they’d spent in the area, that life towards the head of the valleys was relatively insular. It was noticeably different to that of the cosmopolitan feel in the cities or larger towns.

Rhymney and the surrounding small towns and villages were largely populated by generation after generation of the same families and that could quite easily lead to some residents feeling resentful towards outsiders who would almost inevitably want to carve out their own niche and live their own lives.

‘The visit was useful, guv,’ said Lewis. ‘Nathan had a study period so he was at home. He said that their teachers have made them aware of adverts on sites like Snapchat and TikTok about something called the *LookAfterYourself* website. Every pupil was given a leaflet to hand to their parents, explaining what it was about. In fact, he gave me one.’ He handed Jemima a glossy leaflet.

It was an initiative adopted throughout Wales, appearing to be an extension of pastoral care. Offering every pupil the opportunity to online advice and allocating them DBS registered mentors to help them with any difficulties they might experience.

If, as she feared, there was at least one malign influence behind this initiative, it could affect every pupil of high school age. If left unchecked, it had the potential to prematurely end some lives and ruin so many others in the process. She couldn’t help but shiver at the thought of James taking up the offer of such help, only to be callously manipulated.

‘Nathan’s best friend is a lad called Farhan Laghari. He started in the high school about a year after the others when his parents moved to the area. According to Nathan, Farhan reckons he heard that a boy named Thomas Sidhu used that website when he was being bullied.'

'He was one of the suicide victims,' interjected Nancy.

'Rumour has it that Thomas was texted a code which took him onto the dark web. And after that, Thomas seemed to change. He isolated himself from his friends. Lost interest in things.'

'Excellent work, Lewis. You too, Zoe.' Both young officers were buoyed by the DCI's praise.

'Where's the file on Thomas's death?'

Levi shuffled through a pile of folders and extracted one. 'This is it, guv.' He handed it to Jemima.

Turning page after page, she soon found what she was looking for. 'Well at least the investigating officer obtained Thomas's phone records.' There was a list of telephone numbers for calls made and received. Text messages had been retrieved. Most appeared to be innocuous enough, apart from a series of about twenty or so, covering a three-month period, leading up to the day he killed himself. These texts were from a withheld number. Each message comprised of eight characters in length, with no intelligible word amongst them. With various combinations of letters, numbers, and other characters, they could be nothing more than randomised access codes. Whoever was behind this had gone to a great deal of effort to cover their tracks.

'Right, everyone, grab a couple of folders. We're specifically looking for text messages that look as though they could be randomised access codes. They'll look something like these,' said Jemima, as she pointed to what she'd just found.

The room fell silent as everyone concentrated on the task. There was a new sense of urgency and optimism, as every officer in the room was aware that they were quite possibly on the verge of connecting the suicide cases. Events which until now had been written off as a series of isolated incidents but might ultimately have been brought about by a malign actor. An unknown puppet master who had remained out of sight but had selected victims and driven them to commit suicide.

Less than half an hour later, the team had gathered around a table to share their findings, and as Lewis wrote them up on the board, it became apparent that Jemima's hunch had been realised. Eight of the ten teenage suicide victims had received randomised access codes via text messages. A further analysis of those victims revealed that they were from families who had moved into the area.

Someone was targeting outsiders, and the only people they had come across who appeared to dislike outsiders were the members of the Hobby Horses quiz team. Yet, so far, all they had was supposition. If they were going to get to the bottom of it, they needed proof that those randomised access codes were a gateway to a suicide site somewhere on the dark web.

'We're on the right track. At least we now know the killer's preferences, which will help us create an irresistible profile to act as bait. But we must act quickly, and we can't afford to get it wrong. Every second this person is out there, is an opportunity for them to target and kill other victims. Until now we've focused on apparent suicides in this area. But this website is used throughout the whole of Wales. Which means they could have claimed hundreds of victims we know nothing about. Plus, there's nothing to say that they only groom one at a time. It's conceivable they could have multiple ones on the go. We need this monster in custody now. Before they have a chance to claim more lives.'

CHAPTER 30

When Dan's phone rang, he broke away from the group to answer it. Jemima took the opportunity to glance down the other end of the room, and saw that Gareth was on a call too. For the last hour she and the others had been so caught up in searching through the various phone records that she had not given him a second thought. Gareth was on a mission of his own, and any disruption to his thought process could hinder the possibility of him making progress on a task that the rest of them were unequipped to undertake.

Gareth's posture suddenly changed, and he slapped the surface of the desk. 'Oh yes! Yes! Yes! Yes! That's great news. You've pulled a blinder there. Send me a copy of everything you've got and keep a close eye on things at your end. From now on, the moment you spot any suspicious activity, I need you to do everything you can to track down where it's originating from. And I need to know about it. It doesn't matter what time it is. Just call me. And thanks, mate. I owe you one.'

Gareth pushed his chair back and stood up. As he turned to face Jemima, she saw his huge grin. Her heart leapt in anticipation.

'That was Hunter Bryant on the phone. He's the guy who designed and has ongoing responsibility for the *LookAfterYourself* website. As it was a government backed initiative, aimed solely at pupil welfare, he was asked to tick various boxes before he went ahead with developing the site. One of those was collaborating with selected teaching staff from schools around Wales. Now that's where it gets interesting, because one of the names on the list is Daisy Evans.'

'It connects the two cases!' Jemima felt a sense of relief wash over her.

'Sure does, guv. She's an ICT teacher at a Welsh medium school. Given the fact that this website is a Welsh government initiative, they insisted that it had to be bilingual. Daisy fitted the bill on all fronts. She's a fluent Welsh speaker. Computer literate. And get this . . .' He paused for dramatic effect. 'She also has responsibility for pastoral care within her school.'

The moment of relief had quickly deserted her. Her fingernails dug into her palm. There wasn't a case she'd investigated where she didn't feel a sense of anger. Much of the time she managed to keep a lid on it as she knew from experience that it was counterproductive to allow your emotions to cloud your judgement. Solving a case was not enough. You needed to get irrefutable evidence to back up what you knew. Without that evidence the Crown Prosecution Service would refuse to take the case and the perpetrators would not face a trial.

Before speaking, she unclenched her fists and stretched out her fingers to allow the tension to ebb away. 'Can we prove that she's behind this, Gar?'

'Not at the moment, guv. But if we can get a warrant to search her house, and examine every electronic device she has access to, then it's possible.'

'First off, does Hunter have any proof that Daisy has manipulated the program behind the website interface?'

'Not as such. I directed him to that dodgy looking section of code, and he agrees with me. Someone has added that post-website launch. It's safe to assume that whoever did it is extremely competent. Gaining access to the code and inserting a backdoor isn't something anyone could do without risking someone spotting it. It's serious hacking. Takes a lot of skill. Hell, I wouldn't know where to begin.'

'And Daisy has those skills?' If Daisy's skillset was so advanced, she would have been able to make far more money in the commercial sector.

'We'll only know for certain once we've run diagnostic tests on her computers. I'm confident she would have used a VPN to hack into the website. That's textbook stuff. No hacker would dream of poking around in someone else's code and leave themselves exposed. It's far too risky. If they get caught, they could end up with a prison sentence.'

'Well, we've made some headway too. Before we take things further, we need to pool our findings. Update briefing now, people!' Jemima shouted and clapped her hands to get everyone's attention.

Gareth kicked off the briefing session with his recent findings. His enthusiasm energised the team. When he learned of the texts containing randomised access codes, he was unable to hide his delight. 'That's how she got them to access her site on the dark web. I take it that there's no record of who that phone belongs to?' He looked at the others expectantly. Seeing everyone shake their heads he couldn't help but sigh. 'She's not stupid. Must've used a burner phone so no one can trace it back to her. I wouldn't be surprised if she still has that phone somewhere close at hand. If she's grooming someone, she'd need to have access twenty-four-seven. To be effective she'd need to be able to contact them when they're feeling particularly desperate. If she missed the opportunity there'd always be the chance that someone else would find out about their fragile state of mind and she might lose them forever.'

'Has Daisy Evans been brought in yet?' asked Jemima. A few hours had passed since she'd asked for the remaining members of the quiz team to be rounded up and brought in for questioning.

'I'll ring the front desk, and find out,' said Zoe.

'Gar, arrange for search warrants for Daisy's home, vehicle, and school. We need the authority to search and examine every electronic device she's had access to. I know it's going to be problematic when it comes to the school, as God knows how many devices she has access to there. Chances are she does all of this at home, but we don't want to take the risk of missing some vital evidence elsewhere.

'We definitely need a belt and braces approach on this, so, Levi, I want you to try to get a search warrant for Nigel and Kayleigh's house too. But I wouldn't be surprised if it's denied. As yet we don't have any reasonable evidence to link them to the hack on the *LookAfterYourself* website, and to be honest I'm not even sure they'd be capable of doing anything towards it.

'Perhaps more will come to light if Mack manages to round up more of the dead teens' electronic devices.'

'Before we go all out on the suicides, you need to know that I've just spoken to Gary again,' said Dan. 'He told me that the divers have found a quadbike with a trailer, submerged in Rhaslas Pond. They're waiting for lifting equipment and transportation to get them out of there, and Jeanne Ennersley's team are on standby for doing the forensics on them. Though we all know that the chances of there being anything useable after being in the water for a few days are not that great.'

With the recent findings on the spate of suicides, the murders of the quiz team members had momentarily taken a back seat, despite it being the reason they were there in the first place. Though, it wasn't as if Jemima had taken all resources away from the investigation. Gary was up at Rhaslas Pond, and a forensics team would soon be testing the quadbikes and trailers found by the divers. Mike was still doing the rounds in the local towns and villages but hadn't reported in to say if he'd made any progress. Everything that could be done was being done.

At that moment, Gareth's phone rang, and he moved away to answer it.

'Guv,' said Zoe. 'I've spoken to the sergeant on the front desk. He's just been informed that officers went to Daisy's school, but she wasn't there. Apparently, she handed her notice in a while back and finished at the end of last term.'

'Guv! This is urgent!' Gareth's face was flushed. His hand was covering the mouthpiece of his phone.

'What is it?' asked Jemima.

'I've got Hunter Bryant on the line. Someone's accessed the backdoor add-on. Hunter's doing his best to trace things as we speak. It's likely another teenage has been directed there. If we don't act now, there could be another proxy murder.'

CHAPTER 31

The likelihood that at that moment there was another teenager out there being groomed to commit suicide changed everything. There was no time to wait for search warrants.

'Get Mack and Mike on the phones. Do it now! We've evidence that she's connected to that website, and that someone's just used the backdoor to access the hidden add-on. She's grooming another potential victim. God only knows how long she's been getting inside their head. We can't allow her to claim another life. We've got to find and stop her before it's too late.'

'Guv! I've got Mike on the line,' said Levi.

'Give me the phone,' ordered Jemima, as she held out her hand and raced to his side. 'Mike, listen carefully. I need you to drop whatever it is you're doing and get to Daisy Evans' house. Don't bother ringing the doorbell. Force entry and do whatever it takes to get her away from her computer. Do it quickly and if possible don't allow her to shut things down. Whatever link's up and running needs to be kept open. Cuff her and arrest her for murder. We're on our way. I'll get someone to contact Mack. He's in your general vicinity. We're on our way too.' Jemima had disconnected the call before Mike had time to reply.

‘Gar, stay on the line with Hunter, and keep us updated. I’ve no idea how this will pan out, so Zoe, Lewis, stay here in case Gareth needs you. Give Mack Daisy’s address and tell him to get there pronto. We can’t allow Mike to go there without backup. The rest of you, grab your things. We’re off to Rhymney. Let’s finish this thing once and for all. Hopefully before Daisy kills another kid.’

With sirens blaring and lights flashing the two unmarked police cars were driven a speed. Jemima was at the wheel of the first one. Having become familiar with the roads she felt more comfortable going faster than she would initially have done.

When Dan’s phone rang, he was pleased to have the opportunity to distract himself from the speed they were travelling.

Through the speakerphone, the frustration in Mike Hughes’ voice was clear. ‘Mack and I have just forced entry to the property, but there’s no sign of Daisy.’

‘Any sign of her car?’

‘What’s she got?’

‘Hold on,’ said Dan, as he flicked through his notebook, to find the relevant entry. ‘It’s a white Mercedes E-Class.’ He then relayed the vehicle’s registration number.

Moments later Mike spoke again. ‘No. No. Definitely no sign of the vehicle. We’ll knock on some doors. See if any of the neighbours know where she is.’

‘Don’t bother for now. Your priority is to secure the scene and don’t let anyone in,’ said Jemima. ‘Do a thorough search of the place. Look for anything which might tell you where she is. Collect all computers, laptops, phones. Look for SIM cards, and flash drives. Anything which ties her to a website named *LookAfterYourself*.’ She ended the call.

‘What are we going to do now?’ asked Dan.

Jemima thought for a moment. ‘Becca mentioned that Daisy’s parents own a property nearby. What the hell was the address?’

‘No idea,’ said Dan. ‘Shall I call Becca?’

'Yes. No! I'm sure it's—' Jemima reeled off an address and Dan typed it into the satnav as she spoke. With the new destination set, Jemima took a sharp right. They were travelling far too fast, and the tyres squealed in protest. She was forced to yank the steering wheel hard to correct the manoeuvre, narrowly missing the kerb, and somehow managed to avoid disaster.

Dan closed his eyes as he knew they had come within a hair's breadth of flipping the vehicle. Forcing himself not to utter an expletive he spoke far too loudly to mask his anxiety, as he informed Levi and Nancy of their new destination. He only just finished relaying the information when the phone rang again.

It was Zoe. 'Gareth's asked me to tell you that in the last few minutes three other users have entered the add-on, using randomised codes. She's actively grooming four victims right now.'

'Shit!' Jemima slammed a palm against the steering wheel. 'He needs to establish their locations! We've got to get them help before it's too late.'

'He knows that, guv. Gareth and Hunter Bryant's team are doing everything they can but they're on a hiding to nothing. She's thought of everything. It's not like she's one step ahead of them. It's at least a hundred steps.'

Jemima's blood ran cold. Daisy Evans was by far the cleverest psychopath she had encountered. She'd planned her sick game meticulously, all the while hiding in plain sight. What's more, she had been on the state payroll, and they had given her unlimited access to vulnerable school children. Allowing her to cherry-pick her victims and enjoy the sick game she was playing until she murdered them.

'They've tried to shut down the legitimate website, but her code's blocked them,' continued Zoe. 'They're trying to shut down the backdoor access, but the coding's too sophisticated. They can see when someone enters the dark web link but can't do anything to stop it. And once the kids have typed in their access code, they're lost to us. She has total control over them and the entire system. Their only hope is that you find her and shut the operation down at her end.'

Jemima switched off the vehicle's siren, along with the flashing blue lights moments before they turned onto the road where Daisy's parents' house was located. It was obvious that her parents were wealthy. In an area where older terraced properties were commonplace, along with large former council estates, this was one of only two properties.

Jemima pulled up and cut the engine. They needed to take Daisy by surprise. Catch her in the act and stop her from severing her link to the website. Common sense suggested that it was best to proceed the short distance on foot.

The two houses occupied a space which could easily have accommodated a football pitch.

'I think it's the first one, but it'll be difficult to get in,' said Dan. From inside the vehicle, only the roof and upper floor of the property was visible. The lower floor and the ground at the front of the property was hidden from sight by a wall at least six foot high. Entrance to the driveway was via a gate which was electrically operated. A narrower gate, the same height as the wall, was presumably used for visitor access and there was an intercom panel with a small screen mounted into the wall, for the residents to have sight of whoever wanted access, before deciding whether to buzz them in.

'We'll have to go over the wall,' said Jemima. It added another layer of complexity to what she had hoped would be a straightforward forced access to the property. And every second wasted was a moment to Daisy's advantage.

Jemima saw the pained expression on her sergeant's face. Dan wasn't the most physically fit member of the squad and would more than likely require some assistance. 'Has to be done, and we'll need the battering ram. It's a safe bet they've got good-quality door locks. I just hope it's not a steel reinforced door. But before we do anything, I'm going to hoist myself up on the side wall to get a clear idea of what we'll face when we drop down on the other side.'

The others had arrived and were getting out of their vehicle as Jemima headed towards the boundary wall at the side of the property. Thankfully, both properties were located on the same side of the road, which at the far end was a cul-de-sac. It was a small thing in their favour, as there would be little chance of any nosy neighbour spotting them breaking in and alerting Daisy.

Jemima found a small foothold and hoisted herself upwards. It wasn't easy, but it was manageable. A quick glance at the property revealed a large driveway, where Daisy's Mercedes was parked. 'She's here. I can see her car.' A further wall with a closed gate separated the rear garden from the driveway.

However, she realised that their luck had run out when she spotted security cameras positioned towards the roof of the property. It was unsurprising that they were there, given the size and value of the property, as it would undoubtedly attract would-be burglars like bees to a honeypot.

The cameras were problematic, as there was no way of knowing whether the system was switched on. Some could be switched off manually, if a resident only wanted them active at night or whenever the house was unoccupied. Others recorded twenty-four-seven. And from what Jemima could see from her current vantage point, the cameras were angled to cover the entire area leading up to the property. This meant that if they were operational when the team dropped down inside the wall, there was every chance that Daisy would be alerted and would have sufficient time to cover her tracks.

Satisfied that there was nothing else to learn from this recce, Jemima dropped back down to ground level and updated the others on her findings. With each officer clear of their objectives, they proceeded to make their way over the wall.

Jemima led the way, reaching down for the battering ram as soon as she was securely at the top of the wall. Levi gave Dan a leg up, as he appreciated that the sergeant's lack of agility would hold everyone up.

One by one they dropped down on the far side of the wall. Jemima hoped she had called this right as they raced to the front of the property. With no siren breaking the comparative quietness, Dan heaved the battering ram at the door, which proved to be solidly constructed. It took Dan three attempts before it yielded to the assault. Though by that time there seemed little hope that Daisy had remained oblivious to their forced entry, as the battering ram boomed like a cannon each time it thudded against the door.

They split up. Each officer armed with a taser, ready to deploy it to incapacitate Daisy. Dan and Levi went upstairs, leaving Jemima and Nancy to search the rooms on the ground floor.

Jemima headed along a hallway towards the rear of the property, thankful that the carpeted floor masked the sound of her footfall. Having spotted an open door further along she repositioned herself towards the corresponding wall, so as not to make her presence obvious. Any opportunity to buy an extra few seconds before Daisy appreciated that there were intruders in the house might mean the difference between success and failure.

She tentatively peered into the room. It was a home office, though larger than many living rooms. Stepping inside with arms outstretched, she turned her body in a sweeping arc, to enable her to fire the weapon as soon as she had her target in view. But in a matter of seconds she realised that the room was empty.

What caught her attention was a laptop sat upon the oversized desk. As the screen was facing away from her, Jemima was unable to see whether it was active. Racing to the other side of the desk, she stared at a woodland scene with a soothing babbling brook. The imagery, innocuous enough, was displayed on a loop. In the bottom right of the screen an icon showed that the sound was muted. Needing to hear the soundtrack, she moved the cursor and clicked to unmute.

The sound of a soothing, babbling brook gurgled in the background. Its effect was calming, almost hypnotic. Moments later a familiar voice spoke in a calm and reassuring tone. In what was obviously a pre-recorded monologue, of carefully chosen phrases, where Daisy Evans explained why death was the best option:

"Be encouraged that by listening to this you have taken the first and hardest step towards attaining perfect eternal happiness. Your journey's been hard. You've suffered so much and know from experience how cruel life can be.

"There are those who tell you that things will improve. Do not trust them. They are liars. Should your circumstances change in this life, they will change for the worse. Your disappointments will become despair. Your despair will become torment. Your torment will become an unbearable agony. For it is your destiny.

"You are not like others. You are special. You do not belong here. They know you are different and will not allow you to be happy. Better to take control. Forge your own destiny. Take your own path. Be courageous and embrace what awaits you once you have made the ultimate commitment.

"You have suffered in this life, but I know that you are guaranteed to be reborn into a better life. A life where happiness is your divine right. I speak from experience. I have been where you are now. I have lived your pain. I was brave enough to take the ultimate step and was rewarded with a new life. Where I have found love, happiness, fulfilment, and acceptance.

"Believe me when I say that there is nothing to fear. I have nothing to gain but the joy of speaking the truth. Come and join me. Let me guide you along the path towards the life you deserve and know that happiness is within your grasp."

As Jemima stared at the screen and listened to the message the world around her faded away. Unaware of the negative effect it was having on her she failed to notice her legs give way, and she slumped onto the chair she happened to be standing in front of. She had no idea how long she'd been there, but the spell was broken when Nancy, who had entered the room unnoticed, grabbed the mouse and clicked the mute button.

'You all right, guv?'

Jemima stared at the junior officer, until Nancy reached out and touched her shoulder. As she sensed the physical contact it was as though a spell had been broken. Daisy's macabre and dangerous message had somehow blocked out any sense of free will and left her momentarily debilitated.

Daisy's dark message had had such a profound effect on her that communication of any kind seemed beyond her current capabilities. Jemima didn't feel suicidal. As her senses returned, she appreciated the effect a site like that might have had on her if she had encountered it when she regularly resorted to self-harming just to get through the day. The realisation made her feel sick. She had been so emotionally fragile back then, that she might have been brainwashed into believing that vile message was giving her the answer to her problems.

'Not a good idea to listen to that shit,' said Nancy. She reached for Jemima's cheek and gently manoeuvred her face, forcing her to look away from the screen.

Jemima shuddered, as she came to her senses. 'You're right. I don't know what came over me.' As she uttered the words, she could hear that her voice was tinged with shame. She found the resolve to pull herself back to the here and now. Being the officer in charge meant that she had a duty of care to her team, as well as to the four potential victims. This monologue was undoubtedly just the tip of the iceberg. It was designed to lure in emotionally fragile victims who, if they were watching these messages, would almost undoubtedly be on the brink of following through on their suicidal thoughts.

'You're quite tech-savvy, aren't you, Nancy?'

'Yeah, I s'pose so.'

'In that case, ring Gareth, tell him what we've found and work with him to try to establish the location of whoever's watching this. Someone needs to intervene before it's too late. I don't want that bitch killing anyone else.'

Jemima headed out of the room. Despite successfully using a variety of techniques to keep her emotional and psychological problems under control, she knew that she was someone who was vulnerable to the disturbing agenda Daisy was pushing. Of the current team, only Dan knew of her issues, and the lengths she'd gone to get herself back on track. Even Gareth, who was aware of her rape, remained oblivious of the full extent of her troubles.

As she reached the hallway she turned and continued towards the rear of the property. The kitchen was of palatial proportions. All hi-tech top of the range appliances. A dining table that could easily seat a dozen, with room to spare, and a relaxation area with a huge TV. Over the years, it had become increasingly noticeable that many of the perpetrators they encountered lived privileged lives. Yet for some reason, the media relished highlighting crime amongst the less well off in society. Playing up to the stereotype of what they wanted you to believe a criminal should be.

Sensing movement from the corner of her eye, Jemima's grip on the taser tightened, as she raised her arm to the firing position and turned to confront whoever was there. Her heartrate increased as she prepared for a confrontation. Scanning her surroundings, she ascertained that the movement had not come from anywhere in the kitchen. Nor indeed had it come from anywhere within the house. Instead, it had occurred inside a large modern outbuilding, located at the far end of the sprawling garden.

Having been so focused on the inside of the house she had failed to spot what was clearly a building large enough to serve any number of purposes. Whether it was utilised as another home office, a gym, or even housed a swimming pool or sauna was yet to be ascertained. What Jemima did know for certain was that a light was visible through a small glass panel in the door. There was no evidence of this at the window as it appeared as though blackout blinds were drawn. If Daisy was anywhere at this property, it was inside that structure.

Dan entered the kitchen just as Jemima was looking around for the best way to get out of the house without being seen. 'Upstairs is clear,' he said. 'Levi's been roped into helping Nancy. She's liaising with Gareth and it's all hands to the pump, so to speak.'

'I think Daisy's in that outbuilding,' said Jemima. 'There's a light on and I'm sure I spotted some movement.'

'Do you think it's some sort of office and maybe she's got another computer on the go?'

'I hope not, but it's possible she could be actively grooming four potential victims. I'm not tech-savvy enough to know how these things work. But we don't have time to speculate. We need to end this now,' said Jemima.

There was never any intention of heading outside via the bifold doors, as the large panes of glass were visible from the outbuilding. Looking around for another option, Jemima spotted a closed door, which at first sight she had presumed was a cupboard. When she opened it, she discovered that it was the entrance to a large utility area. At the far side was an unlocked door leading to a small courtyard and from there to the rear garden. Being at the side of the property, they could remain close to the boundary, where various shrubs and trees might provide shelter. It was by far their best chance of reaching the outbuilding without being seen.

Moments later, as the two officers stood outside the building, it was apparent that the internal light had been switched off. With minimal natural light inside the building, they would enter the structure blind. This would inevitably give Daisy an immediate advantage.

With her taser at the ready, Jemima reached out to open the door. Butterflies fluttered in the pit of her stomach as she readied herself for the confrontation. As she tried to press the handle, it remained firm. The door was locked, and Dan was no longer carrying the battering ram. There wasn't any time for him to retrieve it, as Daisy must know they were there. Being more agile and a competent kickboxer, Jemima stood the best chance of them effecting a swift entry.

'Give me some room,' she ordered as she identified the sweet spot and lined herself up. Seconds later she kicked the door with a strength and accuracy that would have floored many a seasoned opponent. It helped that the door and frame was not of as high a specification as the property's front door.

Jemima's increased adrenaline level made her ready for whatever she was about to face. The first thing she noticed was the smell of bodily fluids. She wrinkled her nose in disgust as Dan held a torch in one hand and swept it around the room in an arc. They established that there was no sign of Daisy or of any other computer. But the sight which confronted them made them appreciate just how much they had underestimated the former teacher.

CHAPTER 32

Determined not to waste valuable seconds in searching for the light switch, Jemima made a bee-line for the window. She reached for the roller blind. Gripped it firmly and ripped it away from its housing. As it clattered to the floor, light flooded the room. Only then were they fully able to appreciate the horrendous sight which confronted them.

In the far corner of the room was a person. Though, dead or alive, young or old, it was impossible to tell. With limbs and torso securely tied to a chair there had never been any chance of this victim being able to defend themselves against the vicious attack they had endured.

Having seen blood flowing from a laceration across the wrist, Broadbent hung back.

Knowing precisely how this was affecting her sergeant Jemima took charge of the situation. 'Snap out of it, Dan. You're going to have to deal with this.'

The victim's head was slumped forward, chin resting on their chest. Being this close, she established that this was a woman. Placing two fingers on the victim's neck she felt for a pulse. She held her breath as she concentrated, repositioning her fingers to find the point she was after. All the while, willing the woman to be alive. When she found it, she let out a sigh of relief. It was faint, erratic, but it was there.

'She's alive! Call for an ambulance!' Dan did as he was told as Jemima struggled to undo the rope that bound her. The restraint was soaked in blood, which hampered her efforts which at first were clumsy and unsuccessful. It was as though her fingers were no longer under her control, becoming as useless for the task as a string of raw sausages.

This woman's life was quite literally in her hands. If she was to prevent her from bleeding out before help arrived, she needed to free the woman's arm, tie it above the elbow to restrict the blood flow and raise it above her head.

Working as quickly as she could, she hoped she'd be able to make a difference before the inevitable moment she'd pass responsibility to Dan. This injured woman wasn't Daisy Evans. As despite the swollen, lacerated, discoloured features it was clear that this unfortunate creature was someone else. She was slim, dark-haired and petite. The antithesis of the former teacher. There were boxers that had gone ten rounds with Mike Tyson who had been carried out of the ring in a far better shape.

'Ambulance is on its way,' said Dan. He looked away from them as he spoke.

Jemima had already freed the woman's injured arm. 'Give me your tie, Dan,' she ordered.

'Eh?' Dan thought he must have misheard her.

'Give me your fucking tie! I need to stop the flow of blood.'

Coming to his senses, Dan removed his tie and held it out to Jemima.

'You're gonna have to man up, Dan. I need you to hold her arm while I make a tourniquet. Then you're going to have to stay with her keep her arm up and her airways clear until the medics arrive.'

'Why me?' In that moment he looked and sounded like a little boy.

'Because I'm going after Daisy.'

'There's no sign of her. She's long gone.'

'She's here somewhere, Dan. The light was on when we headed out of the house. She didn't come out of that door, so there must be another way out of here. Plus, where the hell are her other computers? She's getting off on killing those kids, and she's working on four of them now. There's no way she'd just take off and miss out on that.'

As Jemima spoke, she paced the floor, searching for another way out of the room. But there was no obvious doorway or window other than those which you could see from the house. As she glanced down, she spotted a rug, spread haphazardly on a section of floor. It was threadbare and soiled in places. Scruffy and utilitarian, unlike the other more luxurious furnishings. For despite this being an outbuilding, it was used as a relaxation area, and it was apparent that no expense had been spared when kitting it out. Jemima guessed that even the chair upon which the victim was tied cost more than her monthly salary.

Using her foot, she tried to slide the rug across the floor, but it did not move. Crouching down, she grabbed the nearest edge and tried to lift it, but it was secured in place. A further examination revealed that its purpose was to obscure a trap door. As Jemima stood and pulled the edge of the rug upwards, the trap door opened, revealing a staircase.

'Wait for backup,' pleaded Dan. 'Remember Finlay. Don't take any chances.' His concern was not lost on Jemima, as their colleague had lost his life in the most awful of circumstances. It was something they would never forget. One moment DS Finlay Ashton was alive. The next he was dead. He'd proceeded without backup. Hadn't appreciated the danger he was in and never stood a chance.

'There's no time. I'm going after her.'

'In that case, I'm coming with you.'

'No stay put. I need you to take care of the victim.' Jemima glanced at Dan and smiled, hoping to show him that she knew what she was doing. From the expression on his face, he didn't seem convinced.

'Nancy'll have to manage on her own for a while. I'll get Levi to take care of this one then follow you down,' he said. As he fumbled for his phone Jemima headed into the unknown.

This was no ordinary staircase, as despite being the access to what must be a basement, it was of a similar quality and appearance as the one she had walked past inside the house. The walls were skimmed and painted. The lighting bright. As goosebumps erupted along Jemima's arms, she realised that the low rumble she could hear was an air conditioning unit, which was keeping the temperature low.

At the bottom of the stairs was a short corridor, at the end of which was a door with a glass panel. It allowed Jemima to see beyond into a room with two rows of workstations. From the restricted vantage point, Jemima counted ten. At the far end was another door, which was shut.

There had been no sign of movement in the short while she'd watched the room. It was safe to presume that Daisy was no longer there. Jemima took a deep breath, reached out and opened the door. As she made her way across the room, she kept glancing from side-to-side. Common sense told her that there was nowhere for Daisy to hide. But Jemima was determined not to let her guard down.

The first thing she noticed was that each workstation had an active laptop. Four of them had live web feeds. Yet there was no sound.

'Can you hear me?' Jemima was practically shouting to get their attention. But when there was no response of any kind, she appreciated that there was no microphone link to them. Yet she was convinced that Daisy had set up a way to communicate with her victims as they each appeared transfixed by something.

A cursory glance at the other six screens, confirmed that they did not have active webcam links. However, it appeared that despite no one operating them, they were actively posting messages. Though about what, or to whom, there was no time to ascertain.

Jemima reached the door on the far side of the room when Dan burst through the first one. 'Daisy's heading for her car. She's making a break for it!'

'Update Gareth on this lot!' shouted Jemima as she took off at breakneck speed. She skidded to a halt, but far too late as the corridor she was in changed direction. Her shoulder slammed into the wall. Years of kickboxing allowed her to rise above the discomfort. Cursing herself for being so clumsy, she winced and continued at full stretch.

Ahead was another set of stairs with a metal fire door at the top. Jemima took the stairs two at a time, pushed down on the bar and rushed outside to find herself at the far side of the house.

The one thing in her favour was that Daisy had parked her car at the front of the property, inside the gates. As Jemima had noticed earlier, they were large, solid, and could only be opened remotely. Though it appeared that perhaps they had not been routinely maintained. They groaned and grated as they slowly slid across a track.

Up ahead, Daisy was at the wheel of her car revving the engine and drumming the steering wheel as she waited for the earliest opportunity to get the hell out of there. As Jemima ran towards the vehicle, she noted the registration mark, along with the make, model and colour.

She saw Daisy glance in the rear-view mirror and knew that she'd lost the element of surprise. With arms pumping and her strides at full stretch she hoped she could reach the car in time to prevent her from getting away. She was within three paces of the vehicle's rear when Daisy floored the accelerator and the car skidded out of the driveway sending clouds of dust and loose chippings everywhere. Jemima's cheek stung, and as blood trickled down her face, she realised that one of the stones must've hit her. A few centimetres higher and it could have had her eye.

The injury hardened Jemima's resolve. It was first blood to Daisy, but Jemima was more determined than ever that she was going to be the one to take her down. Without breaking stride, she was out of the gate in a flash, reaching the car in time to see Daisy take a right. With no time to lose she fixed her seatbelt, turned the key in the ignition, and floored the accelerator.

The chase was on.

CHAPTER 33

With the blues and twos alerting unsuspecting members of the public of the possibility of imminent danger, Jemima activated the hands-free radio. 'All available units in the immediate vicinity, be advised that an officer in pursuit of a vehicle is in need of assistance . . .' She continued to relay details of the car she was following. 'This is an ongoing situation with an immediate threat to life. Suspect is a white female. Daisy Evans. Believed to be responsible for multiple murders and false imprisonment. Unknown whether the suspect is armed. She must be taken alive as we need to establish the locations of four victims whose lives are in imminent danger.'

Having turned right at the junction, Jemima could just about see Daisy's vehicle up ahead. Not used to a high-speed pursuit, the woman was driving erratically. Jemima had the advantage of having trained for the pursuit of other vehicles.

Daisy ploughed through a zebra crossing, narrowly missing a woman with a toddler, who was already part-way across. Daisy swerved, but mounted the pavement, toppling a wheelie bin which shed its contents onto the carriageway. There was a moment when Jemima thought that the former teacher was about to collide with another pedestrian, this time on the pavement. However, she pulled the vehicle back onto the road not a moment too soon.

Thankfully there wasn't much further to go before they left the town behind them. Though where Daisy was heading was anyone's guess.

Providing a running commentary of her route, Jemima was relieved when she heard that other units had joined the pursuit. It gave them options, and the possibility of cutting her off from various routes. If handled correctly they could bring the chase to an end before anyone got hurt.

Jemima watched as Daisy's car fishtailed. The backend of the vehicle swung out as she turned onto another road at too high a speed, leaving trails of rubber on the road. Daisy was going for broke, with no regard for human life, whether her own or someone else's. Yet somehow the young woman regained control of the vehicle which set off up a steep incline.

This road was narrower, with sharp bends that if you were unfamiliar with the layout, could easily take you by surprise. Jemima gripped the steering wheel so tightly that it felt as though her hands were melded to it. Her adrenaline level had raised, as had her heartrate, as she remained entirely focused on the pursuit. She maintained a running commentary, calling out directions to ensure that the other units were kept informed.

As Daisy reached the top of the incline, she swung a right. Jemima relayed the change of direction to the others.

Mike Hughes' voice came over the radio. 'I'm on that road about quarter of a mile ahead. Stinger deployed. I repeat stinger deployed . . . I have sight of her. She's not slowing down.'

Daisy had no reason to suspect the stationary unmarked police car that had pulled off the road up ahead. She glanced in the rear-view mirror and smiled, as she realised that the female police officer was never going to catch her. Daisy held all the cards. She knew this area like the back of her hand and her car was way faster than Jemima's.

If she hadn't have glanced in the mirror, she might have seen the police stinger stretched across the carriageway. Though, given the speed she was travelling it was unlikely she could have successfully made an evasive manoeuvre. The tyres burst before she knew what had happened.

As the car careered off the carriageway at speed, momentum propelled it onwards. The unevenness of the terrain caused the vehicle to jolt and lurch from side to side. Daisy had no control over the vehicle's trajectory, no chance of avoiding any hazard in its path. The underside of the car skimmed across the top of a low-lying rock. Sparks flew, and there was an ominous screech as metal scraped and ripped apart. The fuel line ruptured. It continued its forward momentum for a few seconds more. Now at a forty-five-degree angle. But as the rock's height increased, the inevitable happened. The car flipped and rolled, eventually coming to rest upside down.

Jemima floored the accelerator as she watched the scene play out up ahead. Even from this distance she could see the sparks. It was inevitable that this would be a life-or-death situation. She skidded to a halt and raced out of the vehicle.

Another car which had followed hers, stopped abruptly too. It was Mack's. Having been at least a minute behind her, he had a lot of ground to make up as he ran towards the crash site.

It was probable that Daisy Evans would be injured, possibly even trapped. And there was no way Jemima was going to allow the murdering bitch to die inside a burning vehicle.

That would be the easy way out, and Daisy didn't deserve easy.

As a result of her actions, four teenagers now teetered on a metaphorical precipice. Forced to the edge. A moment where their only choice was between life or death. They needed to be found. Stopped before they ended it all.

Then there were the grieving families of Daisy's other victims all of whom deserved to see justice done.

'Stay back, guv. It's going to blow!' Mack was running flat out to catch up with Jemima and stop her from putting herself in danger.

Jemima heard his warning but ignored it. She carried on going. There was too much at stake to hesitate. She needed Daisy alive and talking. She was the first of the three officers to reach the vehicle. It was a good call. Daisy was alive. At least for the moment. But for how long was anyone's guess. She'd managed to release the seatbelt and was crouched on what would be the inside of the roof.

Despite manipulating so many others into taking their own lives, it was obvious that Daisy was desperate to live. Panic was etched across her face. Her eyes were wide as she spotted Jemima only a few feet away. She frantically kicked at the glass, but the cramped, damaged interior hindered her efforts.

With the restricted space filling with smoke, she coughed and spluttered. If the flames didn't get her, the carbon monoxide sure as hell would.

Despite knowing that it was futile, Jemima reached out and tried the door handle. The metal was hot to the touch but not yet so hot that it would burn the skin. She tugged the door, giving it her all. But it remained fast. Daisy's face was tight to the side window. She pushed as Jemima pulled.

It was a waste of time, which was something neither of them had. The door was damaged. Impossible to open. She needed a different approach. As she scanned the immediate area, she realised that there was nothing readily available with which she could break the glass. With Mack and Mike still twenty or more yards away, they would be of no help. It was down to her, and her alone, to bring about a successful resolution.

'Move away from the window and cover your face!' she yelled. Her legs were stronger than most people's. Through years of intensive training, she had learned how to put the maximum amount of power into her kicks. It was the only realistic option. If she couldn't break the glass no one could.

The flames grew in intensity, strengthening by the second. Any minute now the vehicle would be engulfed. Seconds later an explosion would follow. With smoke stinging her eyes she took aim and kicked, powering through the action as forcefully as she could. There was so much at stake. She had to see this through. Get Daisy out of there and save those teenagers.

The glass proved to be resilient. But on the third kick it finally shattered.

Mack and Mike reached her side. Daisy was still. The smoke had got to her.

'Out of the way,' ordered Mike, as he and Mack reached in, grabbed the unconscious woman, and hauled her out of the vehicle.

Jemima appreciated the moment's respite, but as soon as Daisy was free, she helped the others carry her as they raced away from the danger zone.

The blast was ferocious. Debris flew into the air and lumps of metal landed yards from where they had stopped. Daisy was still unconscious.

'Oh no you don't!' yelled Jemima as she felt for a pulse. 'You don't get to die on us. Not after we've risked our lives. Not like this.'

Mike was already speaking to the emergency services as Jemima and Mack performed CPR. It took two minutes before Daisy gasped and spluttered. Their determined efforts had brought her back. Now she would answer for her crimes.

CHAPTER 34

While they waited for an ambulance to arrive, Jemima allowed herself a few moments to catch her breath before calling Gareth. In an ideal world she would have interrogated Daisy. Forced her to give them the names of the four teenagers they knew she'd been interacting with. But anyone could see that Daisy was too far out of it to be able to cooperate.

Gareth picked up after the fourth ring. 'Guv?'

'What's the latest, Gar?'

'I'm at the parent's house now. I've accessed her site, but so far, I'm unable to shut things down.

'Are the four kids still online?'

'Yeah, but we've no way of communicating with them. It looks as though she had contingency plans. Whatever she did before she made a run for it has stopped us shutting things down. Hunter and his team are trying to come up with a workaround.'

'Are you saying that whatever brainwashing crap she's exposing them to is still happening?'

'Yes. I've managed to get into the system to allow me to hear the messages at this end. It's vile stuff. At least one of those kids is on the verge of ending it all, and there's nothing we can do to stop it. I just hope someone walks in and stops her before it's too late.'

'Keep at it, Gar, and don't let it get to you. It might not seem like it but you're doing great.' It was a pointless thing to say, but Jemima wanted to buoy her sergeant's spirits.

While Jemima had been speaking to Gareth the paramedics had arrived. 'How's she doing?' she asked. She glanced down and saw that Daisy had an oxygen mask on.

'We'll take her in. She's suffering from smoke inhalation and concussion. The doctors will assess her, but it's odds on she'll be kept in overnight for observation. They'll patch up the abrasions and treat the burns, but they're only minor so shouldn't cause any problems. Might need some stitches too, and she's got a sprained wrist.'

'One of my officers will go with her,' said Jemima.

'That won't be—'

Jemima was in no mood to argue. 'It's not up for debate. This woman is suspected of committing multiple murders. There'll be an officer with her at all times.'

'I'll go, guv,' said Mike. 'I know a couple of the local plods. Trustworthy. I'll arrange for them to stand guard. It'll be better coming from me. They won't want to argue.'

'Make sure you're cuffed to her, Mike,' said Jemima. 'No matter what they say, you're to stay with her. Watch her like a hawk. No visitors, or access to electronic devices of any kind.'

As Jemima and Mack walked back to their vehicles Jemima had an idea and called the station. 'Zoe, this is time-critical, as there're four lives on the line. I want you and Lewis to contact every high school in the area. Tell them they need to check their attendance records and explain that we have reason to believe that there is a credible threat to the lives of absent pupils where one or more family members are not Welsh. We need names, addresses, phone numbers of parents. Daisy Evans has four live feeds to other potential victims. If they're not reached in time, we'll have more deaths on our hands.'

Alone in the car, she pressed speed dial as she set off for the station. This was a call she was not looking forward to. As it rang out, she took a deep breath. Having kept Superintendent Olsen in the dark about the investigation into the suicides, there would be an inevitable confrontation. He'd be keen to slap her down. Make her acknowledge who was boss. She'd known all along that there would be consequences and was prepared to be disciplined. Though not yet. Not when at least four more lives were at stake. She'd eat all the humble pie Olsen could serve up, after they'd shut Daisy's vile operation down once and for all.

Olsen's roar filled the car. The man's fury was so palpable that Jemima flinched and jerked the steering wheel causing the car to swerve.

'Sir, we can do this later!' Jemima had to shout to be heard but was not prepared to allow her superior officer to rant on until he had worn himself out. 'Sir! You need to listen! There is a credible threat to life, and I need your help! This suicide website is piggybacking on a government initiative available to every school in Wales. There could be any number of vulnerable teenagers out there, ready to end their lives.' Her persistence and serious tone got through to him. He cleared his throat and instructed her to apprise him of the situation. Ten minutes later she disconnected the call, reassured that Torsten Olsen would organise a team of officers to contact every school in Wales to advise them of a potential threat to life of some of their pupils.

When she arrived at the station, Jemima's first stop was the front desk to establish whether Kayleigh Bevan was still at the station. The officer hadn't long come on shift and rang through to find out the answer to her question.

'Sorry, ma'am. I've just been informed that they were unable to locate her. They checked with her employer, I believe she's a carer?'

'She is,' said Jemima.

'Apparently, she didn't turn up for work. They've had various people contact them to say that she hasn't made scheduled home visits.'

'And no one thought to let me know about this?' Jemima felt like screaming. It appeared that there were too many officers at this station who were not meeting even the most basic standard of operational competence. But that was a problem for another day.

Right now, she needed to establish if Kayleigh had got wind of them questioning every member of the quiz team and had gone to ground because she had something to hide. Or whether the woman was in danger. After all, two of the team had already been murdered, and they were no closer to establishing the identity of the killers.

'Inform whichever officers were assigned to bring her in, that I want to see them in the incident room in the next fifteen minutes. I don't care where they are, what they're doing, or if they've finished their shift. They need to get their sorry arses back in here now. If they haven't reported to me by then, there'll be hell to pay.'

The desk sergeant was under no illusion about how serious the threat was. As she turned to walk away, Jemima heard him pick up the telephone handset and make a call.

Back at the incident room, Jemima barely had time to switch on her computer before the door was opened with such force that it hit the wall. She looked up to see Mack laden with bags of evidence. Dan and Levi, who were a few steps behind him, were carrying things too.

'What with everything going on I forgot to tell you that we found all of these at Daisy's,' he said, as he dropped the various packages on the nearest desk. 'The surprising thing was that for someone so comfortable carrying out murders online, we found a case she'd stashed beneath the sofa. She'd kept records. Names. Photos. You name it. Could be details of her victims.'

'How many are we talking about?' Jemima dreaded hearing the answer.

'Gave up counting after twenty,' said Mack.

'We've got a handful of flash drives too. God only knows what's been downloaded on them. Bet you anything they've gotta be trophies.'

'Great work. Gareth can take the lead on the flash drives when he gets back. But right now, we've another problem.'

said Jemima. 'Kayleigh Bevan's missing. It could be she's linked to the suicide website and has gone to ground. Though there's the possibility that she might have been abducted. Let's face it whoever killed Ben and John made it obvious that they hated the Hobby Horses team. Why else slice off their tattoos? And those tattoos link the five friends.'

'Any idea who's behind it?' asked Mack.

'We know three things.' Jemima proceeded to count them with her fingers. 'Firstly, the quiz team is made up of a group of friends who, according to them, share a love of the Welsh language. Secondly, we've heard that other Welsh speakers choose to avoid having anything to do with that group, as they're wary of their extremist views. And finally, we have proof that Daisy is behind the suicide website, which we believe is targeting non-Welsh speaking teenagers.'

'This is so fucked up,' said Levi.

'It is, and I've a horrible feeling that some grieving family members somehow managed to link that quiz team to their child's death,' said Jemima.

'Vigilantism?' asked Mack.

'If I'm right, then yes. The act of desperation by people who've been let down by this police force. They must have felt the only way to get some sort of justice for their loved one, was by killing those they believe to be responsible. And if that scenario turns out to be correct then as far as I'm concerned, it's a moral dilemma, because if I was in their shoes and one of my kids had killed themselves, I'd go after the bastards responsible for grooming him and take whatever—' Jemima stopped short as a uniformed officer entered the room.

'Ma'am! I got the message you wanted to see me and came as quick as I could.' The officer was red-faced, sweating profusely, and his words were rushed. 'I did my best to find Kayleigh Bevan. Tried her house. Contacted her employer. Got the list of her clients and even went to their homes. But no one had seen her. It's as though she's vanished into thin air.'

'Why didn't you let me know that you'd been unable to locate her?'

'Sorry, ma'am. I s'pose I should've done, but no one told me to.' The officer appeared to shrink under Jemima's withering gaze. 'And while I was out and about, I got distracted by this old man who was really upset. He couldn't remember where he lived. Well, I had to help him. I couldn't leave him to it. Turned out he had dementia. Got out of the house when his daughter wasn't looking. When all's said and done, I just didn't think, ma'am.'

Just as Jemima was about to respond her phone rang. She nodded at Dan, who answered it. Frustrated, but appreciating that she did not have the time to push the constable further she decided to just get the information he had and move on. 'Not your finest hour, Constable. You need to buck your ideas up. Give Detective Mackintosh the details of your enquiries, and we'll leave it at that for now.'

As she glanced towards Dan, she noticed that he had a hand over the mouthpiece of the phone and with his free hand he was frantically gesturing at her. She dreaded what she was about to learn.

'It's Nigel Davies. He's frantic.' Dan all but thrust the phone into her hand.

'Chief Inspector Hux—'

Nigel interjected before Jemima had finished speaking. 'It's Kayleigh! Something's happened to her. She hasn't turned up for her shift. She always turns up. She's not answering her phone and her car's been found. The keys were in the ignition and the driver's door was open. I'm telling you, something's happened to her. You need to get officers out looking for her before it's too late. I don't want her ending up like Benno and Jonno! She's a good person. She's done nothing.'

'Calm down, Mr Dav—'

'Don't you dare tell me to calm down! Someone's taken her, and if she gets hurt, I'll make it my life's mission to hound the lot of you out of the force. If you know what's good for you, you'll get off your arses, get boots on the ground and find her!' Nigel's fear was emphasised by the fact that his entire rant had been conducted in English.

‘Nigel, I assure you that locating Kayleigh is my priority. As soon as I finish speaking to you, I’ll organise a search team. I’ll hand you back to Sergeant Broadbent. He’ll take the details. Tell him exactly where Kayleigh’s car was found and give him her phone number.’ She handed the phone back to Dan. There was no need for her to tell him what to do. As a seasoned and competent detective, this was bread and butter to him.

She turned to see Mike standing close by, listening to things play out. He had just returned from the hospital. Seeing the look of surprise on her face he said, ‘Don’t worry. I’ve two very competent officers guarding her. I’d trust them with my life. As for looking for Kayleigh, I know the area better than anyone. I’ll organise the search and get out there myself.’

Jemima was reassured by this. He was a good copper and would be a safe pair of hands to organise and lead the search for Kayleigh.

‘Mack, for the time being make a start on the records from Daisy’s house. See if you can match any of them to our current list of teenage victims. You said you’d stopped counting at twenty, so there’re going to be other victims we don’t know about,’ said Jemima.

‘I’m on it, guv.’

‘Levi, give him a hand.’

The two officers set about their task without complaint.

CHAPTER 35

Gareth and Nancy arrived back at the station. 'Took the opportunity to come back. Hunter and his team are working flat out. We've brought back the laptops and can just as easily work here,' he said.

Jemima's thoughts were racing. With at least four young lives at stake, they needed immediate breakthroughs, now more than ever.

'Dan, you're with me. We need to do a deep dive into the families of those teenage victims.' Splitting the list of victims into two, she allocated him five.

'What are you hoping to find?'

It was a reasonable question. One for which Jemima didn't have an answer. 'I've no idea. Start by checking out all family members between the ages of fourteen to seventy on the PNC. I know it's a significant age range, but it's possible that they could have the physical strength required to overpower Jenkins and Prosser and hoist them up on that contraption.'

Jemima's skills were best suited to figuring out who was responsible for the capture and subsequent murders of John Prosser and Ben Jenkins. Whichever way she thought about it, grieving relatives of the teenage victims had to be at the top of the list of potential suspects.

Given the fact that the letters aitch-aitch had been gouged into the foreheads of both men, and the Hobby Horse tattoos had been sliced from their shoulders, the only logical conclusion was that those mutilations had been an act of rage. It hadn't been a sufficient punishment to just kill the men. They were sending a message to the other members of that quiz team. Showing them how much they were hated. Telling them what fate awaited them.

As for Kayleigh's disappearance, to find a vehicle abandoned in the middle of the day in a built-up area such as this, would be an unusual occurrence. If it had been stolen by a joyrider, it would most likely have been dumped in an out of the way location. Not left with the keys still in the ignition on a residential street.

Glancing up, she saw Mike was just picking up his phone. Before he had a chance to make another call, she shouted over to him. 'Mike! When you speak to whoever's at the scene, ask them if Kayleigh's car still has fuel in it.'

'Will do, guv. I've just arranged for some uniforms to go house to house in the area. Find out if anyone saw what happened.'

Jemima gave him the thumbs up. Confident that a search was underway to find the young woman, she turned her attention back to the potential reason behind Kayleigh's disappearance. Until she'd disproved her theory, the grieving relatives were top of the list of suspects.

Jemima picked up the first of the case files and opened it. Luna Watson and her family had moved to the area three years before the teenager's death. They were an English, bi-racial family.

Luna had been fifteen years old when her nine-year-old brother found her lifeless corpse with her wrists open. Since that moment the boy had suffered from selective mutism and a disengagement from the rest of the world.

The parents had insisted that Luna had given them no reason to suspect that she was still struggling emotionally. The school had informed them that their daughter had been encouraged to use the *LookAfterYourself* website. But that had been more than a year prior to her death. With the passage of time, Luna had appeared to grow in confidence, and they had come to believe that her problems were behind her.

Luna's mother was devastated by her daughter's death. The shock of what had happened, and the effect on their youngest child had resulted in her becoming clinically depressed. The GP had prescribed anti-depressants, and she was seeing a counsellor.

The father was struggling too, having described his daughter's suicide as the moment that the entire family unit died. Aware that he needed to be strong for his wife and son. Yet endeavouring to come to terms with his own grief.

It was unlikely that Luna's father was involved in the murders. The man had more than enough on his plate. Let alone having time to plan and carry out the execution of two men and the abduction of a woman.

For now, she would categorise the Watsons as highly unlikely to have been involved in the murders. Though, this was a work in progress and her initial assessment might change.

She picked up the next file. Thomas Sidhu had been sixteen when his body was discovered hanging from a tree in the garden of his family home. He'd used a belt to suspend himself from a branch.

Thomas had been a victim of bullying. Teaching staff at the local school he attended were aware of problems and had taken measures to deal with it. They had even gone as far as excluding two of the offenders. Thomas went to counselling sessions and had been referred to the *LookAfterYourself* website.

It was on record that over the years, Thomas's father had reported a few racist incidents, and had been frustrated that the police hadn't taken his complaints seriously. Indeed, one unnamed officer had even gone as far as suggesting that perhaps Mr Sidhu was blowing things out of all proportion, and it might be beneficial if Mr Sidhu took the initiative to try to fit in, by not being so obviously an outsider.

Jemima couldn't believe her eyes. It was highly offensive. But knowing that it had been said by a serving police officer to a man who had complained about racist behaviour, beggared belief. It was obscene. 'Why the hell haven't Neanderthals like that been drummed out of the force?' she growled, more to herself than to anyone else.

With regard to his son's suicide, Mr Sidhu had stated that he would have to live with the guilt. Having known that his son was being bullied and having had first-hand experience of the authorities not treating the abuse of non-white residents seriously in that locality, he had advised his son to rise above it. Suggesting that some things never changed, and it was an unpalatable fact of life that Thomas needed to come to terms with.

Thomas had told his parents that things had improved at school once the two boys had been excluded, as most of his classmates accepted him for who he was and treated him no differently to anyone else. But what neither parent had appreciated was that their son was being bombarded with a relentless campaign of threats and obscenities on social media.

Jemima thought it possible that Thomas's father could have snapped and taken revenge. Yet, further enquiries revealed that shortly after their son's death the Sidhus had emigrated and could not in any way be responsible for the deaths at the Bent Iron.

The next file on Jemima's desk was that of Jack Fernández, and she noticed that he had attended the same Catholic school as Luna Watson. He had been two years above her and had killed himself when he was seventeen. He too had been referred to the *LookAfterYourself* website. And like Thomas Sidhu, Jack had hanged himself.

As she continued to read through the notes, and learned more about Jack's family, Jemima's heart rate increased. His mother, Mandy, was born in the area, and her parents still owned the smallholding where her brother, Dean Walters continued to live. She and the other officers had been so focused on the family names of the deceased teenagers that no one had thought to check out any other surnames linked to those families, and it was an oversight which might end up costing another life.

Jemima knew little about smallholdings, but thought it was possible that such a business might have the need for a quadbike or two.

As she turned the page, the final pieces of the puzzle fitted together. Jack's elder brother, Rick, ran a local tattoo parlour.

It had bothered Jemima that the tattoos had been cut away from John's and Ben's shoulders. When she had visited the murder site and saw the corpses hanging there, both victims had been fully clothed. Yet one sleeve had been torn away to expose the tattoo, while the other remained intact. But for that to happen, at least one of the killers had to have known which shoulder was tattooed, and that both men had the same tattoo.

'Mack, Levi, have you found any evidence that Daisy was linked with the death of Jack Fernández?'

'Yes,' said Mack. 'She had his photograph, and there's also a log of the randomised codes he would have used to access her site. She was meticulous. We've got dates, times, and a record of file names. Presumably the videos and audio messages she used.'

'In that case I think I might have found the killers, and one of them just happens to be a tattooist,' said Jemima. 'It all makes sense. If I'm right, they've got the perfect place to keep Kayleigh until they're ready to dispose of her. At this point in time, I've no solid proof. But they have a motive. It's likely they have the means. And Jack Fernández's uncle lives on a smallholding, which would enable them to have had the opportunity.

'While I make a call, round up as many officers as possible. We'll be searching three properties.'

CHAPTER 36

As Jack's grandparents and uncle lived on a smallholding it was likely that they would have shotguns. And as keen as Jemima was to get up there, she wanted to have a clear idea about what licensed weapons, if any, were likely to be on the premises. As she ended the call, it was obvious to the others that all was not well. Having been entirely focused on the recent conversation she was surprised to see Dan, Levi, and Mack assembled in readiness to search the smallholding. There were a number of other officers there too.

'Take it, it's not good news?' asked Dan.

Jemima shook her head. 'No, there're two registered firearms at the premises. Hardly surprising. Business related use. Shotguns for foxes and other predators which might go after their livestock.'

'Just what we need,' said Mack.

'Could be worse,' said Levi. 'We could have turned up there without checking it out. At least this way, we're going prepared.'

'All three of the family's properties must be searched at the same time. If they've snatched Kayleigh, the smallholding's the most likely place they would have taken her, as it's out of the way. But if Jack's family are responsible for the

Bent Iron murders, it's possible there could be vital evidence at Jack's parents' house, and his brother's place too.'

It was a reasonable supposition, and everyone nodded their agreement.

'Realistically, those firearms could be at any of the three properties that we're going to search,' said Jemima. 'It's a fair bet that the people we're going to bring in for questioning will be used to handling a shotgun. It's a way of life for anyone whose business is rearing livestock. And just because those weapons are registered for use on the smallholding it would be naive to think that a family member wouldn't have taken one, or even both, to another location.'

'They could have unlicensed firearms too,' added Dan.

'Everyone taking part in these searches needs to be mindful of the potential danger they're facing. I don't want anyone getting injured, and certainly don't want any fatalities. Until we have evidence to the contrary, we treat these suspects as dangerous. They are desperate and hurting. They're a family who've had their world ripped apart. They believe that the police's failure to investigate the spate of suicides ultimately led to Jack's death.

'Let's remember, Jack's death was written off as a suicide. Whereas evidence we've uncovered today suggests that Daisy Evans set out to encourage Jack to kill himself.

'There's been no justice for Jack or any of Daisy's other victims. Which is why, when his family thought they'd figured out who was behind their son's death, they felt they had no option but to take the law into their own hands.'

'Are you saying that all the members of that quiz team are complicit?' asked Mack.

'Not at this stage. But it's something we will investigate. After this morning's findings, all we know for certain is that Daisy is behind it. It's an open secret that people believe that the group of friends that make up the Hobby Horses quiz team dislike anyone who's not Welsh.'

'You mean they're racists,' said Levi. He glared at Jemima. 'Don't sugar-coat it, guv. Call it what it is because that's what we're talking about here.'

'Yes, I apologise,' said Jemima. 'If the people who know that particular group are to be believed, then that is exactly what we're talking about.

'Jack's family would have been looking for answers. Answers to questions that this force had no intention of looking into. It's a dereliction of duty and abhorrent. But let's face it, there are a lot of people in this area who were aware of their racist views. Yet they were quite prepared to look the other way. Distance themselves by justifying that those five individuals were nothing like them. But by looking the other way they ultimately played an unwitting part in those teenagers' deaths.'

'The families didn't stand a chance of getting justice. They must see us lot as the enemy,' said Dan.

'Exactly. But just remember, as things stand there's a credible threat to Kayleigh Bevan's life, and we must do everything in our power to see that she comes out of this unharmed. Whatever our feelings, we cannot and must not let them get in the way of doing our job. It's not our place to judge. We're here to uphold the law.'

It was agreed that a team of officers would undertake a search of Jack's parents' home and bring them in for questioning. Mike was to lead another team to find and bring Rick Fernández in for questioning too. As well as undertaking a search of the tattoo parlour and the living quarters above the business premises. Due to the credible and immediate threat to Kayleigh Bevan's life, there was no requirement to wait for search warrants to enable them to enter the three properties.

CHAPTER 37

The Walters' family smallholding was in a sorry state of repair, located in an isolated spot less than two miles from the Bent Iron. It was the ideal location to hold someone against their will. With no neighbours nearby to notice comings and goings, anything could go on there, without raising suspicion.

It would have been easy to miss the turning off the highway. But as they were specifically looking out for it, they spotted it in time, turning sharply to proceed along a poorly maintained narrow track. The surface played havoc with the vehicle's suspension. Jemima realised it would be prudent to go slowly, as the size and number of potholes caused the vehicle to jolt and tilt precariously. On more than one occasion Dan swore loudly as his head collided with the side window. The other police vehicles following on behind fared no better.

A satellite view of the area had shown that the smallholding had only one vehicular entrance. And as they were in the middle of nowhere, it was guaranteed that the sound of any approaching vehicle would be heard by whoever happened to be at the property.

After travelling along the track for a while, a steady whisp of smoke became visible in the distance. It was too controlled to be anything other than from a chimney. Jemima cut the engine. Mack, who was driving the other car pulled up behind her, and a few yards further back the van driver did the same. With insufficient room to open the doors to their full extent they were confident that no one further down the track would be able to drive past them. Even a motorcyclist would struggle to negotiate a way through.

'Levi, you're with me, as are you.' Jemima pointed at two of the four uniformed officers who had travelled in the van. 'Now, we know from satellite imagery that there's the house and one large outbuilding, presumably a barn. So, we treat this the same as any other raid and enter both structures simultaneously. My team will take the barn. Dan, you head up the other team and take the house,' said Jemima.

'Before we head on in, have you all got your Kevlars on?' She looked around and watched each of them nod. 'Good. Now remember your training and work as a team. We need a fast and successful resolution. You've batons, tasers, and CS spray. Use them if you need to. We need those shotguns found and secured before one or more of us end up staring down the wrong end of the barrel.'

They ran down the track, two abreast. Jemima's team to the right. Dan's to the left, keeping low to minimise the possibility of being seen. As the smallholding came into view they stopped before making the final approach.

Jemima exhaled deeply as she steadied her nerves. She had done things like this many times throughout her career. But the frequency with which you did something didn't make it any easier or less fraught with danger. In recent years she had become more aware of her own mortality. As had Dan and Gareth too. They'd lost one of their own on what should have been a routine search of a property. A life snuffed out in the blink of an eye. They all appreciated the fine line they trod every time they went on shift. Being a single parent added to the weight on her shoulders. Her boys needed her to guide them into adulthood, and she was determined to be with them every step of the way.

She scanned the courtyard ahead to ensure it was clear for them to proceed. When she was satisfied, she gestured for them to move forward in their respective directions. Keeping low and moving fast was no mean feat, but the teams made it to their respective buildings without giving themselves away. As she was about to give Dan the signal to breach the house, an agonised scream came from somewhere within the barn. There was no time to lose. The scream was undeniably human, and sufficiently high-pitched to be recognisably female. Giving Dan the thumbs up to proceed, both officers turned their attention to focus entirely on their own mission.

Jemima held a finger to her lips to indicate that they proceed with stealth. With no idea of the competency of the two uniformed officers accompanying them, she needed to ensure that they did not make their presence known. She was confident of Levi's ability, his understanding of the situation, and his capabilities.

As luck would have it, the barn door was already open. It meant that it didn't risk alerting the suspects to their presence. This would inevitably have been the case as even if the large door hadn't creaked, the opening of it would have allowed a significant amount of light into what would have otherwise been a dark and dingy interior.

Ahead of them were bales of hay stacked high. Along the nearest wall, an array of hooks, some rusty and well-worn, were used to secure farming paraphernalia. There was no doubt in Jemima's mind that any of these pieces of equipment could effectively be used as a makeshift weapon.

She turned and whispered to the youngest of the officers. 'Stay here and guard this lot. We don't want to have them used against us.'

As he nodded, Jemima recognised a sense of relief wash over his face. The lad clearly thought this was the easiest option. How wrong he would be if things were to suddenly go south. It would only take someone to unexpectedly enter the fray to put him to the test. He could quickly find himself overpowered. And if they were to get hold of one of those agricultural implements, he'd have his work cut out to bring the situation under control.

There was another bloodcurdling scream, which left them in no doubt of the pain someone was feeling.

'Shut it, you racist bitch! Jack killed himself because of you and your friends.' The voice was filled with hatred.

'I-I don't know any Jack. I didn't do anything.' Kayleigh's voice was unnaturally high.

'Don't you lie to me! You and your friends as good as put that noose around my brother's neck. I did those tattoos for you. Hobby Horses, my arse! Aitch fucking aitch, more like. That's what you lot are about. You hate outsiders. Want everyone to be like you. A bunch of fucking neo-Nazi clones hiding behind the Welsh language!'

Jemima was in no doubt that it was Rick Fernández issuing the threats. After all, he was Jack's brother and a tattooist. She was about to break cover when another man spoke, and she signalled for them to remain where they were.

'Jack was the apple of my sister's eye. My mother's too. The youngest grandchild. You destroyed our family. When my mother heard about Jack, it brought on a stroke. She was as strong as an ox until then. But now she can barely talk let alone walk. We have to spoon-feed her and wipe her arse. You and your friends turned her into a fucking cripple. A woman who was born in that house not twenty yards from where we are. She's lived her entire life here.

'My mam's more Welsh than the likes of you will ever be. There's so much goodness in her soul. She'd give her last penny to help anyone out and go without herself if she had to. It wouldn't matter who they were, where they came from, or what fucking language they spoke. She'd do it because she's a decent human being. She's full of love. She doesn't have it in her to hate.'

CHAPTER 38

The layout inside the barn meant that they couldn't see what was up ahead, but it was likely that there were only the two men with Kayleigh.

With the only natural light source coming from the open door, it became progressively darker the further into the barn they went. Squinting to get a clearer view of the rafters Jemima spotted what must surely be a rope, hanging down about twenty feet from their current location. It seemed likely that the two men were prepared to carry out their threat. It also meant that they had an exact location of where everyone was.

With her voice no more than a whisper, Jemima prepped the other two officers. 'We hit them now. Go in hard and fast. They're about to lynch her and we can't allow that to happen. The priority is to disable them before they hoist her up on that rope.' She pointed ahead.

'Have your tasers ready to deploy. We don't issue a warning. Any comeback and it'll be on me. You're both just following my orders.'

With limited room to manoeuvre without bumping into anything, Jemima led the way. The blood rushed in her ears, and every cell in her body was on high alert. They had one chance, and one chance only. Spotting a narrow clearing between some machinery and sacks of animal feed, she held out her taser and kept low. Levi was directly behind her, standing taller, but still crouching. He had a clear line of sight above her head.

In the seconds it took them to reach the clearing where Kayleigh Bevan was being held, Jemima's confidence grew. The men were still ranting at Kayleigh, which meant two things. Firstly, she was still alive. Secondly, they had no idea that anyone else was in the barn. But Jemima's optimism was short-lived, as the constable, whose name she didn't know, knocked against a spade that was propped against a bag of feed. The implement clattered to the ground before he could stop it, and just like that their cover was blown.

There was no time to lose. Jemima and Levi broke cover. Levi deployed his taser, hitting Dean squarely in the chest. However, there was no clear shot for Jemima to take, as Rick, was positioned directly behind Kayleigh.

Rick was gripping a clump of her hair so forcefully that his knuckles were white with effort. It forced Kayleigh's chin upwards, exposing her throat, against which he held a knife.

'If you don't back off, I'll fucking do it!' Spittle sprayed from his mouth as he spat out the threat. He was both dangerous and unpredictable.

There was already blood running down Kayleigh's arm. Her sleeve was torn from the remainder of her tunic, and an ugly section of skin was hanging loosely down in a grotesque flap. Having been sliced away on three sides, Rick had almost managed to completely remove the tattoo. The injuries reinforced Jemima's certainty that the blade he was holding was sharp enough to sever the woman's carotid artery. The slightest movement and it would all be over for her. She'd bleed out and they'd never be able to save her.

'I'm putting my taser down,' said Jemima. She lowered the weapon to the ground, then held her hands up, palms out to emphasise that she was no threat.

'That's better, now back off! Or I swear to God!'

Jemima took a few steps back. 'You're in charge, Rick.'

'He tasered my uncle.' Rick nodded towards Levi.

'We had no choice.'

'You don't understand. He's got a dodgy ticker. He could die!'

It was only then that Jemima realised that she hadn't heard Dean Walters make a sound since he'd been hit by the weapon. Glancing across she saw that the man was prostrate and unresponsive. 'Shit! Start CPR, Levi! Someone call for an ambulance, and go get the defibrillator from the van! Now!'

There was the sound of movement as the uniformed constables sprang into action. Levi didn't need telling twice. His training kicked in and he set about doing everything he could to save Dean Walters' life.

Despite the severity of this unanticipated emergency, Jemima couldn't allow her attention to waver from Rick and Kayleigh.

'My officers will do everything they can for your uncle, Rick.'

'I'm not going to allow this bitch to live when she's responsible for my brother's death, and most likely my uncle's too.'

'You're wrong, Rick. Kayleigh's not responsible for anyone's death,' said Jemima. Her voice was soft. Non-confrontational. She wanted him to listen. Allow the words to sink in.

'Don't mess with me. You lot are all about mind games. But me and my family are the victims here.'

'Kayleigh wasn't behind the website, Rick. She had nothing to do with what happened to Jack.'

'Yes, she did. They all did.'

'What website?' The terror in Kayleigh's voice made the words sound ethereal.

'Daisy Evans was the one that created an add-on to the *LookAfterYourself* website, Rick,' said Jemima. 'Her background's in ICT. She hosted the site on the dark web. Piggybacking off the government's pastoral care initiative.

The company which designed the main website didn't even know that her add-on existed. We found it earlier today. It was all down to Daisy. Nothing to do with the others.'

'But . . .'

'But nothing, Rick. You and your uncle got it wrong.'

'But the tattoos they got me to do. The Hobby Horse. Aitch-aitch. They were taunting us. They're racists.'

'Apart from Daisy, we all had family links to the brewery. We were honouring our heritage, that's all,' whimpered Kayleigh.

'But you're friends. You must've known what she was up to!'

'Daisy was the posh kid. The one with money. The rest of us had nothing. We were a bunch of misfits. Everyone treated us like losers, so we stuck together. Daisy joined us later, but since we left school, we only ever saw her at the quiz nights.'

'But we kill—' Rick couldn't bring himself to finish the sentence as the implications of what he'd just been told began to sink in. His eyes narrowed and he shook his head, dismissing it as a lie. 'No, no. This isn't right. It's a trick. You're trying to get inside my head. You want me to let this bitch go, that's all. Well, it's not happening. Do you understand me? It's not fucking happening! It's either me or her. Your choice.'

'It's not an either-or choice, Rick. I'm telling you now, she's not—'

'Shut the fuck up! You've put your taser down, but I can see your baton. Question is, can you cosh me before I slit her throat?' Yet again he tugged down hard on Kayleigh's hair, exposing her throat.

'Think about it, Rick. Kayleigh's a carer. She's been a carer since she left school. Which means she works long hours. She doesn't get to pick and choose who her clients are. She helps whoever she's told to help, regardless of who they are, or where they were born. I bet she's knackered when she gets home. I doubt she'd have the time or energy to focus on anything else.'

'My mother used to b-be a-a c-carer,' stuttered Rick. The hesitation in his voice was noticeable, as an element of doubt crept in.

This was the first chink in his armour and Jemima needed to capitalise on it. 'And I bet your mother worked ridiculously long hours and was exhausted whenever she finished her shifts.'

Rick nodded.

'Would she have had the time or energy to commit to something else?'

He shook his head. 'It was all she could do to cook dinner. Most nights she'd be asleep in front of the telly before nine o'clock.'

'And I bet that's what it's like for Kayleigh.'

'It is,' she whimpered.

'Come on, Rick. Put the knife down. Daisy Evans was the person behind your brother's death, and a lot of others too. We've got the evidence to prove it. So let Kayleigh go. She's got nothing to do with what happened.'

As Rick began to cry, his grip on the knife loosened, and it fell to the floor. He let go of Kayleigh's hair and scooted back to distance himself from her.

Extracting her handcuffs Jemima wasted no time in securing them around his wrists. Rick Fernández offered no resistance. Instead, he stared blankly into space. A young man broken, bereaved, and bewildered. The siege was over. Kayleigh Bevan was safe, though traumatised and injured.

'Can't . . . keep . . . this . . . up,' gasped Levi. He was still performing CPR on Dean. The effort of chest compressions was exhausting.

'Move over,' ordered Jemima, as she got into position and took his place.

'Defibrillator, ma'am!' called one of the constables, as he hurried towards them carrying the equipment. 'Ambulance is on its way and we're moving the vehicles to give them a clear run.'

It was a start, but Jemima hoped it wouldn't end up being a case of too little too late. Levi set up the defibrillator while Jemima continued with the chest compressions. With everything in place and the machine fully charged, Jemima ordered the others to stand clear. She insisted on being the one to do this. Not because she wanted to play the hero if it started Dean's heart beating again. Heroism was the last thing on her mind. The truth was that she had no real expectations of it being successful, and she didn't want Levi to carry an additional burden of guilt should it fail.

CHAPTER 39

Levi and Mack remained at the smallholding to secure the scene and wait for the arrival of the forensic team.

Having been read his rights, Rick Fernández was transported to the station to await interview. Kayleigh was treated at the scene by the paramedics then taken to hospital. There was relief all round when Levi and Jemima learned that Dean Walters had a fighting chance of survival. Their perseverance had paid off.

When the defibrillator had restarted his heart, Jemima could have cried with relief. Instead, she swallowed hard as she fought to keep her emotions under control and had reassured the junior detective that everything was going to be all right. This bravado was partly because she wanted to show the rest of the team that she was unfazed, but also because in the coming days Levi might need her support. And she didn't want him to see her vulnerability.

She had led the raid on the barn and had been the one to order the use of tasers. Yet despite following her orders to the letter, and subsequently doing everything he could to stop Dean Walters from dying right there on the filthy floor of the barn, the detective came within a whiskers' breadth of killing a suspect in the line of duty. This was something no decent person would want on their conscience.

'I'll drive,' said Dan, as they were about to leave the smallholding. His voice was firm, with no room for negotiation. He held his hand out for the key. Having heard what had happened inside the barn and taken one look at Jemima, he knew that she'd been to hell and back in the short time they'd been apart.

The search of the house had turned out to be the easy option. Textbook stuff in fact. Dean's parents had been the only people at home. The old lady was in a bad way, with legacy signs of a stroke, and the husband who had been feeding her offered no argument or resistance when they entered the building.

The shotguns were found, securely locked inside the metal cabinet, specifically designed to house them. And the old man hadn't objected when they confiscated the weapons for immediate safe-keeping. Having undertaken a thorough room-to-room search of the entire property, Dan and his team had found no evidence linking back to the double murder or the current abduction.

* * *

Jemima and Dan returned to the incident room to find Gareth and the others huddled around a desk, listening to an audio feed.

'What's happening?' she asked.

'We identified that particularly vulnerable teenager. The one I thought might end it all at any moment. Managed to get an address and a team are on their way there. I called in a favour, and we've got a live feed. With all the shit that's going down we just need some good news. How's—'

'At the property now.' An officer's voice came through loud and clear. A doorbell rang out repeatedly, as someone pounded on the door.

Jemima grabbed a chair and sat with the others. Suddenly, her legs felt too weak to support her body, and her stomach was doing somersaults.

'Force entry!' They heard the thud as the door gave way, then the sound of running feet.

Time stood still as they waited in silence. Then came the worst possible news.

'Oh, Christ! We're too late.'

Jemima turned away and surreptitiously wiped her eyes. She pretended to cough. It bought her a few seconds. As she turned around, she saw that Zoe was in floods of tears and Lewis appeared shell-shocked.

'W-we were t-too late.' It was Lewis who spoke. The young officer's eyes were glazed. He seemed punch-drunk. Broken. Whereas Zoe was sobbing so hard that it was doubtful she would be capable of stringing a sentence together.

'Shall we get the details up on the board?' Jemima appreciated that her approach might sound harsh to the two young officers. But there were still more victims out there. People they might have a chance of saving. And as such, it was business as usual.

'I'll write it up,' said Lewis as he struggled out of his seat. 'Her name's Janelle Adebowale. Youngest so far. No more than a kid. Turned thirteen last week. What a fucking waste of a life!' As he walked to the whiteboard, Lewis kicked out at a nearby wastepaper bin.

'Listen to me. You've all done your best. It's all any of us can do. No one could have done more. You're not responsible for Janelle's death.'

'Doesn't make it easier,' said Lewis.

'You're right. It doesn't. But unfortunately, that's the way it goes. You'll remember this for the rest of your lives. But hopefully you will turn the hurt and anger you feel right now into something positive. Use it to motivate you whenever you're on shift to do everything in your power to make your patch a safer place for everyone. Open your eyes to what's going on out there and do something about it.'

'I did everything I could to try to find the location in time. But I couldn't,' said Gareth. 'This is so messed up. I don't advocate for capital punishment, but Daisy deserves to hang for what she's done. I know it wouldn't bring the victims back, but it might, just might, help their families. An eye for an eye and all that.

'I've already instructed the team leader to bring the laptop and anything else that might be relevant back to the station. It'll form part of the evidence chain and we'll examine it once we're certain that those other kids are out of danger.' Gareth sighed. His eyes were bloodshot. He looked done in but was determined to keep going.

'Get you a cup of coffee?' asked Dan.

'That'd be great. I think Nancy could do with one too. Right now, I need the caffeine. Anyway, better get back to it. There're still three more kids out there.'

As Dan sorted out the coffees, Jemima turned her attention back to Lewis and Zoe. 'I appreciate it's hard, but you need to put Janelle's death out of your minds. There're still kids out there, and there's every chance you can make a difference. So, get back on the phones and see if we can find them before it's too late. Once the schools have shut for the day, we've lost the chance of them giving us the names of any absent pupils who fit the profile. The clock's ticking guys.'

They continued working for a few more hours, well past the end of the shift. No useful information came from the schools, but Hunter Bryant's team somehow managed to trace two of the teenagers, while Gareth and Nancy traced the third. They all sat in silence, waiting for news as officers were sent to the home addresses. Thankfully, in each case, all three teenagers were still alive.

'As far as Daisy's concerned, we wait until she's discharged. She's being kept in until tomorrow, and will be guarded until then,' said Jemima.

'Gary and I will head over to the hospital first thing, and bring her in ourselves,' said Mike. Jemima nodded her approval. 'We'll approach this fresh tomorrow, after we've got all our ducks in a row and also had a few hours to put some distance between us and these godawful events. We all need to spend some time with our loved ones. Have as normal an evening as possible. What I don't want to happen is for us to be so worked up that we allow our emotions to get in the way. The last thing we need is to allow her to get off on a technicality.'

'Does that mean it's early doors for us too?' asked Dan.

'Not just yet. We've got Rick Fernández to interview. Which should be relatively straightforward, as we've body-cam footage of what went down in that barn.'

'I know he's killed two people, and was about to do the same to Kayleigh, but I've got some sympathy for him,' said Dan. 'Rick and Dean were driven to this by officers from this force doing fuck all about Jack's death.'

'I agree. I'll be contacting Professional Standards. Get them to take a look at what's gone on here. There are too many instances of malpractice coming to light for the higher-ups to keep burying their heads in the sand, insisting it's just a few rogue officers. Something needs to be done about it, because if bad practice and wilful neglect goes unchecked, we'll soon reach the stage where no one trusts us. There must be consequences.'

'Couldn't agree more,' said Dan.

'But whatever the provocation, we can't have the public resorting to taking the law into their own hands,' said Jemima. 'It's a kangaroo court mentality, which would quickly result in anarchy.'

CHAPTER 40

After interviewing and charging Rick Fernández Jemima headed home, weary and shellshocked by the day's events.

At the end of a shift, every serving officer had their own way of dealing with things. Tried and tested methods for putting the stresses of the day behind them. Alcohol was frequently the favoured method for dulling the senses. There were some who distanced themselves from reality by immersing themselves in a computer game. Others focused their attention on a lover. Some found other ways to unwind.

But what every parent amongst those who had worked the case had in common was that they each hugged their children a little closer that night. Regardless of their age, and whether the kids wanted to or not. Determined that from now on they'd keep a closer eye on them. Study their moves. Watch out for signs that all was as it should be. Because if this case had taught them anything, it was that you couldn't take your child's life for granted.

Even when it was your job to hunt down murderers, it was still a shocking realisation to learn that a teacher had been responsible for so many deaths. Daisy Evans had hidden in plain sight and would undoubtedly have gone on to kill countless other vulnerable teenagers had they not discovered what she was up to.

It made Jemima wonder; how many more twisted individuals were out there in positions of power? Destroying lives. Playing God. Furthering their own sick agendas.

There were certain professionals the public were conditioned to trust. Parents rarely questioned a teacher's fitness to spend time with their child. It was taken for granted that they had been, educated, trained, assessed. They had passed supposedly rigorous DBS checks. Yet the bottom line was, no one knew what went on in anyone's mind. What they really believed. What hidden agendas, if any, they had. Society had conditioned parents to accept that at a certain age they handed over their progeny to the education system. Most parents, having no other viable alternative, accepted wholeheartedly that it was for the best, and did just that.

Yet Daisy Evans' insidious agenda had gone unnoticed. Allowing her to prey like a vampire, metaphorically, and in some cases, actually draining teenagers of their life's blood. Having been co-opted onto a government initiative, she had set out to groom and subsequently kill vulnerable children.

In the community where she lived, it was an open secret that she held extreme views. Even others passionate about the Welsh language, a sector of society she self-identified with, did their utmost to avoid her. Yet despite recognising that she was potentially dangerous no one raised their concerns or questioned her fitness to influence young impressionable minds. It was a shameful indictment that people had looked the other way. As if by distancing themselves from their fears it absolved them of being complicit. Whereas, if they had acted responsibly and raised those concerns, they might have saved some lives.

It was barely 5 a.m. when Jemima returned to the station. Despite a night of broken sleep, she felt energised and eager to move the case to a satisfactory conclusion. Thoughts about the suicides had been running through her mind all through the night, and she was determined to have everything to hand before she interviewed Daisy Evans.

She had never despised someone as much as she did this woman and was determined to do everything in her power to give the Crown Prosecution Service the best possible chance of ensuring that Daisy went down for a long time.

As she walked into the incident room she stopped in her tracks. She thought she'd be the first of the team to arrive, but it wasn't the case. Gareth was already sat at the meeting table tucking into a bacon roll, as steam rose from a mug of coffee. Jemima's stomach growled. In her eagerness to make a start she had left home without having breakfast. The bacon smelt so good that her mouth watered.

'What time did you get in?' she asked.

Gareth turned mid-munch and held up a hand to indicate that he was unable to speak. His jaw moved rapidly as he chewed then swallowed. 'Not that long ago. Didn't get much sleep. Found it difficult to switch off. Wanted to make a start while there was less distraction.'

'I know the feeling,' said Jemima. 'Canteen quiet?'

'Yeah, good time to get in and out without standing in line.'

'In that case, I'll be back shortly to join you. We'll eat together then make a start.' Ten minutes later Jemima returned and they sat together while they ate their food.

Having finished, Gareth was the first to speak. 'I've Janelle's laptop here. Came in after we left. I'll see what I can find.'

'Anything else there that I can go through?' asked Jemima.

'Those bags are items collected from her bedroom,' said Gareth. He pointed to a pile of evidence bags on a nearby table.

Jemima sat down and began to systematically work through the evidence bags. She discounted most of it as not being evidential, until she came across an A4 size hardcover notebook. 'What the . . .' she muttered. As she scanned page after page of what appeared to be a detailed log containing dates, times, websites, file names, and paths taken to access the files, her heartrate increased. She was so focused on the potential implications of Janelle's log that she almost jumped out of her seat when ten minutes later Gareth shouted.

'Got you, you bitch!' He did a drum roll on the desk. 'There's no way she'll walk away from this. When we accessed Daisy's machines, they were spewing out those suicide images and messages. Well, I've just proved a link with Janelle's machine.'

'That's brilliant news, Gar! And take a look at this. I think it might help too,' said Jemima, as she handed him Janelle's handwritten log.

Gareth stared at it in disbelief, then smiled broadly. 'I'll check this out, but I'm already pretty certain that Janelle's done the hard work for us. It's a reasonable presumption that Daisy thought she was covering her tracks, as once the link was broken it'd be all but impossible to check it out, as she was using a VPN. But what she didn't count on was that one of her victims would keep a comprehensive written record of every interaction she had online. It's given us an indisputable link between Daisy and Janelle. A link that remained unbroken when she eventually took her own life.

'We've got her bang to rights, guv. Whatever else we find will be the icing on the cake. We've bloody got her.'

Jemima had a good feeling about the day ahead. After yesterday's physically and emotionally gruelling shift, things seemed to be coming together.

'Next up is taking a look at Daisy's flash drives. They're encrypted so it might take a while.'

'I'll leave you to it,' said Jemima. Knowing she could be of no help to Gareth, it was time to get her ducks in a row to ensure that when she questioned Daisy, she allowed the woman no wriggle room to worm her way out of the case they were building against her.

It was approaching nine o'clock when Gareth called Jemima over. Nancy had been working alongside him since the start of her shift, and the two officers looked like the cats who had just got the cream.

'We've cracked the encryption,' said Gareth. 'It was only a matter of perseverance, time, and some luck. But those flash drives really are the ultimate payload. The files will hang her out to dry. We've got a copy of the code she created to piggyback on the original site. We've also got copies of every image she sent, and every interaction she had with each victim. What's more, and this is the really sickening part, she kept score.'

'What do you mean she kept score?' Jemima shuddered as she anticipated what she was about to be told.

'There's a file containing the personal details of each victim. Race appears to be the overriding factor. She had a scoring system.'

'She allocated a points system to potential victims. Take a look,' said Nancy.

Jemima couldn't believe what she saw as Gareth opened the relevant computer files. In setting up the add-on site Daisy's sole intention had been to groom already vulnerable non-Welsh teenagers residing in Wales and encourage them to kill themselves. This was backed up by the evidence they had already uncovered. But what came as a surprise was how much she apparently hated people of English and Japanese origins.

Daisy had compiled an extensive list of nationalities where if she had been successful in her efforts to get them to commit suicide, she would award herself ten points. However, if her victim was an English teenager residing in Wales, she awarded herself fifty points. As far as they knew she hadn't groomed a Japanese victim, yet she had decided to award herself one hundred points should she do so.

'What do you make of the scoring system, guv?' asked Gareth.

'I can't say that her animosity towards the English is a great surprise. People like her will deny that they hold such views, but it's practically part of their racist psyche. For some reason Welsh kids are normalised into believing that anyone or anything English is bad. It's done in a joking way by parents, teachers, politicians. But it's vile and insidious. Though as for her hatred of anyone who's Japanese . . . Frankly, I've no idea. Hopefully that will come to light soon.'

'She also kept a league table of how many interactions, how many images, and how much effort it took for her to eventually persuade them to end their lives. She used the data to hone her efforts by assessing which approach was the most efficient to reach the final goal,' said Nancy.

Throughout the years on the job, Jemima had encountered many warped and dangerous individuals. Yet this schoolteacher was by far, the most heinous of them all.

CHAPTER 41

Mike and Gary were at the hospital long before Daisy Evans was discharged, ready to accompany her to the station.

Later that morning, Jemima and Gareth walked into the interview room, laden with more than enough evidence to put her away for a very long time.

Dan had already made some enquiries about Daisy's lawyer, Rhys Llewellyn-Morgan. The man was on a retainer by Daisy's father. He had well-publicised links to some high-profile Welsh nationalists, and never wasted an opportunity to advocate for the use of his mother tongue.

Jemima had already asked Gareth to take the lead throughout the interview for two very good reasons. Firstly, though he chose not to use it, he was a fluent Welsh speaker. Secondly, given his role throughout the case because of his expertise on the IT side of things, he was by far the most appropriate person to question Daisy and see this through to the end.

Unsurprisingly, Rhys Llewellyn-Morgan, a man known for being a zealot, had decided to play the language card. He was a small man, with a bulbous nose covered in unsightly veins. His voice was sonorous, the tone pompous, as though he resented having to spend time breathing the same air as them. He began by insisting, in perfectly spoken English, that the interview must be conducted in Welsh.

The interview would inevitably take longer as Gareth would have to translate for Jemima's benefit. But on the plus side, it might help to unsettle Daisy, as she would quickly begin to realise that Gareth was a match for both her and her lawyer. And before they walked into the interview room, he had already ensured that Jemima knew the Welsh for '*no comment*'. As it was likely to be Daisy's most common response.

As Gareth began questioning Daisy using her preferred language, Jemima's attention was focused upon the former teacher. She spotted a flicker of uncertainty in her eyes. Many of the hardened criminals that Jemima had interviewed were used to playing poker with the best of them. They sat opposite her with expressions of stone. Bluffing it out. More often than not using the common tactic of responding to every question with the same two words, '*no comment*'.

Gareth proceeded to arrange a series of photographs on the table in front of Daisy. Instead of looking at the photographs the young woman stared resolutely ahead.

'I want you to look at the photographs, Daisy and tell me who these people are.' The photographs were of each of the teenage victims, taken during happier times. When Daisy refused to look, Gareth's voice hardened. 'I said, look at the photographs, Daisy!' He pushed each of them towards her in turn, naming each victim as he moved their photograph.

'For clarification, each of these photographs show a person that you murdered.'

'I murdered no one!' Apart from stating her name at the start of the interview it was the first time Daisy had spoken.

'You did, Daisy, and we can prove it. Now look at the photographs!' He slammed his fist on the desk.

'Really, Sergeant, there's no need for such aggression,' said Llewellyn-Morgan.

'You're skating on thin ice, Mr Llewellyn-Morgan. I will not allow you to disrupt this interview,' said Gareth. He turned his attention to Daisy once more.

'What links your victims is the fact that they each came from families where at least one, or both of the parents were not born in Wales. This is Luna Watson. She was fifteen when you killed her. She attended a local Catholic school. Both of her parents are English.

'This is Sophia Tang. She was seventeen when you killed her. She also attended a local Catholic school. Her mother is Italian. Her father Chinese.

'This is Lexi Cook. She was sixteen when you killed her. She was a pupil at the local high school Her mother is Canadian. Her father English.

'This is Jack Fernández. He was seventeen when you killed him. His mother is Welsh. His father Spanish. Jack was a pupil at a local Catholic school.

'This is Oliver Palmer. He was fourteen when you killed him. His mother is from Senegal. His father is Welsh. Oliver was a pupil at the Welsh medium school where you used to teach.'

Jemima noticed that the lawyer was carefully studying his fingernails, looking less composed. Daisy remained silent.

All the while, Gareth continued naming the list of victims. 'This is Thomas Sidhu. He was sixteen when you killed him. His mother is English. His father, Indian.

'This is Joshua Booth. He was eighteen when you killed him. Both of his parents are English He attended the local Catholic school.

'This is David Haque, he was also eighteen when you killed him. His mother is Scottish. His father, Indian. David attended the local high school.

'And finally, we arrive at the victim you murdered only yesterday. Janelle Adebowale had only recently had her thirteenth birthday. Both of her parents are Nigerian.'

As Gareth pointed to the final photograph, the solicitor edged away from his client.

'Why did you kill them, Daisy?'

'I didn't.'

Despite Jemima not understanding the words of this conversation, she knew implicitly what had been said. She nodded to Gareth, who proceeded to place a photograph on top of each of the live shots. This time each image showed the teenagers as corpses.

Llewellyn-Morgan made a strange noise. The man looked as though he was about to throw up. Instead, he took a deep breath, extracted a handkerchief from his jacket pocket, and dabbed his forehead to rid it of perspiration. 'Shall we cut to the chase? Although these images are undeniably upsetting, what evidence, if any do you have to link my client to these unfortunate deaths?'

'We have plenty of evidence, Mr Llewellyn-Morgan, and I'll take you through it step-by-step,' said Gareth.

Just as he was about to move on to the next phase of setting out the evidence discovered on the laptop and the flash drives, there was a knock at the door. Mike stepped into the room and whispered something in Jemima's ear. She suspended the interview and rose to step outside. Before switching off the machine, Gareth repeated what she said, for the sake of everything being spoken in Welsh.

Having closed the door, Jemima walked a short distance down the corridor with the inspector. 'What have you got, Mike?'

'I've been doing some digging, and I discovered that Daisy was once engaged to a classmate of hers. His name's Bleddyn Cadwalader. They'd even set the date for the wedding. Two months before the big day, he called it off. Daisy was devastated. Turned out he'd fallen for a young accountant who had recently joined his firm. It was a whirlwind romance. They're married with kids now. Her name's Hanako Takahashi. Her family relocated to Cardiff, from Japan, when her father was appointed to head up one of the major electronic plants in Bridgend.'

'Any idea when this happened?' asked Jemima.

When Mike answered, Jemima realised that it was six months prior to Daisy's involvement in the schools' pastoral care initiative.

'But that's not the best bit, guv. I've just taken a call to say that the woman discovered at Daisy's parents' house, who is still unconscious and hanging on by a thread, has been identified as Hanako!'

'I'm glad someone's found out who she is. When we came across her yesterday, she was so badly injured that it was impossible to know what she originally looked like. I was worried that if she didn't pull through, her friends and family would never know what had happened to her.'

'Bleddyn had reported her missing, but our lot wouldn't do anything until the usual amount of time had passed.'

'Figures.'

'He'd given up and was ringing round the hospitals asking if she'd been admitted. To be honest it was pure luck that he contacted Prince Charles Hospital when he did. Otherwise, they might still not have known her identity.

'Anyway, I've spoken to Bleddyn, who claimed that towards the end of their relationship, Daisy became increasingly unhinged. It started when she lost out on two jobs she applied for shortly after they'd got engaged. Both vacancies were filled by English candidates.

'Bleddyn said she took it badly. Even found out where one of them lived and poured paint stripper over their car. Kept obsessing over ways in which she'd like to kill them. At first, he thought it was just sour grapes on her part. But after a while, he began to realise her behaviour wasn't normal. He was scared of her. He'd been looking for a way to end things with her, and when Hanako came along he knew he couldn't put it off any longer.

'Anyway, he's prepared to give a statement about her racist tendencies but doesn't want to leave Hanako's side.'

Daisy's actions were not the actions of a rational person. But it was believable that Bleddyn's rejection of her exacerbated her hatred of people who hadn't been born in the area. As warped as the logic was, she was projecting the hatred she felt towards Hanako, on to every non-indigenous Welsh person who settled in the area.

In Daisy's mind, a young Japanese woman had stolen her "*happy ever after,*" therefore every non-Welsh person was a threat. She had not stopped to consider the likelihood that Bleddyn had a choice in the matter. Indeed, had he been happy and committed to his relationship with Daisy, he would have remained with her.

It made Jemima wonder if, given Daisy's privileged upbringing and possible narcissistic personality traits, it was inconceivable for her to acknowledge that Bleddyn chose to end their relationship.

'Thanks, Mike. Head over to the hospital and take a statement from him. Find out how Daisy dealt with the humiliation of being dumped so close to the wedding, and if she's caused them any problems, or issued any threats prior to the kidnapping and torturing of Hanako.'

Jemima headed back to the interview room, buoyed by this latest revelation. It was something she intended to bring up in the interview. Get Gareth to throw it in there, sit back and see how Daisy reacted. It was a time in her life when she had been publicly humiliated. Something she would not want to have to speak about. If Gareth were to unsettle her, all sorts of revelations could come out.

Jemima called Gareth out of the room to update him on this latest development. Glancing at Daisy and her lawyer, she saw them exchange a worried look.

'When you push her on it, don't break the flow by translating things for me. You're the only one that can do this, and I trust your judgement, Gar.'

'No pressure then,' he laughed.

'If you can break her, it'll go down well for future promotion prospects. The most important thing is for you to keep piling on the pressure. It's our best chance of getting her to lose it and say something incriminating. When this goes to trial, I don't want there to be any doubt about what she's done. I want the jury to see that psychopath for what she is.'

When they returned to the room the interview resumed. Gareth questioned Daisy about how she hacked into the website via a backdoor. How she selected and systematically groomed her victims. But Daisy resorted to uttering the words, '*no comment,*' to each of his questions. The short break in questioning appeared to have given the young woman time to compose herself.

Jemima glanced at the wall clock and decided that they had spent more than enough time trying to get her to answer their questions. It was time to shake things up. Beneath the table she gently tapped Gareth's shoe with her own. It was to let him know that it was time for him to change tack.

'What was it like when everyone laughed at you because Bleddyn dumped you for a Japanese woman?' asked Gareth. The question was phrased in a blunt, unsophisticated way to provoke a reaction.

Daisy had not anticipated the question. Her hands bunched into fists. Her expression darkened. 'He didn't dump me! No one dumps me! I dumped him!'

'Not what I heard. Bleddyn said it was love at first sight when he met Hanako. Said she outclassed you in every way.'

Jemima watched the monumental meltdown, as Gareth pushed Daisy further and further towards the edge.

'That Japanese bitch turned his head. But I know Bledd loves me!'

'You're deluded, Daisy. Bleddyn doesn't love you. How could he possibly love you? He chose to spend the rest of his life with Hanako. Not you! He didn't want you then and he certainly doesn't want you now. Not after you all but beat his wife to death.'

Both officers spotted a flicker of fear in Daisy's expression. Determined to ramp up the pressure, Gareth continued.

'That's right, Daisy, the penny's dropped. You didn't quite go far enough with Hanako. It's one thing grooming kids and bombarding them with your vile messages. Breaking their spirit little by little until they feel so hopeless that they kill themselves. But it's quite another thing to kill someone with your bare hands.'

As Gareth paused, they watched Daisy. The young woman closed her eyes as she concentrated on containing her anger.

'Well, Hanako survived, and your DNA is all over her. Then again, it would be, since you beat her half to death. We've an officer at the hospital now. He's gone to take a statement.' It wasn't a lie, just a misdirection. Daisy didn't need to know that Bleddyn would be the one giving a statement.

'That bitch is alive?' Daisy's eyes widened.

'Sure is. Now where was I? Ah yes, apparently Hanako wasn't interested in Bleddyn at the start. Not when she knew he was about to get married. But Bleddyn was going to call off the wedding anyway. He finally appreciated that you weren't just a Welsh patriot. You were and still are a racist. It was you losing out on those two jobs that did it.' Gareth continued to push and push as he drip-fed the latest information.

'He wasn't going to call off the wedding!'

'He was, Daisy. Bleddyn convinced Hanako that you meant nothing to him. Said he'd only wanted to marry you because your family have money.'

'That's not true.'

'This is inappropriate questioning! It has nothing to do with the charges my client faces,' said Llewellyn-Morgan. It was noticeable how his posture stiffened, as though struck by a bolt of electricity. The solicitor's facial expression darkened to reveal a scowl that was almost maniacal.

It was obvious, even to Jemima, without understanding what was being said, that this man was concerned that Daisy might let slip some incriminating information should Gareth continue goading her in this manner.

'It has everything to do with the charges your client faces,' asserted Gareth. 'Daisy couldn't handle the fact that the man she was about to marry ended their relationship two weeks before their wedding. It was the final straw for her. She was angry. Humiliated. In her mind it was bad enough that she'd missed out on two jobs. Jobs that were offered to people who were English.

'Bleddyn's told us she's a racist.'

'That's just hearsay,' countered the solicitor.

'That's as maybe, but what isn't hearsay is that Daisy set up that site on the dark web to groom non-Welsh teenagers to kill themselves. We have a trail of evidence linking her to each of those deaths.

'You're going down, Daisy. Our case is watertight. You'll rot in jail because they'll give you a whole of life sentence. There'll be no parole. Bleddyn and Hanako will still have their happy ever after, with their beautiful bi-racial kids, and no one will ever think of you again.'

Daisy's jaw dropped as she finally lost all semblance of control. 'I hope that motherfucker and his bitch rot in hell! Foreigners like her and their mongrel brats have no business being in our country. They're parasites. This is our country. Not theirs. They should ship the fuck out and get back to where they came from.'

Gareth forced himself to remain silent as he listened to Daisy's racist tirade. It was vile, sickening, and troubling to know that there were people employed in positions of power and influence who held similar extremist views.

As Daisy's energy waned, he eventually spoke. 'It's noticeable that the teenagers you groomed, and encouraged to take their own lives came from families who were not entirely or in some instances, not at all, of Welsh heritage. Is that why you set out to kill them?'

'There's no point in me denying it. Not after you,' she jabbed her finger at him, 'managed to access my code and my records. There're not many people capable of pulling something like this off. I'm more intelligent than any of you. I wanted those fuckers dead. Why shouldn't I? I've done the world a favour. I just wish I'd had the time to kill more of them.'

'You're a racist, Daisy. A shameful, pathetic, inadequate, racist.'

'I'm not a racist. I'm a patriot. But the likes of you are traitors. I love my country. You might have stopped me, but there're others out there who've taken up the cause. We've got a lot of support, and it's growing every day. People prepared to do whatever it takes to rid our country of invaders intent on diluting and ultimately destroying our Welsh heritage. We'll do whatever it takes to win. Believe me, there's a war coming, and if I were you, I'd make sure you end up on the right side.'

With more than enough to charge her, and a confession to boot, Jemima shut the conversation down.

Daisy was formally charged, and as she was led from the room, the former teacher was unashamedly defiant, and sang the Welsh National Anthem as loudly as she could. *'Mae hen wlad fy nhadau yn annwyl i mi.'* Which translated meant, *'This land of my fathers is dear to me.'*

Jemima listened in stunned silence until Gareth spoke, this time in English.

'She's off her bloody rocker, guv.'

'You're not wrong there, Gar,' she replied, as they packed up their documents and headed out of the interview room together.

EPILOGUE

You are cordially invited to the wedding of,
Mr Gareth Dylan Peters
to
Mr Ryan Blake

So much planning had gone into this day. Agreeing a date. Finding a venue. Inviting guests. Agonising over seating plans. Sampling menus. Selecting readings. And so, the list went on. For two busy people who wanted to be hands-on with every minute decision, it had eventually come as a relief when the moment arrived.

'You look a million dollars, Gar. Now relax and enjoy the day,' said Jemima. She and the rest of the team had arrived early to scope out the venue. She could tell her sergeant was on edge, and it wasn't just down to pre-wedding jitters.

'I am relaxed,' he replied. But as he spoke his eyes kept darting about as he searched for any sign that his father was there.

'Try telling your face that,' laughed Jemima. 'Now, take a deep breath. I promise you nothing will go wrong. I've circulated your father's photograph. There're a couple of guys from traffic watching the entrance, and we've got it covered here. He'll not get anywhere near you.'

It was the perfect setting for a wedding. A country hotel. Magnificent grounds. Row upon row of seats, arranged to face an arbour, laden with sweet smelling flowers and luscious green foliage. The sun was pleasantly warm, though not too hot, and many of the assembled guests wore sunglasses. Every member of the team was aware of Gareth's fear that his father would arrive uninvited and cause a scene. It was the reason that Jemima, Levi, Mack, and Nancy had decided not to take their seats. Opting instead to stand at the edges and act as impromptu security guards. They each had every intention of watching their friend and colleague take his vows as he committed to the love of his life. But the four were determined that no one would have the opportunity to disrupt the service.

Dan was centre stage, supporting Gareth. He'd been chuffed to bits, and very emotional when he'd been asked to be his best man. It was all he seemed to talk about in the weeks leading up to the big day. So much so, that his wife, Caroline claimed that he was more enthusiastic about Gareth's wedding than he had been about his own.

Gareth and Ryan had written their own vows. A harpist performed as the guests were seated, enhancing the magical feel of the occasion. The couple had opted to make an entrance together. Each with their best man at their side. And as the registrar was given the sign that they were ready to approach, he signalled for everyone to stand. The chatter died down as everyone turned to watch the grooms and groomsmen approach.

Both men had kept the choice of entrance music a secret. Though, in retrospect, anyone who knew them well should not have been surprised when Queen's, *Crazy Little Thing Called Love* blasted out of nearby speakers. The energy and beat were infectious. Such a contrast to the ethereal mellifluousness of the harp. The hi-octane energy was joyful, infectious, and within seconds guests were tapping feet, singing along, and clapping hands in time to the music.

Gareth beamed from ear to ear as he strutted his stuff towards the arbour. As did Ryan and his best man. Dan tried his utmost to get in the swing of things, but clearly felt inhibited at being thrust into the spotlight in such an unexpected manner. Especially as he lacked any natural sense of rhythm. It hadn't occurred to him that there would be an expectation for him to do anything other than to accompany Gareth, as they both walked sedately towards the arbour.

With the ceremony underway, Jemima began to relax. They'd all been given a photograph of Gareth's father, to enable them to recognise him, should he make the mistake of turning up.

As it turned out there had been no need to worry, as everything went off smoothly.

Later that evening, as everyone took to the dancefloor, Jemima glanced across at Gareth and Ryan, and thought that in all the years she'd known him, this was the happiest she'd ever seen her sergeant.

'They make a lovely couple,' said Caroline Broadbent.

'They certainly do,' replied Jemima.

'Come on, Jem, time to show everyone what you're made of,' said Mason. He grabbed hold of her hand pulling her onto her feet. They reached the dancefloor just as *Your Song* by Elton John began to play. Mason swept her into his arms and held her close. She rested her head upon his shoulder and followed his lead. Closing her eyes, as they swayed gently to the music.

'If only it could always be like this. The perfect end to the perfect day,' whispered Jemima.

'Life's what you make of it, Jem. Anything's possible. It really is that simple.' His lips brushed her cheek as they continued to dance the night away.

THE END

A NOTE TO READERS

Thank you so much for joining Jemima and her team in their latest investigation.

I set this book in and around Rhymney, as it's where I spent the first nineteen years of my life. It's an area of Wales that few non-Welsh people have heard of and are even less familiar with. Located at the head of the valley, approximately thirty miles from Cardiff, it's a world away from the advantages and opportunities of the city.

I attended Rhymney Comprehensive School, located at The Lawn. They were old, dilapidated buildings, which have subsequently gained Grade II listed status. There was a spectacular Monkey Puzzle tree dominating the quadrant. It was large, imposing, and I hope it's still there. Some of our lessons were taught in portacabins sited throughout the grounds, and our sixth-form building was on the upper floor of a small ramshackle house known as Tre York. It was basic, to say the least, but I loved my school days. I have never been to the Idris Davies school mentioned in the book, as it was erected whilst I was at university.

It was inevitable when writing about Jemima's latest case that I'd incorporate some childhood memories into the text. Over the years I heard many stories about the brewery as my father worked there. First, as a drayman, and latterly as the warehouse manager. While the brewing side of the business was operational, it was easy to tell when it was about to rain. The wind would change, bringing with it the distinctive smell of the hops. Clouds would gather, followed closely by the rain.

There is a conversation in the book, where Billy James reminisces about falling off his bicycle on the wet cobble stones. This happened to me on numerous occasions. It was a bumpy ride at the best of times. But when the ground was wet, it became treacherous. It was impossible to remain upright, as the wheels would slip, I'd skid and end up on ground. Just the thought of it makes me wince. I had so many bruises.

The street that Daisy Evans lives in is where my family home was located. We lived with my grandmother whose first language was Welsh. My mother was bilingual, though my father and I only knew a few Welsh phrases.

Most days after school, I'd walk my dog, a beautiful Norwegian Elkhound, down Carno Street to join a footpath at the side of the river, where we'd continue our journey until we passed the tennis courts and the railway station. I'd wait for my father to finish his shift and we'd have a lift home in the car.

Back then, if you walked past the brewery warehouse and looked up to the hillside, you could see the Bent Iron in the distance. I haven't visited the area in such a long time, so things would inevitably have changed. Though, from carrying out research on the internet, I know that the original Bent Iron was replaced by a more ornate structure.

Back in those days, summer holidays and better weather meant longer walks. I'd head up the Barrack's Level Road and stroll along the lower bank of Butetown Pond. During dry periods, there was no overflow and it was possible to head across the moorland in the direction of Fochriw. The ground was rough, littered with animal droppings, and occasional carcasses of livestock. It wasn't unusual for sheep, cows, and horses to roam the moorland, stray onto the carriageway, and occasionally wander through the streets.

As part of that circuit, I'd head for the minor road where Jemima and the others parked when visiting the crime scene. In those days there weren't many vehicles travelling along that carriageway, so the risk to pedestrians was minimal.

Despite this being a favoured walk, I didn't stray towards the Bent Iron. Though, I skirted the edge of Rhaslas Pond. Soon afterwards I'd start of the decent of what we called, Red Hill, but now appears to be named Hill Road. It was exceptionally steep and challenging for tired legs. Once I reached Pontlottyn, I'd call in to see my auntie who lived not far from the Lord Nelson pub, then set off again on the final part of the circuit towards home.

I hope you've enjoyed reading *The Rhymney Valley Killings*, book 6 in the Detective Jemima Huxley series. The seventh book in this series will be set in the Newport Wetlands.

Finally, it would mean a lot to me if you would be kind enough to take the time to leave a rating and possibly a review on Amazon, Goodreads, or Bookbub.

Diolch yn fawr. Thank you.

THE JOFFE BOOKS STORY

We began in 2014 when Jasper agreed to publish his mum's much-rejected romance novel and it became a bestseller.

Since then we've grown into the largest independent publisher in the UK. We're extremely proud to publish some of the very best writers in the world, including Joy Ellis, Faith Martin, Caro Ramsay, Helen Forrester, Simon Brett and Robert Goddard. Everyone at Joffe Books loves reading and we never forget that it all begins with the magic of an author telling a story.

We are proud to publish talented first-time authors, as well as established writers whose books we love introducing to a new generation of readers.

We have been shortlisted for Independent Publisher of the Year at the British Book Awards three times, in 2020, 2021 and 2022, and for the Diversity and Inclusivity Award at the Independent Publishing Awards in 2022.

We built this company with your help, and we love to hear from you, so please email us about absolutely anything bookish at: feedback@joffebooks.com.

If you want to receive free books every Friday and hear about all our new releases, join our mailing list here: www.joffebooks.com/contact.

And when you tell your friends about us, just remember: it's pronounced Joffe as in coffee or toffee!

ALSO BY GAYNOR TORRANCE

DI JEMIMA HUXLEY SERIES

Book 1: THE CARDIFF KILLINGS
Book 2: THE BRIARMARSH CLOSE KILLINGS
Book 3: THE CAERPHILLY MOUNTAIN KILLINGS
Book 4: THE LEIGHTON MEADOW KILLINGS
Book 5: THE MARQUESS CLUB KILLINGS
Book 6: THE RHYMNEY VALLEY KILLINGS

Printed in Dunstable, United Kingdom

66310438R00160